## DATE DUE

| | | | |
|---|---|---|---|
| | | | |
| | | | |
| | | | |
| | | | |
| | | | |
| | | | |
| | | | |
| | | | |
| | | | |
| | | | |
| | | | |
| | | | |
| | | | |
| | | | |
| | | | |
| | | | |
| | | | |
| | | | |

DEMCO 38-296

# Cactus Blood

*A Mystery Novel*

Lucha Corpi

Arte Público Press
Houston, Texas
1995

through grants from the
(a federal agency), the Lila
and the Andrew W. Mellon

*Recovering the past, creating the future*

Arte Público Press
University of Houston
Houston, Texas 77204-2090

Cover design by Gladys Ramírez

Corpi, Lucha. 1945–
    Cactus Blood / Lucha Corpi.
        p.    cm.
    ISBN 1-55885-134-8
    I. Title.
    PS3553.O693C3    1995
    813'.54—dc20                                    94-38164
                                                         CIP

The paper used in this publication meets the requirements
of the American National Standard for Permanence of
Paper for Printed Library Materials Z39.48-1984. ∞

# Acknowledgements

I would like to thank Officer Steven Fajardo, from Oakland Police Services, for his technical advice and patient instruction in the handling of weapons; Pat Haggerty, Director of the Dimond Branch, and the staff of the Oakland History Room and the Main Branch of the Oakland Public Library for making my search for early California history materials painlessly successful; Carlos Gonzales and Mark Greenside for the benefit of their *suspicious* minds; Chuff Afflerbach for sharing his knowledge of baseball and its jargon with me; Sally Headding, *clairvoyant extraordinaire*, for sharing her *"gift"* so generously with me, and José Novoa for his invaluable suggestions. I am forever indebted to my publisher, Nicolás Kanellos, and to my editor, Roberta Fernández, for their inexhaustible energy in support of my work.

L.C.

...we have been the foreshadows of your dream
guided at times
      by nothing more than instinct

Still
      without our collective voice
      yours would have remained
         a soft cry
            a whisper
    in some indifferent stranger's ear.


I
for one
lay claim to have done only this:
provided the soil where your dream took roots.
Nothing else.

> From "Dreamroots"
> and "Dolores"
> by Delia Treviño

*in memoriam*

*Miguel Angel Corpi Aguirre*
*(1915-1971)*

*César Chávez*
*(1927-1993)*

# Cactus Blood

## A Mystery Novel

# Foreshadows

The sun had begun to set and a sliver of waning moon peered from behind a hill. The snake in front of me coiled up, rattled its tail and made two short, swift thrusts in the air—rehearsals for the longer, deadly strike. I backed away slowly, but a thicket of prickly-pear cacti behind me barred my retreat. The prickles drove into my right leg and shoulder, and my blood left its mark on the fleshy leaves. Clenching my teeth, I held back a scream. I sensed a presence behind me, but I didn't dare turn, for the rattler was now drawing closer.

I saw a clearing in the thorny thicket. Like the snake, I recoiled to gather strength. I jumped through the clearing an instant before the rattler lunged forward. I shivered at the thought that its fangs had passed a fraction of an inch from my ankle and stabbed the leaf at precisely the spot where my blood was still present. Rubbing my shoulder and leg, I worked my way carefully around a huge, old cactus.

That's when I saw her. The woman. Naked. Her arms stretched up, tied to the fleshy leaves. Her legs together, bound to the stem. A slumping female Christ with a prickly-pear cactus cross on her back, shrouded in blood, bathed in amber moonlight.

Ever since, she haunts my vigil and dreams. I know I will not rest until I learn for whose sins she was sacrificed.

# One
## Fields of Vision

It was Friday, October 13. With the first of seven games scheduled for the next day, the main topic of conversation in Oakland was the "Battle of the Bay," as fans called the 1989 World Series between the Oakland A's and the San Francisco Giants.

Justin Escobar and I were in his van, traveling east on Fruitvale Avenue, headed towards his office a few blocks away. On the radio, a sportscaster was interviewing Bay Area baseball personalities and fans trying to predict the outcome of the "Battle." My interest in the sport was due mainly to my late husband's and my daughter's passion for baseball. I enjoyed a game every so often, but I was too sporadic a fan to find radio talk shows about the sport intellectually stimulating. So I soon tuned out, and my eyes scanned Fruitvale Avenue then moved up the Oakland hills.

I was looking at the effect of the rust-colored, late afternoon sunlight on the hills, which made them glow as if they were on fire, when Justin took the call from Leo Mares on his cellular phone. Leo was a friend of Justin's and a liaison officer between the police department and the Spanish-speaking community in Oakland.

Justin lowered the volume and listened to Leo in silence. When he hung up, he made a couple of calls on his phone, but whomever he was calling wasn't available and he placed the receiver back on its base. He made a U-turn at the first opportunity and we headed back the way we had come.

"Where are we going? What's going on?" I asked. When I got no answer, I looked at Justin. His face was pale and his gaze fixed. His hands clutched the steering wheel and his knuckles began to turn white. I didn't have to think long or hard to guess that the news he had just received wasn't good.

Something happened to my mother or my daughter and he doesn't know how to tell me, I thought. Adrenaline rushed through my veins and reached my heart in seconds, leaving in its wake the prickly sensation of fear on my skin. It was an irrepressible fear that quickly rooted in the soil of my conscience, already filled with sorrow and guilt. In the span of three years I had lost my father to cancer, my husband Darío to a heart attack, and my best friend, Luisa Cortez, to a bullet intended for me. I knew my extreme concern for my mother's and daughter's safety was irrational, but my fear seemed real at the moment and the only way to deal with it was to confront it.

"Who's dead?" I demanded, and my breathing quickened in expectation of his answer.

"Sonny Mares is dead," Justin finally said. He gave me a quick glance. Surprise more than sorrow nestled in his usually bright gaze. "Leo says Sonny killed himself." Justin repeated his last statement not so much for my benefit, but as if he himself were trying to grasp the significance of Sonny's action.

"Can't be," I said, then added, "I just saw him a week..." I stopped in midtrack when I realized how utterly meaningless my comment was. Disbelief and denial usually followed the news of someone's death. I knew those feelings well. But suicide always raised questions that no one—surely neither Justin nor I at that moment—could answer with any degree of certainty.

Ten minutes later we arrived at Sonny's apartment in Jingletown, near the small residential area where I had grown up in Oakland. He and some other artists had bought an old three-story building in partnership, and had converted it into adequate working and living space for each of them. The coroner's wagon and another patrol car were pulling out as we arrived. A second patrol and a police van were parked a few feet up the street from us.

"Over here," Leo Mares called out as soon as Justin and I stepped out of the van. Sonny Mares had been four years older than Leo, with approximately the same height and weight, the same olive skin, light brown hair and eyes, and the same Pancho Villa moustache. At present the resemblance was uncanny. Anyone who didn't know them well could easily have mistaken one brother for the other.

"I'm sorry, *carnal*," Justin said to Leo as they hugged and patted each other's backs a few times. Both men cleared their throats, trying not to give in to the emotions swelling up in their chests. But the pain in Leo's throat refused to break up, and he coughed.

The only two Chicanos at the police academy, Justin and Leo had met and become friends in 1975. Before he decided to become a private investigator, Justin had accepted a job with the San Jose Police Department while Leo had taken a position in the Oakland Police Department's Community Services Division. Seeing that his hope for advancement to homicide detective, or for bringing about any change in the department's attitude towards people of color, was nil, Justin had left the police department after only five years of service. But he and Leo Mares had remained good friends and had helped each other out professionally from time to time. I was beginning to get the feeling this might be one of those times.

Justin pointed at me with his open palm, and with a scratchy voice said to Leo, "Do you remember Gloria Damasco? She's my new associate."

"Of course," Leo said as he stretched out his hand to shake mine. "We met at your friend Luisa's funeral." He paused. I could sense his pain in his trembling, sweaty palm, and in the way his voice thinned over the word "funeral."

My heart went out to him. "I am now learning to live with my loss. I pray you do, too," I offered as condolence. He nodded and shook my hand again.

Carrying a heavy case that looked like a plastic tool box, a uniformed female technician stepped out as we entered the apartment. Justin handed me a pair of latex gloves, then joined Leo, who had stopped at the door to talk to the lab tech officer—M. Holstein, according to her name tag. "Unless the coroner says otherwise, there is no evidence of foul play so far," Officer Holstein told Leo. "But I'll have more for you later on." Forcing a smile, Leo nodded.

"Any preliminary report on the cause of death?" Justin asked.

Officer Holstein glanced at Leo. When he gestured his approval, addressing Justin, she said, "Unknown substance, orally introduced, most likely self-administered. That's the coroner's preliminary report."

I left Justin, Leo, and Officer Holstein talking in the hall and stepped into Sonny's flat. The two floors above us had served as storage for a paper company. The downstairs space, Sonny's flat, had housed the offices and had been divided into two smaller open areas with no set boundaries between them. The first section comprised the living and dining quarters and a small kitchen area. The second, a working area, was occupied by bookcases along the wall, a desk and a chair. Next to the chair was a table with a computer, a printer, a phone and a FAX machine. A drafting table, a reading chair with a pile of books next to it, a VCR, and a console TV completed the room. A third section, the only area separated from the rest by walls, was Sonny's bedroom and the bathroom next to it. The large windows, which ran the length of the outside wall in the living and dining areas, provided natural lighting for the flat.

Through the windows, a patio and chalk garden enclosed by a
tall wooden fence were visible in their entirety.

I was immediately drawn to the working area, as I
noticed that the TV was on. Soundless images flickered on the
large screen. "Odd," I said under my breath. "Why would Leo
or Officer Holstein turn on the TV and then leave it on?" But
it wasn't a regular TV program, I soon found out. It was a
video-taped documentary. Of what? I asked myself as I gazed
at the screen, trying to figure out what was going on.

Tall, gruff, thick-set men, some shirtless, others wearing
vests over hairy chests, hard hats and heavy work shoes or
western hats and boots held bunches of grapes in their hands
and taunted or gestured with their arms at either the cameraman or someone behind him. Their mouths spewed grape
seeds, as well as spit, slurs and lewd words that even with the
sound off came across loud and clear.

These vociferous men looked like the wild chimpanzees I
had recently watched in a *National Geographic* program,
which, feeling threatened, ran towards the camera but
stopped at a safe distance from it. They flapped their arms,
made shrill sounds, and gnashed at the photographer to give
the impression that they surely were fearless beasts, determined enemies to be reckoned with.

The boisterous, aggressive behavior of these men made
me curious. Why the bravado display? What could this film
have to do with Sonny's suicide? I slipped my latex gloves on,
found the remote control, rewound the tape, pressed the play
button, then turned up the volume. The men's vicious insults
slapped my ears. "C'mon! C'mon!" they yelled. "You're just a
dirty Mex'can! A fucking commie! You're not an American!
You're a slimy commie!"

Suddenly, the cameraman swept around and focused on
the action going on behind him. I could no longer see the belligerent men, although I could still hear them. Then I saw the

object of the goons' hostility: a small, dark man flanked and followed by hundreds of other men and women. The camera zoomed in for a closer view, and César Chávez, surrounded by members of the clergy and other official-looking people, came into the field of vision. He headed a picket line of men and women—farm workers and strike sympathizers, carrying the-black-eagle-on-red United Farm Workers' flag and banners bearing the image of the *Virgen de Guadalupe*.

The camera refocused on the men. The Teamsters, I thought, as I paused the tape. This was a film about the United Farm Workers' strike. Back in 1973, I remembered, the teamsters had been brought in by the grape growers at sixty-five dollars a day per man to break the farm workers' strike.

Luisa, Darío, and I had supported and participated in one way or another in the UFW's 1973 grape boycott. Sonny Mares and his best friend, Art Bello, who were also Luisa's fellow poets, went a step further. They made the 1973 strike their exclusive personal and political commitment. Was Sonny watching this film before he killed himself? I couldn't figure out what, if anything, this film had to do with Sonny's death on Friday, October 13, 1989, sixteen years after the UFW's grape boycott. I decided, nonetheless, to watch the rest of the video tape.

As I hit the play button again, the filmmaker shifted perspectives. Since his field of vision was wider and unencumbered, I surmised that he was filming from a higher structure, perhaps from the roof of a van or a camper. The camera focused on a number of helmeted cops bearing the insignia of the Kern County Sheriff's Office on their sleeves. They were peacefully arresting striking farm workers and putting them into large buses to transport them to the county jail. But a minute later the scene drastically changed. The same sheriffs were suddenly macing and dragging, beating and choking

Mexican American men and women with their sticks while they battered the farm workers' spirits with a barrage of dirty slogans. "Beaners, Frito-banditos, greasers" were among the least vicious.

As if they had been thrown personally at me, the racial slurs thundered in my ears and pierced my heart. A visceral anger rose slowly from deep within me and hit the walls of my throat. I hadn't felt such impotent rage since the 1970 Los Angeles National Chicano Moratorium march and riot, when the police had attacked us as we peacefully assembled. "Stop! Stop!" I heard myself cry out, softly at first, then louder. "You're killing them!" I yelled as I had done back in 1973, when Luisa, Darío, and I had witnessed first hand the deputies' brutality.

I sat on Sonny's reading chair and for a few seconds relived that sweltering summer day when all of us marched behind the coffin of a field laborer brutally beaten and dragged, then left to die in a ditch by Kern County Sheriff's deputies. Before that summer of 1973 came to an end, a second farm worker died. Many others were seriously injured by either teamsters or deputies. A Mexican American family's home went up in flames. And thousands of farm workers ended up in jail.

A sudden change of scene in the film caught my attention again and brought me back to the present. I wiped my tears as I wondered who had filmed or edited this documentary—if that's what it was. What was his intention in patching together all this material with no narration to help the viewer along? As I watched the perspective shift again, it occurred to me that this film might be only a personal document. Was it Sonny's personal record of past struggles and glories?

The camera's eye was now sliding over vineyards and fields. It finally locked on the graceful flight of a seemingly large bird. An eagle, I thought, or a hawk. Given the field of vision and the angle, the camera had to be on the roof of either a building or some other tall structure.

In the distance, three people—one of them a woman, I guessed—seemed also to follow the bird's flight down to the pole of a high-wired fence. As the camera closed in, I realized the bird was one of three turkey vultures. "Unusual," I reflected as I realized I had never given any thought to vultures and had no idea if it was natural to find them at that particular place. The other two buzzards perched on top of a big cylindrical container stamped with a large decal of a skull and crossbones inside a fiery red diamond. Since it was a table-grape farm, I surmised the tank contained a pesticide or some other deadly inert agent. I watched the vultures spread their wings to take in life-giving sunlight before devouring something behind the tank. "How chillingly fitting. Death's inert agent and its beneficiaries, side by side," I said as my mind grasped the filmmaker's intention. Through his vision, my eyes also lingered over the gruesome scene.

Seeing the vultures keep vigil, the cameraman must have reached the same conclusion I just had, for he kept scanning the area. Through his eyes, mine were ever observant of the slightest shadow or the smallest mass. The three people who had seen the bird fly had had the same idea and also seemed to be heading for the tank. Whatever the buzzards watched lay hidden behind something the camera couldn't peek through.

A large shadow was reflected on the ground, cast by someone just outside the narrow field of vision of the close-up lens, and the filmmaker followed it up to a large man walking away wearing levis, a plaid long-sleeved shirt, boots, and his long hair loose under a big Indian hat. The man turned briefly to look over his shoulder toward the tank and the vultures, then stepped up his pace to a trot as if someone pursued him.

The camera retraced the man's steps back to the tank to find the pursuer, but no one was following him.

The three vultures perched on the hazardous tank, still in dead calm. In some bizarre way, the filmmaker and I found solace in the peacefulness of the scene, in the split second of truce between life and death. But not for long.

The explosion of the tank was so unexpected that the camera jumped as high as my stomach and heart, and the hand holding it quivered for a few seconds before regaining control. For the first time, I heard the filmmaker speak. Although I had expected to hear Sonny's voice, instead I heard Art Bello say, "He did it! That S.O.B. did it!" I could hear the tremor of fear and excitement in his voice while his eyes and mine watched the burning, which neither the tank nor death's winged beneficiaries survived.

# Two
## Fields of Desire

It was rather warm inside Sonny's apartment, but my hands felt cold and cramped. Surely my reaction was the effect of the emotions triggered by Sonny's death and Art Bello's film. I had the feeling, nonetheless, that something else was at work in me. A bittersweet desire pulled at my heart and mind. I realized that in the span of Art's film I had grown politically nostalgic. I knew I was wallowing in wistfulness, wishing that things were the way they used to be in the late sixties and early seventies.

Intellectually, I realized it was foolish to long for the most oppressive and repressive times we, as Chicanos, had experienced. But I had the feeling I didn't miss the activism as much as the innocence that had underscored our political zeal and the newness of our commitment. I connected our harrowing experience—the violent repressive actions of the police against us at the 1970 National Chicano Moratorium march in East Los Angeles and during the 1973 United Farm Workers' strike and grape boycott—with the loss of that innocence.

Sunlight streamed into Sonny's living room through the large window. Drawn to it as to a lit fireplace in winter, I moved towards the window and leaned on it for an instant. Then, stepping back from the window, I looked through the glass at the inside patio and chalk garden surrounded by a tall picket fence. I gazed upon Black Sophie, Sonny's cat, sitting on her hind legs next to the gate. She was very still but seemed to be looking intently at a place on top of the fence. I raised my eyes and glimpsed something brown—perhaps a bird or the tail of another cat—drop behind the pickets and disappear.

I closed my eyes and saw the fangs of the rattler in my vision coming at me. The image seemed so real that it made me shiver. My nape felt hot, as if a feverish hand were resting on it. Cold sweat trickled down my back. I shuddered again and opened my eyes. Without knowing why, I turned around, expecting to find someone behind me. No one was there. I fought the temptation to curse every one of my ancestors from whom I could have inherited my clairvoyance—my dark gift, as I called it.

Knowing that the only way to remain sane was to keep focused, I headed towards the sleeping area as Justin and Leo were walking into the flat. On their way to the working area, they glanced in my direction but didn't indicate they wanted me to join them. So, I went into Sonny's bedroom as planned. A while later I heard the voices of the teamsters. Leo and Justin were viewing Art Bello's documentary film.

Looking at Sonny's bed, I noticed that all the covers had been pulled down and lay piled in disarray on the floor. I assumed Sonny had been found lying there, on the right side, as the impression of his body on the bottom sheet indicated. The depression on the pillow where he had laid his head was still visible. Approximately ten inches below the pillow, on the left at about the level of Sonny's chest, were two hardly notice-able small cuts. The sheet was an old one and showed a few other signs of wear here and there. But the two tiny slits that had caught my attention looked like incisions made by slim, sharp blades; they had clean, unfrayed edges. On closer scrutiny, I saw that the incisions cut deeply into the mattress.

Scissors, I thought. "Sharp, slim scissors," I said aloud, then noticed the smear of purple—possibly lipstick—around the edge of the upper cut. "A woman," I murmured to myself.

A glimmer of a recollection began to form in my memory. It quickly passed, but I couldn't dismiss the feeling it left behind—the certainty that I had heard or read about someone stabbing a bed with a pair of scissors. Not just someone, but a woman. "A woman would use scissors instead of a knife," I said, thinking aloud. "Scissors. Scissors," I kept repeating the word, as if by incantation I could conjure up the memory. But it eluded me.

I turned my attention to a couple of dried wet spots. They looked quite recent. They glared at me, confirming my suspicion that a woman had laid with Sonny in the not-so-distant past. His sex partner had bled or was either beginning or ending her menstrual period, as the spots had tinges of fading crimson on them.

Grief is a strange companion, especially for the suicide who has already begun to mourn himself while alive. Still, would a man who is contemplating suicide have lovemaking on his mind? It was somewhat unusual but plausible, I thought as I remembered my overwhelming desire to have sex with Darío the day of my father's wake. Perhaps it was my need to be comforted, to quiet my own fear of dying, or simply—like a drink to the alcoholic—the way into oblivion.

Which of those was Sonny's reason? "No way to know for sure," I said under my breath. Still, I felt I had stumbled upon something significant, as important as the explosion scene on the film. The way all these minor but bizarre details and events fit together wasn't obvious to me yet, but they mapped Sonny's last hours among the living. On the other hand, I reminded myself, they could be just a number of coincidences. The police seemed to believe they were just that, but I doubted these seemingly insignificant facts were a mere accident.

Perhaps my grandmother, Mami Julia, had been right when she said that there were no coincidences in life. Unless we thwarted fate's efforts with our willfulness, she often told me, meeting certain people was predestined, the course of major events in our lives already charted. As I walked around to the night table on the other side of the bed, one thing seemed certain: that coincidences ceased to be a series of random events when an intelligence made sense of them. I had always wanted to be that intelligence. I still do, I said to myself as I peeked in the drawer looking for a pair of scissors and closing it when I saw none. Instead, I noticed a relatively recent water stain on the night table which, by its size, might have been made by a tumbler. Since the glass wasn't there, I assumed Officer Holstein had taken it.

Fifteen minutes after Justin and Leo had gone into Sonny's studio, I saw them come out and head towards the kitchen. I followed them. Justin was carrying a large plastic bag with the video cassette in it. Leo opened the refrigerator and took out a bowl full of dark purple table grapes—the kind that Mami Julia used to call "black beauties."

"You see?" Leo commented to Justin, who gave him a knowing look. "What would Sonny be doing with grapes?" Without waiting for an answer, he added, closing his hands and pointing at himself with both thumbs the way Sonny used to when he talked "heavy" Chicano. "*No, cabrón*. Don't even think about it. Me and Art are probably the only *carnales* who have honored every grape boycott called by César." Leo chuckled, caught for an instant in the memory.

"Yeah. That's what Sonny'd say, *ese carnal*," Justin said, smiling. He had referred to Sonny as *carnal*—blood brother—although I knew he and Sonny hadn't been very close. Justin was lost in thought for an instant, then commented, "You're right. Sonny wouldn't have bought grapes, not even organic."

"That's right," Leo said.

"Someone must have given him the grapes then," I said to myself. "Someone Sonny wouldn't beat to a pulp for doing so." I peeked at the grapes in the bowl, which Leo was still holding. But I noticed nothing strange. Then I smelled them. "Maybe they were given to him by someone who intended to kill him. But why didn't she remove the grapes when she left?" At that point, it occurred to me that the scissors I was looking for could be kitchen shears, and I began to look in the drawers.

"Why do you say it was a woman who gave Sonny the grapes?" Leo asked, moving towards me.

His question took me by surprise. "Did I say that?"

Both men answered, "Uh-huh."

Smiling but feeling embarrassed, I explained, "There are wet spots and a tiny lipstick smear on the sheet." When I heard nothing from them, I continued. "They look recent. I'm assuming a woman was here as recently as last night or this morning. She could have brought him the grapes."

Leo patted Justin on the shoulder and, pointing in my direction with his thumb, said, "She's good! But let's see how she does under pressure, gifted or not." Justin managed to smile, though he seemed mortified. He put the bowl of grapes back in the refrigerator and headed out towards the workshop area.

I felt upset and swallowed air to keep myself from saying something I might regret later. Leo's attitude annoyed me, but I tried to remain calm. "I assume I didn't tell you anything you and Justin didn't already know," I said to Leo, who gave my comment an assenting nod. "Then you know about the two incisions in the sheet. Do you know if Officer Holstein took the object that was used to make them?"

"No. I don't think anyone gave those two marks a second thought, except you," Leo explained, adding, "and Justin and me."

Since I hadn't seen Justin go into the bedroom, I surmised that Leo had briefed his friend while they talked outside. Judging by Leo's complimentary comment on my skills

and my "gift," I assumed they had talked about me. Not wanting to waste time on speculation, I quickly turned my attention back to Leo.

"I'm not sure myself they are important," the policeman
said. "What do *you* think made them?" he inquired, obviously
referring to the two incisions in the mattress.

"Scissors or shears," I replied, then continued looking in
kitchen drawers for such objects.

"Take a look at these," Justin asked, walking towards us
holding between index finger and thumb a pair of long, slim
scissors. A piece of paper hung from one of the blades. Leo and
I walked over and looked at them. "What do you make of this
note?"

The paper had been torn badly in two. The left half was
missing. A comma and the word "ALWAYS" were written with
an opaque and rather fading purple lipstick on the right half.

"Could be a love message, an old one, judging by the yel-
lowing edges." Both Leo and Justin agreed. "So, we know a
woman was here. She was wearing dark purple lipstick, but...
but why aren't there any more lipstick smears on the sheet or
pillow?" Justin completed my question, then added, "Maybe
the message was written first, pierced through with the scissors."

"Could the note and blades then have been driven into the
mattress?" I wondered.

"Perhaps," Justin responded as he put the message and
scissors in a small paper bag, then inside a larger, reclosable
plastic bag where he had put the video cassette.

We began to walk in the direction of the front door, but I
stopped midway, unable to contain my curiosity any longer. I
turned to Leo first, then to Justin. "Am I to understand you
two are now assuming that Sonny didn't commit suicide?" I
asked.

"No," Leo, who had been very quiet, said. "Only that we have a few loose ends. Too many unanswered questions. Until we, or rather, you two find reasonable explanations for these discrepancies, I can't be satisfied with the OPD's ruling of Sonny's death as suicide."

At that moment I surmised that Leo had asked Justin to look into Sonny's apparent suicide. I looked for Justin's eyes to confirm my assumption. He did.

I also realized Leo had taken for granted that I truly was Justin's associate. I assumed Justin had failed to mention that I had only recently decided to begin my apprenticeship with him to qualify for a private-investigator's license. I was still far from truly being his associate.

"Was there a suicide note?" Justin asked, then briefly looked at me. Leo shook his head.

"Isn't that unusual?" I asked.

"Not really. Not all suicides leave notes. Still..." Leo breathed in and exhaled noisily, then completed the sentence. "Can you imagine a poet not having anything to say about taking his own life?" Leo looked at Justin, then at me. "Can you picture Sonny not having the last word?" The three of us shared a chuckle and a moment of relief.

Leo went around making sure windows and doors were locked. Justin began to rub his nose forcefully. In his case, his gesture indicated the onset of an allergic reaction. When I saw Black Sophie lying on Sonny's bed, I remembered that Justin was allergic to cat hair. Justin took out his handkerchief and covered his nose with it, holding back the sneeze flaring up in his nostrils. Then he turned his attention to Leo, who was looking at Black Sophie.

Leo swallowed hard as Sophie came near him. He caressed her back. Sophie purred. "*Ay, gatita,*" he said. "If only you could talk, you could tell me what *mi carnal* was afraid of these last few days."

Justin and I looked at each other.

"What's all this about Sonny being afraid?" Justin inquired.

"You know Sonny. He got weird when he drank." Leo spoke slowly. "He called me two days ago saying that some dark force was at work around him, that he had found strange things outside the door."

"What kinds of things?" I asked.

"Oh, he found a long strip of skin tied around a bunch of weeds." Leo rubbed his forehead. "Some nonsense like that. I told him maybe Sophie had brought it to him. You know how cats are." He picked up Sophie and said to her, "*Vámonos, bonita.* I'll take you home with me."

"What kind of skin was it?" I asked.

"The kind of skin that snakes slough off in the summer," Leo elaborated. My heart raced as I recalled the rattler in my dream the night before. "I realize," Leo continued, "that I should have paid more attention, but it's...too late...now."

I closed my eyes and saw the images of the woman tied to the cactus and the waning amber moon. Then, a shadowy figure bowed and rose. What, if anything, did it all mean? Who was the crucified woman? What was her connection with Sonny Mares?

I sensed the warmth of Justin's hand near my face. With my eyes still closed, I perceived its presence as a softly glowing, soothing, blue energy. I opened my eyes. His hand was no longer near my cheek, but his eyes observed me closely. I expected him to say something, but he didn't. Instead, he followed Leo out of the bedroom and into the kitchen. He came out a minute later with the bowl of grapes. "I'll take the grapes to Bob Messinger's lab. It won't hurt to have them tested," Justin said to Leo. I knew that Bob Messinger was the lab technician who had worked on forensic evidence at OPD for a long time. Upon retiring, he had opened his own lab.

As the three of us moved towards the front door, Leo
stopped at a table by the entrance and picked up his hat. Outside, concerned with the painful duty of telling family and
friends about Sonny's death, Leo said, "This is going to be so
hard on my mom and my sisters, especially Rosa..."

As if he had suddenly wanted to tell Justin something
important, Leo asked, "Have you seen Art?" Without waiting
for an answer, he continued, "I called him earlier, but he was-
n't home or at the college. And, of course, I didn't want to
leave...this kind of message."

"I also tried calling Art from the van as soon as you told
me about Sonny. But I didn't reach him either. I haven't seen
him for a couple of days," Justin explained. "Don't worry," he
reassured Leo when he saw his friend's frowning countenance.
"I'll tell Art about Sonny." He patted the policeman's shoulder.
"Call anytime, you hear?"

*"Gracias, carnal."* Leo waved and got in his car. I did not
envy either man his painful task.

As soon as we left Sonny's place, Justin tried Art Bello's
number. The answering machine was on. "He's probably away
somewhere, writing." He tried to sound casual, but the tremor
in his voice betrayed his apprehension. His usually bright,
almond-shaped eyes seemed smaller and lusterless now as he
stared at some fixed spot in front of him. I realized then how
much Art's unavailability distressed Justin. I became worried,
too, and found myself also needing reassurance.

Justin's way of working out a problem was to take photos
or work in his darkroom, or carve wood while he listened to
Latin rhythms, blues, or jazz. Seeing him so concerned about
Art's disappearance and Sonny's death, I tried to lighten his
load—and mine. I asked jokingly, "Can I get you anything? A
Sarah Vaughan or Tito Puente CD? A broken chair? An unde-
veloped roll of film?"

He chuckled, and, for an instant, his face lit up. Then we both became quiet again. "I can't postpone my trip to Sacramento any longer," Justin said. "If I do, I'll lose that client. So I'm going to spend the day there tomorrow. But," he continued, "could you call Myra Miranda or anyone else you think might know where Art is? Be discreet," Justin cautioned as he parked behind my car. "We don't want to alarm anyone."

As I drove home, I realized I hadn't talked to Myra in at least eight months. A Chicana poet and a friend of Art's and arch-enemy of Sonny's, Myra was the main editor at Women of Color Press, a publishing house owned by a women's collective. They had published two of Luisa's poetry books. Since Luisa had named me her literary executor, Myra had phoned shortly after Luisa was murdered to ask if I would consider submitting some of Luisa's poetry for publication. Her request included a manuscript my friend had compiled and edited, *The Chicana Experience,* which contained Luisa's interviews of Chicanas who had been involved in the political movement of the sixties and seventies.

A few weeks after Luisa's funeral, I had started sorting through her literary papers, but it had become such a painful task that I had postponed the job for a later time. As soon as Justin asked me to call Myra, I knew that she would again press me about Luisa's manuscripts. I immediately decided to resume my work on them. That way, the manuscripts would also provide me with a good excuse to call Myra. I would then not have to explain about Art's possible disappearance or the circumstances surrounding Sonny's death.

Although we had never become close friends, I had seen Myra off and on during the past fifteen years at poetry readings and other cultural events. Like Art, Sonny, and Luisa, Myra was also a poet; they were all good friends. All of us had participated in one capacity or another in marches and fundraising events to collect money for the farm workers' effort.

Although I had never felt very close to Sonny or Myra, I had always preferred her company to his any time. But from the very beginning I had liked Art very much and had felt very close to him. While Justin and Leo attended the police academy, Leo had introduced Justin to Art, and the two of them had become good friends almost instantly.

Afraid that I would start wallowing in nostalgia again, I tried to concentrate on other things. But despite my efforts, memory was flowing and for an instant I was back in the Napa Valley on that misty winter night when Luisa Cortez had pushed me out of the way and had been hit by the bullet meant for me.

For weeks after she died, I had many death dreams, for I felt as if I had killed my friend. Myra and Art tried to tell me it wasn't so. How could I feel guilty if I hadn't pulled the trigger? But it wasn't so simple, for I would always feel I owed Luisa my life, and there wasn't a chance in heaven or hell that I could ever repay my debt to her. But perhaps, I thought, I could at least begin my reconciliation with my own conscience. I hurried home.

# Three
## *Open Season on Poets*

I could not see her face, but I could hear her voice, slightly accented in Spanish and breathy. "Into the darkness," the woman in my dream was saying, repeating louder each time, "Always, always, always." An instant later she stepped out of the darkness and came closer to me. The voice belonged to an oval, dark face with glossy dark brown eyes and a head of curls. Holding a pair of shears, her hand had risen then struck down, piercing the pillow where my head lay. I turned quickly to the side, trying to avoid being injured. Suddenly, the woman and her shears were gone.

I opened my eyes. Looking at the blue, gray, and pale coral on the eastern horizon, brightly punctuated by the morning star, I gathered that the day was dawning.

Lying in bed, I was sure that this dream and the one from the night before last were not just two more death dreams. I'd had plenty of those nightmares after Darío and Luisa died, but after a while, I'd stopped having them. Only recently had I begun to foresee in my dream the woman tied to a cactus cross.

I was twenty-three when I'd first discovered I had an extrasensory awareness—my dark gift. Since then, I had known that I had no more control over its rhythms than I had over my heart's beating. Nonetheless, I had relentlessly fought not to have my reason clouded by this prescience in me. But I also realized that regardless of how I felt about my heightened perception, once the dreams and visions came I would be committed—like an unskilled cryptographer—to extract meaning from them and to act on the knowledge.

I thought about each of the women in my two dreams. The woman tied to a cactus and this shear-brandishing woman were not the same person. Of that I was certain. But the accent and the breathiness of this second woman's voice, her hair and face, were somewhat familiar. Was she the woman who had been with Sonny the day he died? I wondered. And what about Myra Miranda? Had Sonny finally been able to drive her over the edge? She and Sonny had started as the greatest of friends, then had become the most bitter of enemies.

Back in the mid-seventies when I'd first met them, Myra, Sonny, and Art had started a review to publish Chicano and Chicana narrative and poetry. But Myra and Sonny frequently found themselves at odds with each other about the review. Over the years, Art Bello had often mediated between Myra and Sonny, usually taking her side. As a consequence, she had remained Art's most loyal and steadfast friend. One day, tired of fighting what she considered a losing battle, Myra left the magazine and joined the collective that produced Women of Color Press. A year later, she had become their managing editor.

Myra had told Luisa and me about the time Sonny had gone to see her. Drunk and belligerent, he had tried to seduce her, thinking that Myra would go back to work for him once they'd had sex. Pushing him back, she had rejected his advances. Furious, he had raised his hand to strike her, then backed off, storming out of the room instead. She expected an apology. He never offer one. At a public function a few months after their violent encounter, Myra and Sonny spoke for a few minutes. They seemed to be cordial and pleasant with each other. Then, suddenly, Sonny tried to grab her arm. Whether by accident or on purpose, Myra spilled the wine in her glass all over him. Their cold war began the day after and lasted through the next ten years.

Could *she* have been the woman who was with Sonny before he died? The idea seemed preposterous, but I knew I would probe until I was certain she was not.

I was just getting out of the shower when the phone rang. To my great surprise, Myra Miranda was on the line.

"Lucky coincidence," I said to her. "I was getting ready to call you." Apologetically, I quickly added, "I'm sorry I haven't called you back about Luisa's work, but I've been working on it and I'll have something for you next week for sure."

Myra hardly acknowledged my apology; she had something else in mind. "I heard Sonny died, but I have to tell you, Gloria, I just can't believe he killed himself."

"I know," I answered. "All of us are having a hard time believing it, too, but it might..."

"No buts," she said adamantly, "I hated that *vato,* but I know he would *never* kill himself." She paused then added, "He wouldn't—I just don't believe..." This time, her words trailed then broke off.

"What makes you so sure of that, Myra?"

"I couldn't sleep last night thinking about all this, and suddenly I was afraid, Gloria. In less than a year we have lost Luisa and Sonny. The circumstances were different, it's true, but..." Myra exhaled. Her otherwise throaty voice thinned out.

Her remark reminded me of Sonny's comment to Leo that a dark force was at work around him. Still, I quickly dismissed Myra's pronouncement as nothing more than a normal reaction to the death of someone close. By personal experience, I knew full well how displaced grief made unrelated incidents seem part of some sort of conspiracy to punish us for some unidentifiable transgression. "It would seem that way, but you know it isn't," I reassured her.

Ignoring my last comment, Myra began to talk about Sonny and about their bitter and complicated relationship. "I suppose I've always been angry at *him* for disappointing me. I expected so much more of him because, you see, I knew that other Sonny, long ago. The one I loved deeply was a generous man who sold his car and everything else of value to contribute to the bail fund for farm workers arrested during the grape strikes...That Sonny made his child-support payments, even though the child wasn't even his," she confided, her voice rising in intensity as she went on. "I loved the man who fought for everything we Chicanos...," she muttered, swallowing the last word. Then taking a deep breath, she raced on. "I loved the Sonny who launched the careers of so many Chicano poets, poets who never even thanked him, who probably won't even show up at his funeral." Myra had begun to mourn the enemy she had loved most.

"Not an easy man to love," I offered. Myra said nothing at the other end. "When was the last time you saw Sonny?" I prodded her.

"Eight months ago, at the *Floricanto*," she answered, alluding to the poetry and music festival organized in Luisa's memory by Sonny and Art. "It was a beautiful memorial reading, and so appropriate that Luisa be remembered that way. She was so giving," Myra reflected.

"Yes," I agreed. "It was a lovely way to remember Luisa." After a short pause, trying to concentrate on the business at hand, I asked Myra, "Had Sonny been seeing anyone special lately? Anyone on a regular basis?"

Not answering immediately, she finally responded with two questions of her own. "Why are you so interested in Sonny's affairs, Gloria? What's going on?"

"Because, like you, I want to find out why Sonny killed himself," I replied right away, knowing that it was the only honest answer I could offer without betraying Leo's or Justin's confidence in me.

"I see. You think he would kill himself for a woman," she remarked. "I don't think so. He would not kill himself for any

woman, not even for Diane." She paused briefly, then continued. "Though I must say that he did keep a low profile since
Diane left." Myra suddenly sounded very tired. "Art could
probably tell you more than I can," she suggested.

"Have you seen him lately?"

"Not in the last few days," Myra answered. "He's probably
gone away. He told me he still had to rewrite several of the
poems that he wanted to include in his manuscript," she
offered.

"Did he tell you he was going away?"

"No, not really. But I do know that his manuscript is due
at his publisher's soon."

"Any idea where he might have gone?" I asked, then
added, "I don't think he knows about Sonny."

"Oh, my God!" Myra exclaimed. "You don't think something happened to Art, do you?" she asked anxiously.

"I don't know. Why do you say that?"

"I'm not sure. It's just that you're the second person who's
asked me if I know where Art is." She added quickly, "Why
are so many people looking for him? What's happened to
him?"

"Who else asked you about Art?"

"A woman," she replied. "She said she was a friend of
Art's."

"Did she give you her name?"

"Yes. She identified herself as Carlota Navarro. To tell
you the truth, I just didn't give much importance to her call.
She said we had met at Luisa's funeral..."

"Why would she be looking for Art now?"

"I really don't know," Myra replied. "Will you let me know
when you and Justin do find Art?"

"You'll be the first to know."

"Thanks." Myra then added, "Don't forget to look for
Luisa's poems and for the manuscript on 'The Chicana Experi-

ence.'" She sounded a bit more animated. "We're serious about
publishing her work and her interviews of Chicanas."

"I won't," I promised. "I'll have something for you next
week."

After spending the rest of the morning trying to locate
Art's whereabouts, I prepared a light meal to have with Tania
later. Then I went into my late husband's office, which was
now my study. For the next four hours I reviewed the interviews that Luisa had intended to publish as a collection.

I looked out the window at the MacArthur Freeway
packed with cars and remembered it was Saturday, October
14, the day of the first "Battle of the Bay" World Series game.
The memory of Darío and Tania, our eight-year-old daughter,
wearing their A's caps as they headed towards the Coliseum
for her first baseball game rushed through my mind. I sighed
as I wondered if nostalgia was, in the end, nothing more than
a paler shade of mourning.

A creaking noise behind me brought me out of my reverie.
I knew in an instant that Tania was trying to surprise me
when she entered the house. Instead, she was startled when I
greeted her without even turning to see who was behind me. A
premed student at Cal Berkeley, she lived near the campus
and usually came to see me on Sunday afternoons. Or she
brought my mother with her for dinner on Tuesday evenings.
This being a Saturday, she had assumed I would not be
expecting her.

Hugging her, I pushed her gently by the shoulders
towards the kitchen. Opening the refrigerator door, I showed
her a bowl of guacamole, another of salad, and a six-pack of
cherry-flavored mineral water. When she saw her favorite
vegetarian pizza, with onions, jalapeño, Jack and goat
cheeses, sun-dried tomatoes, and walnuts, ready to be popped
in the oven, her eyes lit up.

"Oh, Mom, I can never surprise you. How did you know I was coming? ESP?" she asked, jokingly. I grinned, so Tania asked again, "Was it really ESP?"

"Tch. Good old mother's intuition," I teased. "I don't need ESP to know you miss your daddy very much." I laughed at the expression on her face. "I knew you would come to watch the first of the A's-Giants game here, so you could feel close to him." I tapped her pointed nose with my index finger and brushed a few wavy strands of hair away from her face. There were four things Tania had inherited from her father and her grandfather, Blás Damasco—their nose and light-brown, wavy hair, their love for medicine, and their passion for the Oakland A's.

"I do miss him very much," she said, and bent down so she could lay her head on my shoulder. At five feet five inches, my daughter was an inch taller than me.

"So do I, hon. I miss him, too," I said and passed my arm around her waist. "Hungry?" I asked, and she nodded. "Go ahead and turn on the TV," I suggested as I slipped the pizza into the oven and set the timer. "It should be ready in about forty-five minutes," I said, heading back to the study where I had been since lunch time trying to organize Luisa's papers. "I'll join you when the game begins."

"You're not going to stay and talk with me?" Tania complained.

"I'm sorry," I apologized. "But I don't want to watch any of the previews. I'll watch the game with you, though."

"I'm not interested in all that brouhaha either. I want to spend a little time with you," Tania explained.

"All right. Then let's go into your daddy's office and we can talk while I look for some material I need. As a matter of fact, you might be able to help me." I headed towards the study and Tania followed.

Tania picked up and began to read the transcribed text of Delia Treviño's interview. Delia was a Chicana poet and Luisa's friend; she was also one of the women included in Luisa's collection, "The Chicana Experience."

I had only one more interview to listen to. Looking at my notes on the other woman's interview, I realized it had been the first text I had heard, about a month after Luisa's death. Aware at the time that I was really in no emotional condition to make the editorial decisions that had to be made, I had abandoned the project. I couldn't recall what this particular text was about. All I remembered was the overwhelming sadness I felt as I listened to the woman's story. Now, I was beginning to feel emotionally taxed, and I cringed at the prospect of feeling that kind of sorrow once again.

"Would you mind listening to this last interview?" I requested. Tania looked up and agreed with a gesture. "You'll have to check the transcription as you listen to make sure they correspond. What Luisa wanted was to document the Chicano Civil Rights Movement, but from the perspective of Chicanas," I explained. "I'm not sure," I continued, "that this interview you're going to hear fits in."

Putting down the text of the interview she'd been reading, Tania said, "You should write about your experiences, too, Mom. Sometimes I think younger Chicanas and other women don't give you and the Chicanas your age any credit for what you did. They think that you sold out, that you only did what the men told you, and that you were not feminist enough." Tania was beginning to get excited.

"Do they? That's too bad." Over the years, Luisa and I had heard every complaint about those of us—we—who called ourselves Chicanas for the first time back in the sixties. At one time, those comments had distressed me, but they no longer fazed me. So, I suggested to my daughter we get back to the task at hand.

Before handing Tania the cassette player and the text, I checked the transcription for a name. I found only the initials C.N. My daughter sat back to listen while I looked for Luisa's address books to find the name corresponding to those initials. Despite my reluctance, I found myself interested in the woman's story, and soon, I, too, began to listen.

What first caught my attention was the engaging manner in which the woman told her story. She spoke in complete sentences, with none of the usual "You knows" or similar phrases the other women interviewed had used to give themselves time to censor what they were about to say. The first time I'd heard her story, I remembered having the impression that she was reading a text rather than simply talking about her experience. Or perhaps she was recounting a text she had memorized. I also noticed the unusually long pause in the middle of some words, as if the thought was suspended but reconnected a moment later without missing a sound. During the many years I worked as a professional speech specialist, I'd heard speech disorders like that when I'd worked with people who suffered from either *petit mal* seizures or a semi-aphasic neurological condition. There was also something else, something very familiar in the quality of her voice.

I asked Tania to turn up the volume. For the next twenty minutes my daughter and I sat next to the recorder, mesmerized by the woman's account of her harrowing journey from her hometown in Mexico to California.

When it was over, Tania turned off the tape recorder and pressed the eject button but didn't remove the tape. "This is so sad, Mom," Tania remarked, wiping away a tear and reaching for a tissue to blow her nose did the same.

"Would you check the tape to see if there's a name written anywhere?" I asked Tania.

"Only the initials C.N.," Tania replied. I picked up Luisa's address book and resumed my search for the woman's name.

"Carlota Navarro, 2911 Mariposa, Kingsburg, California. This is the woman!" I exclaimed as I recalled my earlier conversation with Myra and the pair of eyes staring at me from the memory of my dream the night before. "I am almost positive now."

"What's the matter, Mom?" When I didn't answer right away, Tania inquired again. "Mom, what's wrong?"

"Nothing wrong, hon," I explained. "I just found another—maybe the most important—piece of a puzzle."

"I see," Tania interjected. "You've been having visions again." I could sense her concern when she asked me, "Does it have anything to do with the case you and Justin are working on?" She reached for her baseball hat and her mitt and bat.

"It would seem that way," I answered, trying to tell myself that I shouldn't be so sure my theory was right until I went out and got the evidence to support it. "I still have to prove it though. I have to make sure I'm not just fooling myself. It's the only way I can keep my sanity." I smiled at her. She smiled back. "Would you mind checking on the pizza?" I asked, and she nodded. "I'll join you as soon as I find a box big enough for these two manuscripts." Tania walked back to the kitchen, taking with her all her baseball memorabilia, including the bat.

Ten minutes later, I walked back into the kitchen where my daughter was swinging at an imaginary ball as she listened to Luis Miguel, her favorite Mexican pop crooner, on the radio.

Casually, she turned to me and said, "Mom, you should get a gun and learn how to use it."

As we sat down to eat, I looked at her, open-mouthed.

Seeing the expression on my face, Tania added in a soft voice, "I worry about you. If you're going to be a private investigator, you should know how to defend yourself." She paused, then said, "You're not the only one who has nightmares. I do, too, about you." Her eyes showed quite a bit of concern.

"Is that what you wanted to talk to me about?" I asked her.

"Uh-huh." She sighed.

"Oh, hon. I'm sorry I've caused you any worry," I said. "I'm not going to die, I promise." I tried to reassure her. "I'm not even sure I want to become a professional P.I. yet."

"But, Mom," Tania rebutted, "that's not what I mean. I don't want you to quit doing what you love to do. I know Daddy made you stop your investigation after that little boy was killed in East L.A.," she said, referring to the first case I had ever been involved in, back in 1970.

"Who told you that?"

"Dad did."

"When did he tell you that?"

"When you were ill with pneumonia three years ago. He told me that the last time you'd been that sick was when that L.A. policeman, Matthew Kenyon, died. He also told me that during that time you and Kenyon and Luisa were looking into little Michael's murder. I think Dad was jealous of that policeman Kenyon," she added.

"Did he tell you that also?"

"Well, he didn't say he was jealous, but he said he had never been able to share with you your love for detective work. And Matthew Kenyon had. He also said he'd regretted many times forcing you to stop your investigation because he had caused you all this pain and had made you very unhappy."

"No, hon," I tried to clarify, "no one forced me. It was entirely my decision."

"I don't want you to be unhappy, Mom. I just want you to be able to defend yourself."

"I promise I'll learn to defend myself—with a gun, if it comes to that," I told her, and put the matter to rest. We fin-

ished our meal. While I loaded the dishwasher, Tania went to
the living room and turned the TV on as a sportscaster
echoed, with a jubilant voice, the umpire's "Let's play ball."

I was getting ready to join her in the living room when
the phone rang. Upon answering, I immediately recognized
Justin's hello and asked, "Are you still in Sacramento?"

"I'm on my way back to the Bay Area," he said.

"Have you heard from Art?" I inquired.

"No. It seems quite a few people have been looking for
him."

I quickly related my conversation with Myra and my felicitous discovery of Carlota Navarro's identity.

"This Carlota called me also," Justin said. "She was looking for Art and left a message with my answering service.
When I called the number she'd left, a man there told me the
woman had gone back to the San Joaquín Valley, where she's
from." Justin mumbled something else I couldn't understand,
but before I had a chance to ask him to repeat it, he added,
"You can tell me all about her tonight." He seemed suddenly
pressed. "I've gotta go. Traffic's getting heavier, and people
are driving crazier than ever," he explained. Then he added,
"By the way, I'd like you to go with me to Art's apartment
tonight. That is, if I can get Sarah, his landlady, to open up for
us. About nine?"

"Come by my house at eight-thirty. I've got something I'd
like you to hear before we go to Art's house."

"All right. Eight-thirty then."

# Four
## Moons and Rivers Ago

Justin showed up promptly at eight-thirty, just as Tania was leaving. He asked her for the score at the door. "Five to zero," she informed him, then complained, "It was actually a boring game. The Giants didn't stand a chance; Stew mowed them down," she remarked, referring to A's pitcher Dave Stewart, who struck out every Giants batter. He smiled at my daughter's obvious admiration for the pitcher. Justin and I waved at her from the door as she drove away.

I had already set the stereo tape deck in my living room with Carlota Navarro's recording. Justin sat on the love seat and I took the easy chair next to the stereo. First, we heard Luisa's voice explaining that the woman she was interviewing did not want to be asked any questions. She preferred to simply tell the story of why and how she had emigrated to the U.S. from her hometown in Michoacán, México, and her experiences in California. Static followed the noise of someone clearing her throat.

Out of the corner of my eye, I caught Justin checking the time. I assured him that the narration wasn't going to take long if we listened without interruptions. We would still be able to make it to Art's apartment on time.

"It must have been about six in the evening," Carlota began to say. "But it was still so hot in-(...)-side the car trunk, that every mouthful of air I inhaled felt like an exhalation from the Devil's breath. Pushing back the tears, I tried to think of the Media Luna River running near our village in Mexico. I remembered the weeping willows, bordering the river and dancing in the moonlight like gigantic grass skirts.

My friend Chuchita and I used to help our mothers do the wash at the Media Luna, then bathe and play in the cool water before we went back to our school for storytelling and *labores domésticas*—needlework.

"Inside Dr. Mark Stephen's car trunk, not knowing which was worse, dying or being caught by *la migra* and sent back to Mexico, all I could recall was the suffocating heat of dog days, of that afternoon my parents were crushed by a truck on the road back from Morelia, of how I couldn't shed a tear for them.

"In the trunk of that car," Carlota continued, "on my way to the San Joaquín Valley, to a fugitive's life as an illegal domestic worker for the Stephenses, I cried for my father and mother, wetting the soil in the pot where my *nopalito,* my little Mexican prickly cactus, was growing.

"A few clothes and my family photos in a Mexican burlap shopping bag, together with that tiny, one-leaf, Mexican cactus Chuchita and her mother gave me the night before I left were my only possessions. The next morning, with enough food and water to last me two days and a few pesos in my coin purse, I left my village, walked twenty kilometers to Morelia, and boarded the bus that would take me to Mexicali. There, one of Chuchita's uncles waited for me to take me across the U.S.-Mexico border, where, on a dirt road a few miles from El Centro, California, Dr. Stephens waited for me. The doctor handed Chuchita's uncle an envelope, led me to the car, and helped me into the trunk.

"'*Dicen que florea una flor azul, casi morada,'* I remembered Chuchita telling me as she explained that the cactus flower was a violet blue, that it bloomed in cycles of five years. My grandmother, the only grandparent I knew, died when I was three years old. Just before her death, she consulted the stars and the corn kernels on my behalf. She predicted that my life would evolve in cycles of five years, that I would shed many tears, but that, finally, on the seventh cycle I would find happiness.

"'*No me olvides. No te olvides,*' had been Chuchita's mother's last words to me, reminding me to keep all of them in my heart, and not to forget who I am.

"Buried in the trunk of the doctor's car, unable to get out, I wondered if I hadn't already died. As though to remind me that I was still alive, the cactus pricked my chin. I hugged it closer to my chest. I cried for a long time, then fell into a fitful sleep. I didn't wake up until I felt the car stop. Trying to keep still, I held my breath when I heard the crunching of gravel on the side of the road. Someone approached the trunk and opened it slowly. A large shadow shielded my eyes from the blinding light of the setting sun. Every muscle in my arms, legs, and belly tensed up, aching for release. Still hugging the potted cactus, I got ready to leap out of the trunk. Two hands held me up gently, and I knew they couldn't be the hands of a border patrolman or a sheriff's deputy. Supporting myself on Dr. Stephens's soft, fleshy arms, I stumbled out of the trunk.

"'*Venga al asiento de atrás,*' Dr. Mark Stephens said, indicating the rear door of his Lincoln Continental. I was out of danger for now, he explained in broken Spanish while I sat on the gravel wri-(...)-thing in pain and trying to stretch my legs to restore the circulation in them.

"We should get going soon. Inside the car, I could eat and drink something, stretch out on the back seat, perhaps sleep for a while if I wanted.

"More than anything, I wanted to sleep. I wanted to escape the memory of my parents, my feelings of loss, and the realization that I was all alone in the world. So I did just that—sleep.

"When I woke up, we were pulling into Dr. Stephens's garage in Fresno. Mrs. Stephens's gentle eyes were smiling at me.

"Since I had left my village in Mexico, I hadn't been as happy as I was during the following year, living with the Stephenses in Fresno. I cleaned their house, cooked for them, did their laundry, and cared for their garden. I also took care of their six- and nine-year-old daughters on weekdays, and made sure they did their homework when they came home from school. Then the three of us watched TV or played games.

"Four evenings a week I went to night school to learn English. The class I was attending was part of the Fresno Public Schools adult education program. Although they'd warned that I had to be eighteen or older to attend, I didn't have to show any kind of identification. I was fourteen but already quite developed, so Mrs. Stephens suggested that I claim to be eighteen on the registration form. No one questioned my age.

"'*Eres bonita y sexy*,' Josie Baldomar, a teacher's aide at the school, told me. '*Redondita*—round and soft. With that sensual mouth, bronze skin, and that beautiful, wild, dark, hair of yours, you'll have no trouble landing a good gringo husband—maybe one of the good doctor's friends. Look at me. I'm not as pretty as you, but I landed a European, an accountant. We live in Swedish Town. Swedish Town es el pueblito de Kingsburg, California, about twenty miles south of Fresno.'

"'Phillipe is actually British, not Swedish,' Josie said. Then, pointing at the sky with her index finger, she cautioned, '*Pero no te cases con mexicano*. No, no drunk Mexican husband to beat you up every Saturday and spend your money, like my father.' She sighed, then added, '*Edúcate*. When you have an education, a career, you don't have to take any abuse from anyone.'

"I, of course, understood what Josie Baldomar was telling me, although I didn't know every word she said in English, which she mixed with Spanish. Every day, new phrases and

words in English blurted out of my mouth with greater ease. I
felt proud of myself. One night I even imagined that I'd heard
a man's voice whisper in my ear, 'Oh, my love. You are beautiful, so lovely. Your hair, your eyes, your full mouth.' The next
morning I laughed when I recalled my dream.

"'*Parece de telenovela*—sounds like a cheap soap opera,
*pero al menos,* you're already learning English,' Josie told me
and we laughed. It was a Sunday afternoon. The Stephenses
were going to be at the country club all day, and they let me
spend the afternoon at Josie's house in Kingsburg. Josie had
invited a couple of her women friends and me to a *carne
asada.* Her husband, Phillipe Hazlitt, had come in later. He
wasn't a very talkative man, and obviously uncomfortable
around the Mexican women. After eating some of the *tacos de
carne asada,* he went into the living room to watch whatever
sport was on T.V. Most of the time, he kept looking in our
direction, especially when Josie displayed any kind of affection towards any of her women friends. I asked her about
Phillipe's behavior later, but she said, laughing, '*Así son estos
europeos.* These Europeans get intimidated by our exuberant
spirit.'

"Maybe my romantic dreams were the result of that 'exuberant spirit' Josie talked about. The truth is that even during
the day I had the normal romantic fantasies of an adolescent,
so dreaming about someone speaking soft words of love to me
didn't seem unusual. I was happy throughout the following
day until that night, when the same voice I'd heard before
repeated the same exact words in my ear. This time, something made me wake up, and I opened my eyes. I thought I
saw a shadow walking out of the large dressing closet that
had been turned into the tiny room where I slept.

"For a few nights after that episode, I slept fitfully, waking up three or four times during the night, expecting to see

the shadow by my bed. When no one was there, I began to believe it'd been a dream.

"A month later, on a Friday evening, two days before my fifteenth birthday, Mrs. Stephens and the girls drove up to Monterey to spend the weekend with Mrs. Stephens's mother, who had recently undergone a bladder operation. I had expected to go, but Mrs. Stephens did not take me with her and the girls to Monterey.

"Trying (...) to keep myself from feeling lonely and depressed, I sat in the back porch for a long time listening to the Mexican radio station. I thought I would ask Dr. Stephens if he would let me go to Josie's house in Kingsburg on Sunday to celebrate my birthday and the end of my first year in the San Joaquín Valley. I was wearing a sleeveless housecoat and was fanning myself with the skirt. A soft breeze blew in. I opened my legs and pulled my dress up to let the coolness reach up.

"I looked at my Mexican cactus, which I had transplanted into the rocky, sandy soil in the yard where a saguaro and an agave were already growing. Its first fleshy leaf had grown ten inches in height and six inches across. Other leaves were growing on each side of the large leaf. Mesmerized, I watched the shadows of the saguaro and my little cactus on the wooden fence. Then I scanned the sky, searching for the evening star to wish what I always wished for: someone to love me.

"I didn't hear him approach, so I wasn't aware of how long Dr. Stephens had been standing at the kitchen door watching me. I slowly pulled down my skirt below my knees. Not paying any mind to my reaction, he kept rubbing his left arm as though it hurt badly. Yet he smiled when he came closer and sat on the porch steps. His eyes were bloodshot, and he seemed very tired. I could tell right away he'd been drinking. He drank (...) like that only when his wife was away. He drank alone, not with his friends, almost as though he were trying to show Mrs. Stephens how much he missed her. But she wasn't around to know about it. Perhaps it wasn't her but himself he was trying to convince, I thought.

"'The cactus is really growing now,' Dr. Stephens said. 'And so are you. You're getting to be a lovely girl.' I smiled, but I avoided his gaze. I didn't like the way he had been looking at me lately, the way he would pat my butt, or peck me in the mouth with his wet lips. It's true that he touched Sandy and Remmi, his daughters, that way, too, and that Mrs. Stephens didn't seem to find his behavior odd in any way whatsoever. But I felt ill-at-ease around him. My father hadn't treated me that way when he was alive. More than once I fell asleep folded in my father's arms, but he never touched me the way Dr. Stephens did.

"At some point, I threw a quick glance at the doctor, sitting on the kitchen steps, his eyes fixed on me. I quickly looked away. I got a whiff of his alcohol breath every time he noisily exhaled in my direction, heard the creaking of the wood (...) when he got up and began to come closer. A chill ran up my spine, but I didn't move. I wasn't sure what I should do.

"First, he put his hot, sweaty palm on my face. Suddenly, he tried to force my lips and teeth open, to stick his tongue into my mouth. I was determined not to let him do it.

"I turned my face away, my revulsion for him beginning to stir around inside my stomach. I refused to get sick, so I fought back the nausea. I began to push him away, but he overpowered me and pushed me down on the ground. Pinning one of my arms behind my back with his left hand, he unbuttoned my dress and began to rub my breasts. He twisted one of my nipples so hard I cried out. Not knowing what else to do, I got hold of one of his ears and twisted it.

"Fighting him off made my tears rush out. Oblivious to my cries and pleas, he began to suck and bite my lips harder and harder. The salty, bitter taste of blood mixed with my tears seeped through my lips as I felt his other hand be-(...)-gin to roll my panties down.

. "Die. I would rather die. No. Live! Contradictory thoughts crossed my mind, back and forth. I bent my leg and tried to push him away with my knee, but I couldn't get enough leverage to get him off me. At least my bent leg was making it difficult for him to get my panties off. Nothing was going to stop him, I realized helplessly, as he continued to bite and suck my nipples and pull my panties down.

"Frustrated, he pushed my knee down violently. I heard the noise of his zipper, then felt his fingers searching for the opening to my vagina. I held my breath and tightened up the inside muscles of my thighs. All to no avail, for he forced me open and thrust into me. The burning pain inside me and my rage made me scream. Despair and impotence took over, making me wish for a sudden death. I held my breath for so long that I began to lose consciousness.

"How long he was inside me, I don't know. I vaguely remember his sweaty face and his teary eyes as he withdrew from me. I must have looked quite lifeless, for he staggered backwards as if surprised he had been capable of doing what he'd just done. Zipping his pants up quickly, he disappeared into the kitchen and he came out a few seconds later, holding a wet, soapy washcloth and a glass with a clear liquid. He made me drink from the glass. The mere smell of the vodka made me feel nauseous, and I vomited into the glass and all over his hand. He put the glass aside, wiped the vomit off his hand, then tried to clean my legs with the soapy cloth.

"I was grinding my teeth so hard, my jaw was beginning to hurt. Without saying a word, I pushed him back. Then I slapped him with all my might; I kicked him in the groin and on both his shins repeatedly. I then fell to my knees and started to pray aloud. He reeled back in pain, grabbing his crotch, tears rolling down his cheeks. Then he staggered back into the house. A few minutes later, I heard the Lincoln rev up and screech out of the garage and down the street.

"Holding on to the chair I'd been sitting on earlier, I attempted a few steps, but the burning sensation in my vagina made me bend over, and I had to lean back on the chair. My whole body felt like a large mass of raw nerves. My arms and legs jerked, and my teeth chattered. But I didn't cry. Watching the full moon rise over the neighboring house, I was suddenly (...) very cold. Half crawling, half walking, I found my way to the bathroom. In spite of the burning pain, I scrubbed between my legs, around my nipples, and inside my mouth with very hot, sudsy water to wash every trace of Dr. Stephens's sweat, saliva, and semen off my body. On my tender skin, I applied an ointment I'd seen Mrs. Stephens use on the girls when they got skin rashes.

"After I got dressed, I searched the drawers in the kitchen for Mrs. Stephens's coin purse, in which she kept the spare set of keys and some cash. Then I put my few clothes and shoes, my books, and my family photos into the Mexican burlap shopping bag I had brought with me when I came.

"I went out to the yard and dug out my Mexican cactus. Its prickles cut into a vein in my arm and drops of blood left a trace of crimson on the stem. I planted it into a pot from which, a moment ago, I'd yanked out a favorite gardenia that Dr. Stephens intended to transplant to a larger pot. I tore out the blossoms and mashed them with my foot until the sweet aroma of the fresh blossoms turned into a sickening stench of crushed flowers. Making a wall with my books around it to keep it from breaking, I put the potted cactus in my burlap bag.

"The full moon had risen to mid-sky, shedding its silvery light on every living and dying being. But not on me. I waited in the shadows, my belongings and my potted cactus in the burlap bag beside me. I recoiled deeper into the dark-(...)-ness when I heard the Lincoln Continental drive into the garage. Dr. Stephens staggered up the steps, and once inside the house, he turned on the light in each room, then turned it off. He moved subsequently to the yard, where he must have seen the crushed gardenia and the missing cactus. Convinced I was no longer in the house, he then fell asleep in his bedroom. In his drunken stupor, the doctor wasn't aware I had reentered the house. He didn't hear me take the sharp shears in one of the kitchen drawers or walk up to his bed. He didn't even stir when I deposited next to him on the mattress the sheet of paper on which I had written with Mrs. Stephens's lipstick, "WATCH YOUR BACK, ALWAYS." He didn't move when the cloth and the paper ripped as the scissors pierced and cut through the mattress, a finger's width from his left flank.

"With no more company than the moon, I walked into the darkness before me.

"I headed south, towards Kingsburg, the town where my only friend, Josie Baldomar, lived. I would be fifteen in two more days, but I felt a thousand years old. I was the violated sister, the dark face of the moon. But I would regather myself, I swore, and some day I would get my re-(...)-venge. These thoughts kept me alive while I ran, then walked, and finally dragged myself, my photos, and my Mexican cactus across lettuce and onion fields, passing through vineyards where the sweet but deadly smell of pesticides hung, still fresh, in the air of a hellish dawn."

Carlota paused. "I can't,..." she said at last and sighed. Her breath slowly dissolved into the static of the tape.

Although I had already heard the story earlier that day, my anger had stirred up again. I had been so tense that my muscles were stiff. My arms and legs felt numb. Absentmindedly, I slapped my limbs to get the circulation going again.

I glanced at Justin, who was sitting with his elbows resting on the desk. Knotted into a single fist, his hands pressed

hard against his mouth, making his knuckles and lips turn
white. Tiny drops of sweat were visible on his forehead and
above his upper lip. He stared at the recorder as if he expected
Carlota's voice to come back on, to announce that she had
killed the man who had raped her. I shared in the rage that
made his irises turn jet black, almost glossy.

When I handed him the paper with Carlota's address in
Kingsburg, Justin looked at it. Without saying a word, he put
it in his pocket. Then he rose slowly from his chair and headed
out.

I gathered my things and followed him. We both heard
the click announcing the end of the tape as we stepped out the
door and into an incongruously balmy October night.

# Five
## *Wild Grapes/Bitter Grapes*

Sarah Sáenz Owen, Art's landlady, was expecting us. Justin had phoned ahead to tell her we were coming. When he called, Sarah had informed him that Art had left early on Friday for her house in the Sonoma Valley, a drive of an hour-and-a-half from Oakland. Art had told Sarah that he hoped to finish editing a poetry manuscript he was getting ready for his publisher. This coincided with the information Myra had given me. After her earlier conversation with Justin, Sarah had phoned Robin Cardozo, her house manager in the Sonoma Valley, and Robin had said that Art had never arrived there.

In the Bay Area, Art Bello rented a large cottage behind Sarah's main house in Piedmont, a small city encroached by Oakland proper. The upper-crust professionals with aspirations of wealth and the truly wealthy people lived there.

I suspected that the cottage had been the servants' quarters at some point. But Sarah Sáenz Owen, a banker's widow and a fairly well-known photographer, had converted the quarters into suitable rental space for a single man or woman.

In the early seventies, Art Bello had told all of us that he would do everything he could for *la causa*. Over the years, with laughter underlining a seemingly serious countenance, he had recited his political creed to all of us, pledging that he would spend his summers organizing and helping farm workers in the valleys of California. He had actively pursued the discontinuation of pesticides, herbicides, and fungicides, all of which were responsible for cancer, birth defects, and many other diseases among migrant farmworkers. He had told us that, even at the risk of getting beat up, maced, and arrested by the police, he would join picket lines or participate in marches and demonstrations to support Chicano civil rights efforts anywhere they happened.

Luisa and I witnessed his written promise—in case *Madame Posterity* suspected him of being a *vendido*, a sellout—that he would picket till he dropped, never again eat table grapes, drink Coors beer, or wear Levi jeans. "I'll call myself Latino, but not Hispanic. It's got to be this way or there won't be any of us Chicano *chingones* left," he said with a glitter in his eye.

Art had told us nonchalantly that he intended never to live in Oakland, in a warehouse-turned-studio in Jingletown, like Sonny Mares. Nor would he ever be a resident of the Fruitvale, Laurel, or San Antonio Districts like Justin, Luisa, or me. He had solemnly sworn never to give into the "romantic" idea of living in San Francisco's Mission District. Yet, he had promised us that he would bequeath his art collection to the Mexican Museum in San Francisco.

None of us argued with Art when he rented the cottage from Sarah Sáenz Owen in smart-set Piedmont. Being that Art was charming, caring and witty, and an *employed* poet, Sarah immediately accepted him as a tenant. She lived alone, and was perhaps much older than she admitted. So I suspected she not only cherished Art as a friend, but also liked the idea of having a man around who could help her should she need it.

Ironically, Justin and I were now on our way to Sarah's house, hoping she would be able to help us locate Art.

When we arrived, Justin parked on Mandana Road about half-a-block from Sarah's house. She opened the door as soon as we rang, but we found her speaking on the phone. She asked us to wait in the sitting room, where photo and oil portraits of Sarah's family members were displayed. On various occasions Sarah had told Luisa and me about her ancestors.

Martín and Luis Sáenz, Sarah's great-grandfather and great-granduncle, stared at me from their oil portraits. Business acquaintances of the prominent Vallejo family in Sonoma, the Sáenz brothers had been purveyors of spirits in San Francisco when former General Vallejo established the first California commercial winery in the Sonoma Valley by opening his private cellars to the public.

Sarah's great-granduncle, Luis, had fallen in love with one of the Vallejo girls and had hoped to ask for her hand in marriage. Sarah said her uncle never stood a chance, for just about that time, the general had arranged for his two daughters to marry the sons of a Hungarian winery owner, a pioneer in the wine-making industry who was on his way to wealth and fame.

I was fascinated with the story of Luis Saenz's ill-fated romance, for, as Sarah explained, he had never again loved another woman and had remained a bachelor. But he had fallen in love with the valley and had built a house—Quinta Selena—west of the city of Sonoma. Sarah was now Quinta Selena's sole owner. The quinta was a large California Gold Rush rustic mansion. "A-brick-and-stone-and-*el diablo*'s-spit house," Art had called it, as he marveled at the way it'd been built.

I had never been to Sarah's house in the wine country, but Luisa had told me that the huge stone mansion sat on a hill surrounded by two acres of sloping fruit orchards and a hillside vineyard. The property was bordered by a forest of madrone, oak, and eucalyptus trees. Sarah had said that the Oakland writer, Jack London, had built his house on the next hill. London had renamed Sonoma "The Valley of the Moon" after a legend of the old Chocuyen, the valley's native people.

Whenever Art had needed uninterrupted time to complete a literary project, he'd gone to stay at *la quinta*. I wondered what had happened to Art this last time that had made him not reach his destination as scheduled.

Now, Justin and I were at Sarah's house in Piedmont waiting for her to open Art's cottage for us. Realizing that she was going to be tied up longer than expected, Sarah handed us the key to the cottage and signaled us to go ahead. I assumed she would join us there as soon as she could.

Before entering Art's apartment, Justin and I put on our gloves. At first glance, nothing seemed out of place. Art, like Justin, kept his living space quite organized and clean. But unlike Justin's apartment, which could be described as a study-in-black-and-white-with-splashes-of-red-and-turquoise, Art's Piedmont cottage displayed color everywhere one looked.

The first time I visited his home, I was impressed beyond words. As if I were at a museum, I moved quietly through the house. Nicely displayed throughout the house was Art's collection of prints by Chicano and Latino printers in the Bay Area. *Ofrendas* for the dead and box altars, Mexican folk art and linen decorated tables, corner stands, and softly-lit niches.

My favorite works were large prints by Tony Burciaga, Ester Hernández, and Rupert García depicting Mexican artist Frida Kahlo. These were hung in Art's bedroom, facing each other from adjoining walls.

Unfortunately, this time Justin and I were not there to admire the art. While Justin went to the kitchen, I headed towards Art's study. The door was closed. The instant I put my hand on the door knob, I felt an almost imperceptible electrical shock that sent an army of diminutive prickles marching up my fingers and hand. Getting a shock from metal wasn't unusual, but the door knob I had my hand on was made of glass. Briefly, I sensed danger in the strong presence of someone on the other side of the door. I gulped a mouthful of air, turned the knob, and pushed the door open. Slowly, I went into the room.

"The window," I said under my breath when I saw the curtains flutter. I moved towards the open window and crouched. Then I pulled the curtains open to take a look outside. Someone was out there, I was certain. I could hear the crunching of dry pine needles. "Could be deer," I told myself, but I knew it wasn't an animal. They were soft but unmistakable human footfalls. I widened the opening between the curtains and stuck my head out. I then saw a shadow disappear behind the huge sequoias in Sarah's dimly lit, woodsy yard. I waited an instant, hoping to glimpse the figure again, but whoever had been there was probably gone.

Sarah came into the study and turned the light on, startling me. "What are you doing in the dark?" she asked.

Not wanting to scare her, in the calmest tone I could manage, I said, "Just enjoying a little quiet. You have a lovely place here." Putting my hand on my chest to steady my heart, I turned around to face her. At that moment, for the first time I noticed the empty places on the wall opposite the window. A bow-and-arrow and the red-and-black United Farm Workers' strike flag which usually hung next to it had been removed. As I looked at Art's photo display of contemporary California Indians and farm workers, I noticed two of the photos were also missing.

Unsure the missing items were germane to this case and trying to remain calm, I said to Sarah, "I guess Art got rid of some of his art work." I pointed at the two empty spots and commented, "I don't remember what these photos were about, do you?"

"Art would *not* do such a thing. Those were two of the photos I gave him. I took those photos. He's had them since 1973," Sarah protested, then looked at me. I tried not to show my apprehension, but she must have read it in my eyes anyway, for she asked, "Do you think there is a connection between the disappearance of these things and Art's disappearance?" Gradually, the seriousness of the situation began to dawn on her. "Someone wishes him ill? Who?" she asked. Since I couldn't begin to answer her question, I remained quiet. "He's in *real* trouble, isn't he?" Sarah said, aghast.

"I'm afraid so," I answered, as I pulled a chair for her to sit on.

Sarah sat down. "I was here earlier today," she said, then paused to catch her breath. "I came in here after Justin called me this afternoon. He asked me to look for Art's address book and to check for a number Justin needed. But I couldn't find the book." She got up and went to inspect the wall. "I could have sworn they were still here when I came," she said, referring to the missing photos.

"Do you remember what was depicted in them?" I stood next to her and looked at the rest of the photos.

"Of course I do," she replied. "This smaller one was a group photo. Art and some friends..." Sarah closed her eyes to concentrate. "Yes. Sonny, Art, Dieguito, another man—I don't remember his name—and two women. I don't remember their names either. Farm workers, probably. I took that one in Delano, during the strike." Sarah combed her hair with her fingers, and was lost in thought for a minute.

Justin came in carrying a paper bag. He opened it enough so I could see the bunch of dark purple grapes in a half-carton of milk he had found. In the bag, next to the carton, there was also a resealable plastic bag with something that looked like a strip of beef jerky in it. I put my index finger over my mouth, asking Justin to be quiet. He acquiesced with a nod and walked back to Art's desk.

"Yes," Sarah was saying, confirming her previous statement. "It was in Delano. That photo was companion to these others here." She pointed at photos of César Chávez, and of farm workers being beaten by Kern County Sheriffs and insulted by vociferous teamsters. "Art had them all together because he said he never wanted to forget the summer of '73."

Out of the corner of my eye, I saw Justin pore over the contents in the desk. He picked up an envelope and examined it. Then he pulled out a slip of paper. Turning on the desk lamp, he read what was written on the slip, then took out the piece of paper with Carlota's address that I'd handed him earlier. He compared both under the lamp and put them in the breast pocket of his jacket.

Turning my attention back to the photos, I asked Sarah, "Who was in the larger one?" I put my hand on the spot where the photo had been.

"That's a more recent photo. It was taken in Sonoma. As a matter of fact, it was somewhere in the woods around Quinta Selena," Sarah answered without hesitation. "It's a photo of Dieguito Pa-wah Su'-ma, a descendant of an old Wappo chief—Dieguito claims so anyway," Sarah said as she turned to look at me, then added, "He is a superb dancer, you know? A shaman, too." Leaning towards me, she added in a hushed voice, "The vineyard workers have found all kinds of Indian charms and amulets, small pouches with herbs and ashes in them. The workers swear that they've seen the glow of fires burning in the night, in a hollow between two hills. They've gone to check them—you know how dangerous fires can be in a forest of eucalyptus. They've found cinders and ashes, but no one there. The Indians around there swear it's the ghost of Old Solano, the chief who first met Vallejo when he landed on the Sonoma Coast," Sarah said, her voice ever so soft. "To tell you the truth, this is all folklore nonsense. To begin with, chief Solano and his people lived northwest of Sonoma, far from where my house stands. But Dieguito wanted to see this place where the bonfire had been seen. He danced there to appease old Solano's and old Coton's spirit."

"Old Coton is Dieguito's ancestor. He was a Wappo Indian chief, fierce and unconquerable," I heard Justin say, and I turned to look at him. "The Wappo occupied the Napa Valley and were the only tribe that never submitted to missionary, soldier, or settler, right?" he said as he looked at Sarah, who nodded in agreement. Justin must have seen my inquiring look, for he immediately explained, "No big deal, really. Art has talked to me about the Wappo, and Dieguito himself has told me about Old Coton."

Justin examined the wall. "That photo is missing," he said.

Sarah and I both nodded as we pointed to the other empty spots on the wall.

"Did Dieguito give Art that bow and the arrows?" I asked Justin.

"I don't know. Maybe it was Dieguito. I truly don't recall."

"It wasn't Dieguito," Sarah interjected. "It was a woman who gave Art that bow. Art told me as much," she continued, then closed her eyes to concentrate. "Yes, this woman insisted on giving him a valuable gift. Art had done something for her and she had no other way to repay him. Imagine! That bow was surely a museum piece, beautifully crafted."

"Do you know who the woman is?" Justin asked Sarah.

"No, I don't."

I turned to Sarah. "You wouldn't by any chance still have the negatives of the missing photos, would you?" I expected Sarah to say she didn't. I was extremely surprised when she nodded. "You *do* have them?" I asked.

"I'm sure I have them," she said. "At the moment, I just don't know where. It was such a long time ago." Her eyes swept across the photos on the wall. "But I never throw away a negative. If I don't have them here, they're at Quinta Selena."

"Would you mind looking for them?" I begged.

"Not at all. I'll do anything to help you find Art," Sarah offered. "Dreadful business. Just dreadful!" she exclaimed as she walked out of the study.

"Someone—I don't know who—was here, in this room," I informed Justin as soon as Sarah had moved out of hearing range. "Man or woman?"

"Difficult to tell. A short man. Perhaps a woman. I only saw a shadow moving away. It disappeared behind the sequoias at the far end of the yard," I explained. Justin gave me a brief glance just before he turned off the light in the study, but he offered no other comment.

"Did Art look all right to you before he left?" Justin asked Sarah when we joined her in the living room. "Was there anything bothering him?"

"He seemed to be preoccupied, but I paid no attention," Sarah said. "The artistic temperament often makes one seem sulky or unsociable to other people," she continued. "You ought to know this, Justin, although you refuse—God knows why—to call yourself an artist. Anyone who's seen your photographs and has any taste knows you have the vision."

Just before she switched off the lights in the front room, I saw Justin nod to thank Sarah for the compliment. He attempted a smile. A tinge of red spread over his cheeks as he took off his gloves and put them in his jacket.

Outside, Justin gave Sarah his business card, to which he had added Leo's phone number. "Don't hesitate to call. Any time," he reassured her. "Gloria and ..." Giving me a brief look, he corrected himself, "I'm going to Fresno very early tomorrow, but I'll be back no later than nine in the evening. I'll phone then, all right?"

"Thanks, dear. That'll be fine," Sarah said to Justin. Then she turned to me. "I'm so glad you came along, Gloria. You don't know how worried we were about you, especially after dear Luisa passed away. Art was heartbroken, too. You know,

he always thought of Luisa as a dear, kindred spirit." She
shook her head, then added, "Well, good night." Justin and I
waved and headed for the van.

"Of course I'll go to Fresno with you," I reassured Justin
as soon as I settled myself in the seat. Showing his agreement
with a slight nod, he handed me the paper bag and I put on
the gloves still in my hand before handling the contents.
Then, taking out the milk carton with the grapes, I read the
name of the company on it, "Valley of the Moon Dairy Farms,
Carneros Road, Sonoma County."

"Don't handle the grapes. Just smell them," Justin suggested as he picked up his cellular phone and began to place a
call. "I'm going to have Messinger analyze these grapes, too.
There's something odd here." As soon as Bob Messinger
answered, Justin told him he would be dropping by later on,
then hung up.

"They stink," I told Justin after I smelled them. "But the
smell is strangely pungent. What do you think is making it?"
He shrugged his shoulders. I smelled them a second time.
"There's another smell, though. I think there's alcohol in
them." Pulling up the plastic bag, I looked at its contents.
"What is it?" I asked Justin.

"A skin coil, just like the one Sonny described to Leo.
Remember?"

"What does it mean?" I said to Justin, and felt my neck
stiffen.

"Dieguito once told me that the old Sonomans believed
you would die of poisoning if you ever found a snakeskin near
your door."

I tried to suppress my fear, but it traveled down my veins,
making me short of breath. I recalled the silhouette of the
dancer in my vision. "Could Dieguito be the one who's doing
this?" I asked.

Justin gave me a quick look. "I don't think so," he said. "What reason would he have? He got along well with Sonny, and he and Art are very good friends."

I considered telling Justin about the visions, but decided to wait until I was certain of their significance. "What time would you like us to leave for Fresno?" I inquired.

"Let's say around five in the morning," Justin answered, and began to drive towards my house on Excelsior and Park. From there, I was sure, Justin was going to drop off the grapes and coil at Messinger's lab.

"All right," I said to Justin. "I'll be ready." Putting everything back in the paper bag, I commented, "I'm assuming that you also found a phone message or some note from or about Carlota." Justin gave me a questioning glance. "I'm talking about the paper you found on Art's desk."

Justin laughed. "You don't miss much," his eyes seemed to be saying, but instead, he explained that he had found a slip with a phone number written on it, but no address. "We'll have to check the phone book for both Josie Baldomar's and Carlota Navarro's numbers when we get to Fresno/Kingsburg," he explained. I agreed.

"Were there any puncture marks in Art's bed like the ones we found in Sonny's?" I inquired. He shook his head to indicate there weren't any. Since he didn't mention he had found a video tape, I assumed that Justin had not found a copy of the video documentary we had viewed at Sonny's.

Justin fell silent. His automatic movements as he drove showed me that his mind was somewhere else.

Ever since we'd listened to Carlota's story, he had been unusually sullen. His reaction was not the mitigated anger we all experience over a rape that happened fifteen years before. I sensed that Carlota's tragic experience had stirred up some strong emotions and brought them to the surface. But Justin's anger wasn't a shapeless, nameless rage. I suspected that such strong emotion fed from a terrible experience he'd had. I had no more access to that source of Justin's anger than to the underground source of a spring. I had to admit that I knew very little about Justin's private life.

We rode the rest of the way to my house in silence. When we got there, I saw the full moon rising behind my house, scattering shadows over the facade. For an instant, I thought it wasn't my home, that Justin had driven me to someone else's house. I felt reluctant to go in, and hesitated for a split second.

Intrigued, Justin looked at me and seemed ready to say something but changed his mind. My fear was now weighing heavily on me, and I had to fight the desire to ask him if I could spend the night at his place.

A minute later, I forced myself to overcome my fear. I got out of the van and started towards my house. Whatever had caused my unwillingness to go in was dispelled by the time I unlocked the front door. Followed by my moon-made shadow, larger and darker than me, I entered my house.

# Six
## Green Sentinels

Watching over the boundaries between the coast and the valley, the tall wind-powered electricity generators, like night sentries, queued on the top of dark sloping hills at the Altmont Pass. Farther below, between the coastal range and the Sierra Nevada, lay the vast expanse of the San Joaquín Valley, one of the richest agricultural regions in the world. Carlota Navarro and Josie Baldomar lived in its midst.

Justin had asked me to drive to Kingsburg so he would have a chance to sleep. He was exhausted. The night before, he'd had to drop off the grapes and milk carton at Bob Messinger's lab. I had never seen Justin as concerned as he had been during these past two days, and I was sure he had worked in his woodshop or darkroom until he was tired enough to fall asleep.

Two and a half hours later, as I drove past the huge Scandinavian windmill at the entrance of Kingsburg's main thoroughfare, I looked at the Swedish chalet-type architecture. Then I watched a few tall, blonde, and blue-eyed passersby on their way to church in the early Sunday morning. I realized then why Kingsburg was called California's Swedish village.

I pulled up to the curb in front of a pancake house. Justin seemed to be still fast asleep. Before waking him, I cupped my hands over my tired eyes to rest them. As I closed my eyes, the glowing silhouette of Justin's head and torso—the last thing I'd looked at before closing them—took shape inside my head. Suddenly, a different image surfaced, and I stared at a palpitating gash just below what I somehow knew was

Justin's rib cage. The vision was so unexpected it scared me. I opened my eyes.

I felt the comforting warmth of Justin's hand on my shoulder. "How long have you been having them?" he asked softly. I didn't have to think at all to realize that he was asking me about my psychic visions.

"The first time was a week ago Sunday night, a recurring dream. The second one was yesterday at Sonny's house. They're coming more and more frequently now. Sometimes even with my eyes open."

"Are you sure they're not just dreams?"

"They're visions all right," I assured him. "I'd like to tell you about them, but they may scare you."

"Well...We'll see about that. I don't scare easily," Justin reassured me.

At that moment, I sensed that Justin's anger had subsided, giving way, at least for a while, to something I could only describe as a simmering passion, a blend of emotion and intellect that allowed him to transcend anger and create harmony out of chaos. Luisa had called this mixture "the utilitarian passion," for, without this particular combination, human creativity would be unproductive, she had explained.

Justin reached under his seat and pulled out a small leather traveling kit, some maps of the area, and his note pad. "Why don't you tell me all about your dream over breakfast?"

Seeing him smile again, I was tempted to ask him why Carlota's rape had affected him so, but I kept quiet. There would be other—hopefully more auspicious—times to talk about his personal life. I wasn't used to having a large breakfast, so I ordered a fruit plate with yogurt. I ate only half of it while I told Justin about my dream and the other short extrasensory perceptions, motifs I wove as best I could into the larger tapestry of the vision.

"I see why you were so scared last night," he said. "The snakeskin," he elaborated, but he didn't look at me while he talked. I would have been a fool not to realize that he observed me as much as I did him. I shook my head and smiled. Just the same, I decided not to mention the part where I saw a gash below his ribs, as this could simply be the result of my concern for his safety.

I felt disgruntled at the thought that I might forever have to second-guess myself, to rifle the murky waters of my psyche armed with nothing more than the puny light of my intuitive intelligence to guide me. Not wanting to go over old ground or allow frustration to take over, I went to pay the bill while Justin finished his breakfast.

I tried the number Justin had given me for Carlota in Fresno only to find out the line had been disconnected. I checked the phone book under Phillipe Hazlitt, Josie's husband, and found an address on Union Street. Out of curiosity, I also checked under Baldomar. Although there was no listing under Josie or Josephine, I found a María Baldomar living on Mariposa Street, at the same house Luisa had listed for Carlota in her address book. No Carlota or C. Navarro was listed in the Fresno-area directory.

Although I wasn't sure what good it would do, I checked the White Pages for a listing under Mark Stephens, the man who had raped Carlota. There were three Stephenses, none of whom was the one I was looking for. No Mark Stephens appeared under the physicians listing in the Yellow Pages. Regardless, I wrote down the addresses for all the Stephenses in Fresno. With luck, Josie Baldomar would be able to tell us if the doctor and his family still lived in the area.

"Why you think the Stephenses are involved in Sonny's death and Art's disappearance?" Justin asked, looking over the paper I'd just handed him.

"That whole business with the shears, mostly. And that half-torn message. There might be a connection," I offered as explanation. I shrugged my shoulders as I wasn't really sure why I was suggesting we locate the Stephenses. "What do you think?"

"It's a long shot, but better played than not. At this point, we have to consider every possibility," Justin said. Then, after a pause, he asked, "Do *you* have any particular reason to check them out? I mean—something in your vision?" He pored over his maps and identified the locations of the addresses I had given him. He then established the latitude and longitude of our trek through the San Joaquín Valley.

"Nothing I saw. Just a...hunch," I answered at first, sheepishly. I hated using words like "hunch," so I immediately corrected myself. "An *educated* guess," I said. "Given the puncture marks on Sonny's mattress, I'd like to know what happened after Carlota left the Stephens's household."

"I'm not sure I trust your *hunches,*" Justin said, looking at me on the sly and trying to hide his amusement. "But I *do* trust your visions." He chuckled as he handed me the maps where he had circled the addresses, including those of the various Stephenses in Fresno. "I think we should check that address for an R. Stephens. A doctor and his family just might choose a residential area around a country club to live," he suggested as we got back in the van. We started up towards Josie's house on Union Street.

Unless it was an emergency or he was in a hurry, Justin liked to drive around before approaching a house, to familiarize himself with the surroundings.

"It's probably that house at the corner." I pointed at a one-story, ranch-style house. A Buick Regal was parked in the driveway. A weeping willow stood on the street corner of the dark-green, manicured front lawn with a small fountain in its middle. A few sun-beaten blossoms still clung to a bougainvillaea vine, resting on a large trellis affixed to the house. "If this weeping willow wasn't here before, Josie surely planted it for Carlota."

"Yep. I think you're right," Justin said as we approached the house and checked the number next to the mailbox.

After circling around Josie's house, Justin decided to park about fifty feet up on the opposite side of the street. Turning off the engine, he motioned for me to stay in the van for a couple of minutes, probably to observe the action on the street before we made a move. Had I been alone, as impulsive as I've always been, I probably would have been knocking at Josie's door by now. But Justin and I were a team, at least for now, and that meant mutual understanding and collaboration. So I waited.

Josie had done well for herself, I thought, looking at the houses up and down the block, all with their green, lush lawns and landscaped gardens. I squirmed in my seat as I thought of my rose bushes and lemon tree starving for lack of water, while here, in the valley, people were so casual about the drought.

In a short while, we walked up to the house. The grass was wet, and as we passed the willow I noticed, tied to a very low branch, a thin, black ribbon, which almost touched the ground. The door opened suddenly. I expected a gust of cool air to greet us, but the air coming from inside the house felt unusually warm, as if all the windows were closed. Justin and I found ourselves staring at a pair of large, round, black eyes, surrounded by long lashes and set under two shapely brows. A slim nose, high cheekbones, and a sensual mouth completed the face of the woman we assumed was Josie Baldomar. About forty years old, she looked like María Félix, one of the most celebrated Mexican actresses.

On second look, Josie's beauty was rougher. Unlike María Félix, she had long straight hair and no cleft chin. She was wearing her hair in a braid, and she had on a sleeveless dust coat over a black cotton dress. She was obviously engaged in her daily household chores.

"Josie Baldomar?" I asked, and looked at Justin, who, also recognizing the uncanny resemblance to María Félix, was still staring at her. I helped him get over his fascination with a discreet nudge.

"Yes," the woman answered. "I am Josie Baldomar Hazlitt. What can I do for you?" She seemed pleased with Justin's attention and began to throw furtive glances in his direction.

"May we come in?" I asked.

"Give me a good reason," she said with an edge of defiance in her voice.

"My name is Gloria Damasco," I said. "We're looking for Carlota Navarro. I met Carlota at Luisa Cortez's funeral. Luisa was my best friend." Josie looked directly into my eyes while I talked. For an instant, her gaze softened. She sighed, and I perceived a faint smell of alcohol in her breath.

I couldn't help wondering whether Carlota had idealized her friend when she had made Josie sound like a happy-go-lucky kind of person. Despite her obvious pleasure at Justin's admiring looks, the woman standing in front of us seemed hard, angry, and defiant. Something about her seemed familiar in some ineffable way. I knew it had nothing to do with her resemblance to María Félix. Whatever the reason, it made me feel uneasy.

Josie glared at me, and I held her eyes in mine without reproach or anger. My gesture must have impressed her, or told her she could trust us, for she opened the door wider, staggering back as she did. But she didn't invite us to come in. Next to the door, I noticed a small wreath, a circle of entwined purple and black ribbon, sage, basil, and fading roses, whose mixed fragrances still lingered in a room full of color and light.

Taking her housecoat off, she tossed it on the sofa. Her dress was plain and black, and she wore no jewelry. Black was a good color on her and it was definitely in fashion, but her dress seemed somehow out of harmony with the bright colors all around us. She smoothed her dress around her waist and hips. Although she didn't look at Justin right away, her gesture was meant to attract him.

Justin had taken the opportunity to observe Josie while she and I had had our exchange, and now he seemed to be ready to intervene. Taking out his P.I. identification, he showed it to her as he said, "Carlota's been trying to contact me." Josie took his I.D., studied it, and handed it back to him without saying a word.

"Your friend called me a few days ago, looking for Art Bello," Justin began to explain. "Sonny Mares was found dead a couple of days ago, and now Art Bello has vanished. I thought that your friend might know where Art is."

"I don't think Carlota knows anything about Sonny's death or Art's disappearance," Josie remarked.

Justin and I checked each other's reaction briefly. We both noticed the familiarity with which Josie pronounced the names of the two men. Unless we were mistaken, she had been around both of them for some time. We turned our attention again to her. Her irritability clearly visible in her eyes; she met my scrutiny without batting an eyelash. Then she looked away.

"Just the same," Justin stated perfunctorily. "I'd like to have a word with her."

"Sorry. I can't help you. I'm looking for her myself." With that statement, she put her hand on the inside knob and got ready to shut the door on us.

We would probably have no other opportunity to check the place out, so I asked in Spanish, "May I use your bathroom? We're going back to the Bay Area, and I'm afraid I won't get another chance for some time. You know how men hate to stop." Josie seemed to find my comment amusing. In spite of her reluctance, she signaled me to go ahead.

Justin, who was getting ready to step out the door, turned around when I asked to use the bathroom. He stood just inside the door, giving me a chance to snoop a little; for, as long as Justin was in the house, Josie would want to be where he was. She not only found him attractive but dangerous, as he was the real private investigator. I was only an added nuisance.

"Down the hall, to your left, next to the family room," she said, gesturing with her hands as she explained. She made no effort to accompany me. I took inventory of everything on the way. Unfortunately there wasn't much to see, except a few framed posters and Mexican bark paintings on the walls. Plenty of mirrors decorated the walls. Josie Baldomar or someone else in the family either collected mirrors or loved to see themselves in them.

I didn't go into the bathroom, but I closed its door from the outside. I was more interested in checking the family room next to the bathroom and went into it. Papers lay in piles on the floor. Next to stacked sealed boxes, men's shoes, socks, and ties were strewn around. Pants and shirts still on hangers lay on top of the boxes. A clipboard on a table nearby showed a half-filled-out application to a household finance company. I guessed Josie and Phillipe Hazlitt were thinking of refinancing their mortgage. A trophy topped by a large bronze figure of the goddess Diana stood next to the clipboard.

The rest of the house was so clean that I was surprised to see a messy family room. As I looked around, a display of photographs and diplomas caught my attention. One of the diplo-

mas was a certificate of recognition awarded to Josie Hazlitt
by the school where she worked. The other was a certificate
awarded in 1987 to Carlota Navarro by the Fresno Citizens
for a Safe Agricultural Environment Organization for her
"undaunting" work and service to the community.

A multi-photo mat frame showed a number of family photos. In some of them, a woman, whom I assumed was Carlota,
and Josie stood or sat together. A large photo next to the
multi-photo frame showed Josie and her husband on their
wedding day, and the one next to it showed a group of about
seven people standing next to a tall prickly-pear cactus. "Probably Carlota's Mexican *nopal*," I said under my breath. It was
a three-inch print, a bit fuzzy and out of focus, but I recognized Sonny and Art. I assumed that the tall man with ash-
blond hair was Phillipe, Josie's husband, and that the very
dark man with braids was Dieguito. An extremely thin and
sick-looking Carlota stood next to a man who was holding her
up by the waist in an awkward, almost forced position. Josie
looked on the man with contempt, but he seemed oblivious to
her angry stare. I had seen him before, perhaps in one of the
photos taken from Art's house, I thought, but I wasn't sure.

Quietly, I walked out of the family room. Returning to the
bathroom, I flushed the toilet and washed my hands. As I
approached the living room, I noticed that Josie had put her
dust coat back on and was wiping the dining room table with
a rag sprayed with lemon oil. Bending over to reach a distant
spot, she threw a furtive glance at Justin and smiled, obviously pleased to find him looking at her. She stopped when
she saw me and, without a word, closed the door as soon as
Justin and I stepped outside.

We refrained from talking until we got in the van. Once
we were in the vehicle, I began to summarize my impressions
of our meeting with Josie. "She knows where Carlota is, and is
not telling. She was in a foul mood and was hiding something.

But there's something else. The way she was dressed, the funereal wreath inside the door, the black ribbon tied to the willow. I'm certain someone died, and I'm just as sure that she's having financial problems. There were boxes of men's clothing and shoes piled up in the family room. I think Phillipe Hazlitt is dead," I concluded.

For an instant, my mind wandered back to the weeks after Darío died a year and a half before. The hardest part after his funeral was to gather all his belongings. It took me months to muster up the courage to clear his closet, to give away the shoes he hated but always wore, or the shirt he was wearing when Víctor Trummer, his associate, found him slumped on his desk in his office. Every garment, paper, and toiletry item I touched transmitted to my soul its own set of memories. I was the executor of this legacy of intangibles, the one to decide which moments of our daily life together remained and which were given away. I didn't envy Josie Baldomar Hazlitt her job.

I sighed loudly and turned to look at Justin, who was staring at me in silence. He smiled, a kind of strange but knowing smile. Then he started up the street, took a right at the first cross street, turned the van around, and began to park close to the corner to continue our surveillance of Josie's house. While we waited, another car—a green sedan—parked halfway between us and Josie's house on Union Street. Two men sat in it. The thought crossed my mind that they were also watching Josie's house, but seeing them talk animatedly for a while made me change my mind. I resumed with my description of Josie's family room and told Justin about the photos.

"I suspect that this is the same group in the photo stolen from Art's house. Didn't Sarah say that photo was taken during the UFW's strike, back in '73?"

"Yes, she did." Justin paused, then elaborated, "Something that dates back to 1973 ties them all together. I bet it is related to that explosion in Art's film, but how? Why no repercussions until now?"

"Weren't you also with them at that time?" I asked, remembering that Justin had mentioned once that he had worked with *la unión de César Chávez*, as Chicanos in the Bay Area called the United Farm Workers.

Justin gave me a brief glance. Then, looking in the direction of Josie's house again, he said in a quiet voice, "No, I wasn't. My father died of cancer that year, and my mother fell ill." He looked at me, then turned away again as he said, "My youngest sister was still at home. I was needed at home, so I stayed in Oakland." Silence surrounded us once again. "Three people I loved died in the summer of '73."

His voice trembled slightly and, for an instant, I saw the presence of a relentless anger in his countenance, in his eyes fixing on some unknown point in the distance. Dumbfounded, I didn't know what to say. He had said three people, I was sure. Was Justin expecting me to inquire, to probe into his personal business? Would he shut me out once I started asking questions? Somehow the latter possibility was too painful to risk. I decided to remain silent, to let him open up to me when he felt like it.

Turning my attention to Josie's house, I was beginning to think that Josie was never going to make a move. But suddenly, Justin and I saw her come out of her house. She got in her car, backed out of her driveway, and drove down the street past us. We followed at a reasonable distance. The light-green sedan with the two men in it—which had been parked only a few feet away from us near Josie's house—pulled in front of us, positioning itself between Josie's car and Justin's van.

"*Migra,*" Justin said under his breath. I lowered my head to take a look at the two immigration officers in the sedan.

Since they weren't in uniform, they looked more like ranchers than *la migra.* "She's going through," Justin said. I saw Josie's car go through the intersection as the light changed. The other car followed hers, clearing the intersection a second before the red light lit up. It was too late for Justin and me, and we had to stop.

"They're following her," I said aloud. "My God! That's why she was so suspicious of us." I looked at my casual cotton pants and shirt and at Justin's lavender shirt and khaki pants.

"Do we look like *migra,* though?" Justin gave me an amusing glance.

"I'm insulted," I uttered. "Or maybe she thinks we're cops."

"Regardless, the *migra* might be looking for Carlota," Justin said.

Why? The question got caught somewhere in my mind, swallowed by another thought as I spotted Josie's car, still tailed by the immigration sedan. Two blocks down, she turned left. I pinpointed our location on the map, frantically trying to get an idea where she might be going. We were all traveling west on Conejo, a street in the vicinity both of Highway 99 and the railroad tracks, which Josie's car had just crossed. Visible ahead was the green sign announcing the entrance to 99, but Josie had driven past it.

Judging by the signs in Spanish and the sudden change in architecture, I assumed we were near the area where Mexicans lived. The presence of the Del Monte cannery looming a short distance behind us confirmed my suspicion that we had just entered Kingsburg's Mexican barrio. I looked at the map again. "I think I know where she's going," I said to Justin. He glanced at me, but waited for me to continue. "To María Baldomar's house on Mariposa Street. I don't know for sure, but

I'd bet María is Josie's mother," I said. "If you're willing, we could cut off the posse at the pass."

Justin smiled, then asked, "How?"

I directed him to a house on Mariposa, facing a raisin-grape vineyard and the cemetery beyond it. There, in the front yard, its slender hanging limbs softly ruffled by the morning valley breeze, stood a weeping willow next to a prickly-pear cactus—green sentinels guarding Carlota Navarro's memories of her village in Mexico, lifetimes ago.

# Seven
## *The Devil's Blood*

From the direction of the cemetery, ten minutes after Justin and I parked on Mariposa Street, on foot and looking in all directions, Josie Baldomar emerged from between two grapevines. When she was sure the *migra's* green sedan was nowhere in sight, she crossed the street and rapped softly on the window at María Baldomar's house. From where we were, neither Justin nor I could see who opened the door. Josie went in but came out a little while later. She scurried across the street and disappeared into the green trenches of the vineyard.

"I'd like to talk to the person in that house," I said to Justin, then added. "Alone, if you don't mind..." I expected him to protest, but he readily agreed.

"Bob Messinger gave me the name of a sheriff's deputy here in King County who's a friend of his," Justin explained, as he reached back for the camera bag behind his seat. He began to check his equipment and pointed his camera at the cross rising above a row of grapevines. "This Deputy Carlson might be able to tell me why the *migra* is after Josie and what happened to Phillipe Hazlitt. I doubt very much Josie is going to make a move. But I'd like to see if she'll talk to me once I have some facts. Shall I meet you back at Josie's house?" he proposed while he checked his light meter and refocused.

"All right."

He pointed at the house."I'll wait until you go in."

A few minutes later I was facing an older woman whom I presumed was María Baldomar, although she bore little resemblance to her daughter Josie. Slender and dark, with surprisingly few wrinkles around her large, soulful eyes, she was dressed in a gauzy sky-blue, mid-length dress tied at the waist with a sash. Holding a comb in her hand, she was wearing a towel over her shoulders which soaked up the moisture of her long, salt-and-pepper hair. The only thing she had in common with Josie was the beauty mark on her right cheekbone.

"Mrs. Baldomar?" I asked.

"Sabina," she whispered. "Sabina," she murmured again, and that name sounded like a breath of wind moving swiftly through a row of poplars.

"My name is Gloria," I told her, thinking that she had me confused with someone else.

The aroma of hot chocolate emanating from her kitchen worked its way up my nostrils to a place in my mind where I keep my happiest childhood memories. I was momentarily lost in the enticing, bittersweet essence of nostalgia and mystery lingering in the air of an open door.

María Baldomar didn't seem surprised at all to see me. For an instant, I had the sensation that I had been struggling long and hard to come to this moment and place, to see this woman called María. I felt as if I had come home.

The older woman looked at me. Still holding my gaze, she signaled for me to follow her into the kitchen. Her attitude suggested that in her house we would not talk about anything until after we'd had something to eat or drink.

She guided me gently to a chair. Using a *molinillo*, she beat the hot chocolate until it foamed, then poured two cups and handed me one. In the middle of the table was a basket of fresh-baked *pan de huevo*. She took a large bun and broke it in two with her hands, giving me one of the pieces. Dunking the bread in the chocolate, the two of us ate and drank in silence, except for the little slurps, drips, and sighs of two contented souls. Throughout, I kept wiping tiny drops off my forehead and the area around my lips. The breeze coming through the open window cooled the perspiration, and I began to feel refreshed.

Through the door of the small room behind the kitchen, I could see rows of pots with all kinds of herbs in them, jars full of powders of various colors. Bunches of laurel, sage, sweet basil, and other herbs hung from the ceiling, drying. Two small, flickering votive lamps flanked an altar with a statuette of the Virgin of El Carmen dressed in the traditional brown scapulary dress. Also on the altar was a photo of César Chávez, two photos of Josie Baldomar Hazlitt, and a third one of a woman—whom I safely assumed was Carlota Navarro. A three-legged lava-rock incense burner let out a sweet smell. María got up and went into the room. She took a small amount of coarsely ground *copal*—Mexican incense—and dropped the streamlet of granules into the burner. Its blue, smoky sweetness filled the air. María Baldomar was a *curandera,* a healing woman, I surmised.

The ritual finished, María was the first one to break the silence. "You've come looking for Carlota. I know," she said to me in Spanish, which we spoke throughout our conversation.

I assumed that Josie informed her mother about the goings-on with everyone. Nonetheless, I said, "Yes, we—my detective friend and I—are looking for her, and for our friend Art Bello, who has also disappeared."

"My daughter Josie came to warn me about you," María confirmed. "She doesn't want me talking to anyone, but I know I can trust you." With her hands, she drew the contour of my head as she said, "You have a radiant spirit."

It must have been the cocoa; maybe that's the reason ancient Mexicans called chocolate the drink of the gods, I thought. María smiled, as if she knew what I had been thinking.

"Carlota needs your help and mine," she warned. "I don't agree with my daughter that we should abandon Carlota to her fate."

"Why wouldn't Josie want to help Carlota?" I was intrigued, as I had assumed that Josie and Carlota were very good friends.

"My daughter feels Carlota is responsible for Phillipe's death. Phillipe is my son-in-law."

"I know who he is," I said without thinking. When I noticed María's puzzled look, I explained. "Carlota taped her story for my friend, Luisa Cortez. I recently came across the recording."

María nodded. She resumed her story. "My son-in-law died two weeks ago. No one knows how he died. Josie seems to think that he killed himself, but she will not tell me why she thinks he did." María pointed her right index finger in the air. "And Phillipe's body has not been found. Now, the police suspect Carlota because she went to Josie's house looking for him. Carlota and Phillipe were seen leaving Josie's house together in his car. He never came back. No one has seen Carlota since then." María lowered her eyes as she said the last sentence.

Unlike other older people who have begun to lose their hearing and need to read lips, María had been looking directly into my eyes the entire time, and it seemed odd that she would now take her gaze away. Despite my radiant spirit, I thought, she wasn't quite sure she should make me privy to Carlota's whereabouts. In time, she would tell me. Everything in its due time.

"What exactly did the police find? And why do they think it might be suicide?" I asked.

"All of his personal effects, including his credit cards, were found neatly piled on a beach near Monterey." She paused, then added, "That day, Josie hadn't been feeling well and she had gone to Fresno to see the doctor. My daughter doesn't trust my remedies, you see. The next morning the police stopped by to inform her of Phillipe's disappearance."

"What do you think Carlota and Phillipe were doing in Monterey?" I asked María.

"I have no idea," the older woman answered.

I remembered that Carlota had said in her taped memoirs that Mrs. Stephens's mother lived in the Monterey Peninsula. "I know this may sound strange," I began to say. María gave me her undivided attention. "But I seem to recall that the Stephens family had relatives in Monterey. Do you happen to know where Dr. Stephens is now?"

"I see," María said. She drew in a long breath through her mouth then exhaled it as she added, "Mark Stephens is six feet underground in Fresno. May his soul rest in peace." María raised her right arm and laid it across her chest, then rapped lightly on her left breast with her fist.

"He died?" I exclaimed. "When?"

"The day after he raped Carlota. His heart gave out. I guess he had a weak heart all along. Then, the weight of what he'd done, the alcohol, Carlota's threat, and the possibility of scandal must have strained his heart beyond endurance," she explained.

"How did you know the doctor had died? Did Carlota go back to the Stephenses' house?" I asked.

"No, Carlota did not go back to the doctor's house. Josie read it in the local paper. Apparently someone had alerted immigration and the police."

"Probably because they found the note and the scissors," I said aloud. María looked inquisitively at me. "I told you I recently listened to Carlota's story, which she recorded a long time ago for my friend Luisa," I reminded her.

"Yes, I remember. And yes, Mrs. Stephens had found the note and the scissors. Two Fresno homicide detectives came snooping around, asking us questions about Carlota. They tried to convince us that we would be arrested as accomplices if we didn't produce her. But a few days later, the medical examiner and Dr. Stephens's own doctor said it was a heart attack.

"By that time, the immigration officials had been called in, and they were also looking for Carlota. Mrs. Stephens herself came to Josie's house the day after her husband died. Imagine, that Sunday evening, just a day after the rape, she wanted to talk with Carlota. Mrs. Stephens didn't say how she had found out about what had happened, so we assumed that her husband might have confided what he did. They were Catholic, you see. At any rate, Mrs. Stephens told Josie that she wanted to beg Carlota not to tell anyone about the rape, for her daughters' sake. Then, Mrs. Stephens told Josie that she was expecting another child. No doubt it was true. I don't question Mrs. Stephens's love for her husband nor her grief at the time. But I think the woman's fear of scandal kept her from accepting the pain her husband had caused Carlota. I agreed with Josie when she threw the woman out of her house. Ironically, that day was Carlota's fifteenth birthday. It was a heartbreaking business all around."

"Was Mrs. Stephens really pregnant?"

"I really can't tell you any more about Mrs. Stephens. We never heard from her again," María explained, then continued with her tale. "After the rape, Carlota was very sick for days on end. At dawn, the day after the rape, Josie brought her to me, vomiting, convulsing, screaming. Her skin was red, partly because she had scrubbed herself so hard, but there was more. Carlota didn't know it then, but the fields she went through on her way to Josie's house had been sprayed with the *Devil's blood*."

"Pesticide?" I exclaimed. I had often heard Art and Sonny describe some kinds of pesticides using those same words.

"Yes," María answered. "Pesticide." She lifted her index finger and tapped her lips with it, then closed her eyes slightly. "Parathion or some other nerve gas," she said. "That's what a doctor later told us, that some of those pesticides work by paralyzing the insects. That the poison finally robs them of air, their appetite, everything they need to go on living. The insects choke or starve even though there's food all around them." She lifted her hand up to her forehead and left it there for a moment, then added, "If the pesticide does that to bugs, I can't help wondering what it might do to human beings who come in contact with it."

Paralysis, then asphyxiation. A chill ran up my arms to my shoulders and neck, leaving a trail of goose bumps in its wake, as I remembered the gassings all of us had been exposed to during the civil-rights demonstrations. Fortunately, no deadly amount of nerve gas had been used. It was obvious Carlota had not been as fortunate as the rest of us.

"We tried everything," María said, pulling me out of memory's stream. Then, for no apparent reason, she asked me, "Do you know Dieguito?"

"I don't know him personally, but I know who he is," I replied. "Was he involved in this, too?"

"He certainly was. He and I tried every remedy and every ritual we knew. We bathed Carlota constantly with herbal infusions, trying to clean her skin. We made her drink and eat every herb and root that could even remotely help to flush the poison out of her blood. She had scrubbed herself quite hard after the rape, and the poison had then penetrated more quickly through the broken skin.

"When we couldn't do much for her, despite my objections, Josie insisted we take Carlota to Ramón Caballos, a shaman. A man of magic, he called himself at the time. To tell you the truth, I think he was a quack. Dieguito thought so, too. He got Carlota to sweat in the *Temescal*—the "sweat hut" he had in his backyard. Carlota's skin became so sensitive after the sweating that she could not tolerate anything on her raw skin. She became dehydrated, then she got even sicker thanks to Ramón's medicine. Delirious, disoriented, she had awful headaches and began vomiting again, worse than ever. Ramón had moved her to his house and didn't want anyone to visit her. Josie wouldn't hear of it, so she, Phillipe, and Dieguito went to bring Carlota back to my house. Ramón was furious, but let Carlota go.

"Josie wanted to take her to a hospital, but Carlota had no papers; she had come into the country illegally. She might have been charged with causing the doctor's death, Josie said, and she could go to jail before being sent back to Mexico. We didn't want that to happen.

"Anyway, we hid Carlota as best we could. But she got worse. At that time, Art and Sonny were here working with the farm workers' union. Josie knew them because they had rented a room from her and Phillipe when they had first come to the area to join the movement. Finally, Josie got in touch with Art and Sonny, and they came over. They knew a woman doctor who treated farm workers for different kinds of medical problems. She was also studying the effect of pesticides on them. She's the one who told us that Carlota had possibly been exposed to parathion or some other similar pesticide. César Chávez and his union were already aware of the effect of pesticides on the workers," María said, throwing a glimpse in the direction of Chávez's photograph. "He and the union were trying to have laws passed banning certain pesticides. But very few of those politicians who could change the situation were listening. That's what Art and Sonny told us.

"Anyway, this woman doctor was connected to some large university up north. Art and Sonny took Carlota to her. But by the time the doctor saw Carlota, the pesticide had done some damage to her brain."

"What kind of damage?"

"Carlota has memory lapses that can last one minute or one hour. Now, thanks to the medicine she takes and her endless will power, Carlota has managed to keep to a minimum the length of the lapses. But that is only one of her problems. When she doesn't take her medication, she goes into severe depression. Just before the medication takes effect, she has an incredible amount of energy. She hardly sleeps, and is constantly active. You have to understand that Carlota has a relentless spirit to have withstood the terrible life she's had. She was an orphan at a tender age; she was sold to the doctor by her best friend's—Chuchita's—uncle. At age fifteen, she was raped, then poisoned. And she was pursued by Ramón..."

"Why was Ramón pursuing her?" I interjected.

"He said to Dieguito that he could cure her, that Carlota had been sent to him to test his power. Sent by whom? The man was a charlatan, I tell you. Dieguito talked to him, and he told us that Ramón Caballos wasn't even an Indian, let alone a Pomo Indian, as he claimed. His medicine was a combination of all sorts of rituals and herbs he didn't know well. He'd taken them from the Navajos and the Pomo, and heaven knows who else, but he really had not taken the time—a lifetime it takes—to learn their curative powers, to use them properly."

"I saw a photo at Josie's house earlier today. A man was holding Carlota up. She seemed very sick. Was that Ramón Caballos?"

María sighed. "That's him."

"What did he do after you took Carlota from him?" I asked.

"He didn't do anything at first. But he swore that he would fight the growers—the owners of the farms—who spray their fields with 'the Devil's blood,' and many years later he killed a man and set fire to a storage tank."

I inhaled deeply. I wondered if Ramón Caballos was the man in Art Bello's film who had blown up the storage tank and the vultures, so I asked, "Do you know where that happened?"

"On some farm, near Delano. Josie could tell you more about it. She and Phillipe were there, so were Art and Sonny. They saw it happening," María responded. Then she looked at me and asked, "Is there something the matter?"

"No. Nothing, really," I answered, then added, "I'm assuming Ramón was tried and convicted." When María confirmed my assumption, I asked, "Do you know where he is now?"

"Probably dead by now," María said. "The last we heard was that Ramón had cancer and was dying."

"Did he die in prison?"

"He was first at Folsom, then he was released early, apparently for good behavior. He came looking for Carlota, but she was not here, thank God. Later, Josie found out that Ramón had gotten into trouble and had assaulted a police officer. He ended up in San Quentin." She sighed. "But when he was still at Folsom, Carlota insisted on going to see him. I went with her. I waited for her at the gate; she didn't want me to go inside with her. I don't know what she and Ramón talked about, but after we came back, she began to read about pesticides, then to talk to people about them. She even convinced Father Marino to let her talk to small groups of parishioners about the dangers of pesticides. She was so engaging, and sounded so knowledgeable that people listened to what she had to say."

"Where was Carlota when Ramón blew up the tank of pesticide?" As I asked the question, I realized that I was sounding inquisitorial.

María looked with curiosity at me for a brief moment, then answered, "She was here, with me."

Softening my voice, I then inquired, "What happened to Carlota? In the end, I mean?"

"She was able to get jobs from time to time, but couldn't keep them very long. The fever in her brain didn't let her, and she couldn't get aid from the state. She depended on whatever we could give her. But she was proud and left us for a while, traveled up north. We lost track of her for many years. Later on, when she came back, she told us she had been living in a shack near the city dumps, collecting bottles, cans, anything she could sell so she could buy her medicine." María's voice intensified. "She is one of the bravest women I've known in my life, and a walking miracle.

"Anyway," she continued, regaining her composure, "your friend, Art Bello, saw her one day and recognized her. He took Carlota home with him for a few days and got her plenty of medicine from a Dr. Damasco there."

I felt a knot tightening hard around my vocal cords and I had a hard time forming words and began to clear my throat. María noticed my distress and immediately went to the kitchen to get me a glass of water. I took a large draught then, clearing my throat asked, "Was the doctor's name Darío Damasco?"

"I think so. Why?"

"He was my husband," I said. "You think you know all there is to know about a person, and even after he's dead he keeps surprising you," I whispered.

Of course there hadn't been any reason for Darío to tell me about Carlota. She had probably been a patient referred to him by the Helping Hands Organization, with whom he had often volunteered to provide free medical care for indigent patients.

María took my hand and held it in hers. She didn't say anything, and I was grateful. "I gather you didn't meet Carlota when she was living in Oakland."

"I didn't," I confirmed. "Anyway, tell me what happened
to Carlota after she saw my husband."

"Art's poet friends found things for her to do—gardening,
cleaning. Art and Sonny fixed it so she could start taking
classes at a junior college in the area, where Art—bless his
heart—worked. I'm guessing, because Carlota never said who
got her a fake green card, but I think it was Art. She knew so
much about pesticides and legislation affecting the food-grow-
ing industry that Art even got her some 'gigs,' as she called
them, speaking to small groups about the need to curb the use
of pesticides. Carlota made some money that way. She did as
much as her condition allowed her to do. Then, one day, she
showed up at Josie's door. I'd never seen my daughter so
happy."

"Do you have any idea why your daughter thinks Carlota
is responsible for your son-in-law's death?" I asked her, then
added, "And why is Josie being followed by immigration officers?"

"I didn't know she was being followed, but it doesn't surprise me. She probably called the *migra* herself. She wants
Carlota caught." María shook her head. "Sometimes I don't
understand what moves my daughter. Willfulness, perhaps,"
she said, exasperated. She touched her hair and reached for
the comb on the table.

"I don't think Josie called immigration," I told her.
"Justin Escobar, my detective friend, and I, and the *migra*
officers were following her. Your daughter made sure no one
from immigration was around when she came to your house."

"My poor daughter," María exclaimed. "I really don't
blame her for her willfulness. It's probably the only thing that
has kept her going. Life hasn't been kind to Josie, either. I
tried my best, but Nicasio, Josie's father, wasn't a very good
father or husband. I hadn't wanted to marry him, but he
forced me to go with him one night, and after that my father

felt he had no choice but to marry me to Nicasio. Josie barely
managed to finish high school because she had to go to work
very young. Nicasio drank away every penny he and I made at
the cannery. He slapped my daughter and me around, and one
day I came home and found one of his drunken friends trying
to..." María didn't finish her thought. After a while, she added,
"Nicasio was a despicable man. You can perhaps understand
why Josie and I tried to do as much as we could for Carlota.
My poor Carlota," she lamented.

"I can see that you love Carlota very much," I stated.

María looked at me, wondering where I was leading, then
shook her head. She accidentally dropped her comb. I bent
over to pick it up, then handed it to her. Before I could ask if
perhaps Josie was jealous of the attention she gave Carlota,
María said, "No, Josie doesn't resent my deep affection for
Carlota. She loves her, too."

"I guess after sixteen years or so of knowing each other,
they're like sisters," I commented.

María finished combing her hair. Letting it still hang
loose, she took the towel off her shoulders and folded it. Then
she said, "Josie and Carlota don't love each other like sisters."

"No?" I said. They love each other like mother and daughter then, I was about to suggest, when it dawned on me that
María was trying to tell me something without spelling it out.
"Oh," I said, and nodded. "What about Phillipe?" I asked. "Did
he know how Carlota and Josie felt about each other?"

"Yes, he knew. So did I," María answered. "We never
talked about it, but even blind, we would have known what
was going on. My daughter is very beautiful, and she has
always gotten attention from everyone. I'm afraid that has
made her not only expect but demand to be the center of
attention." She paused briefly, then continued, "I think
Phillipe knew that she loved him as much as she loved Carlota. Phillipe has always been in love with Josie. Like me, he

would never leave her. Killing himself was out of the question. He had no reason to do so, especially now that Josie might be expecting a child."

"Wow!" was all I could manage after these revelations. "What do you think happened to Phillipe? Do you think someone killed him? I mean, if, as you say, he didn't commit suicide, where is he?" Everything was beginning to get quite complicated. My mind was racing, and without giving María an opportunity to answer, I asked again, "Or are you saying that he might have been murdered? Is that what Josie believes? That Carlota is responsible for Phillipe's death?" María had answered every one of my questions by shaking her head, except for the last two. Then she had nodded twice. So I ventured the next question: "Do you know where Carlota is?"

María didn't answer. She lowered her eyes and began to braid her hair. I again saw her hands tremble.

"She's the only one who can give us the answers we're looking for," I insisted. "If it's true that Phillipe was murdered, then all the people connected with him might be in danger. I know it," I said with vehemence.

María Baldomar thought for a moment, then said, "I don't know the name of the place where Carlota is. She didn't want to tell me in order to keep me out of any trouble. My poor Carlota, worrying always about not getting the people she loves in trouble." María sighed. "All I know is that she's in a house somewhere in the wine country. Dieguito is with her."

"Do you know whether Art Bello is with her?"

"No," María assured me. "Art is not with them. She would have told me if he were."

I wondered if the place in the wine country might be Sarah's house in Sonoma. "I think I might know where Carlota is," I said as the image of the woman tied to the cactus surfaced. Although I was now able to see the images in the visions with my eyes open, I instinctively closed them to conjure the woman's countenance and to see it clearly. Despite my concentrated effort, I still couldn't identify the woman's face since her head—seemingly lifeless—hung down and rested on her chin. I could only sense that she wasn't María. I opened my eyes to see María gazing at me with more intensity now than ever.

"What you know will always cost you, Sabina."

I stopped in my tracks. "Why have you been calling me Sabina? Who is she?"

"She was my friend, a young woman of great power who could see the past. She died in 1946, forty-three years ago."

"And you think I am Sabina?"

"I don't know that you are her, but you could be. You have the same radiant spirit she had. I see it in you. I know you can also see the past."

"The past?"

"To look into the past, Sabina and I were taught, is to look into the future. But it takes a certain kind of talent, a great gift, to see how the past will become the future. That's what your gift is all about. Mine is to alleviate the pain, to mitigate the sorrow, make the body and the spirit be in harmony with one another." She was lost in thought for a moment.

"You make it sound so simple," I said. "It hasn't been that simple for me."

"Only because you doubt yourself so much. It is hard to be who you are," she said after a while. "People make fun of you—they don't understand," she continued, speaking in a soft voice, almost as if confessing something to herself. "They taunt you, unable to see the nature of your gift, afraid of it many times. After all these years, Josie still feels embarrassed when someone asks me what I do and I tell them the truth." Her voice thinned out, and her pupils narrowed suddenly as if a blaze of sunlight had burned into her gaze.

The thin, double-edged blade of anger and loneliness was now beginning to carve into my heart, and I rose slowly from my chair to keep it from cutting too deep. But the memory of my father's reaction when my mother tried to explain my clairvoyance to him had already surfaced, and his words left a blazing trail across my mind. "Is my daughter now going to become one of those Madames so-and-so with their crystal balls, or those gypsies who read palms for a buck?" he had asked, not knowing that I was within hearing range.

Trying not to dwell too long in the house of pain, I turned my attention to María again. She was now standing next to me, waiting. We began to walk toward the front door. "One day, soon, you will find the strength to let everyone know who and what you are. I know you will," María said, already at the door. She held both my hands. I held back the tears. "Take care of Carlota for me," she begged. "Promise me you'll look after her. She needs someone to help her now more than ever."

I promised with a nod, not sure what Carlota's fate was at this point. I swallowed my words and decided not to tell María that Carlota would be the prime suspect should Justin's and my investigation reveal that Sonny hadn't killed himself.

I wrote my address and phone number on a piece of paper and handed it to María. "In case you need to get in touch with me."

Stepping out, I saw Justin's van parked up the street and figured that either he had gotten nowhere with Josie or she'd given him the slip, too.

As I walked towards him, past the grapevines, I noticed that the leaves had begun to turn yellow, ochre, and brown. In the time I had spent with María, autumn had finally arrived.

# Eight
## "Wrecked Upon Infinity"

As I got closer to the van, I was surprised to see that Justin was reading *The Review of Existential Psychology and Psychiatry*. Even though I knew he had a master's degree in psychology, since we'd met I had been aware only of his interest in reading criminology, sociology, and photography books. In his personal library I'd seen photo essays and novels. Occasionally, I had also seen him read poetry books. As soon as I got in, he laid the *Review* between the seats, underneath the Fresno map.

"What did Josie have to say?" I asked.

"Well," Justin began to explain, "she didn't say much, really. She was gone for a long time. When she came back, she showed pretty much the same attitude and was as tight-mouthed as before. But I did get the feeling that she'll be fleeing the coop as soon as she shakes the *migra*. I don't know how she's going to do it, though; they're really dogging her." He paused. "I'm almost sure one of them is with corrections; the other is *migra*."

"How do you know that?"

"I saw them over by a church near city hall. They seemed to be waiting, so I parked, took out the map, and pretended to be looking for a street. I knew Josie wasn't in that church because I had just left her at home. Anyway, I asked them to show me the fastest way to get to Fresno through the back roads."

"And they did?"

"*Simón*—they sure did. Those guys are experts on back roads. They boast they will get to know a valley this size like

the palm of their hand in one day flat," Justin replied. "I'm
sure they can do it, too."

"But how do you know one of them is with Corrections?"

"His I.D. was clipped to his paperwork; it said 'Department of Corrections.' That seemed odd, because he carried
himself more like a prison guard than a probation officer.
Anyway, he's operating far from home; his name tag showed
he works at..."

"San Quentin!" I interjected. Taken by surprise, Justin's
mouth opened but no words came out. "How do you know?" his
eyes seemed to say. So I offered him an answer immediately.
"It's all speculation on my part, but I think they're probably
looking for a Ramón Caballos. He's the guy who killed a man
and blew up that tank of pesticide and the vultures to
smithereens back in 1973. Remember? Art's film? The video at
Sonny's place?" Not quite realizing why Justin's mouth was
still a bit open, I looked straight at him to see if he understood, and he nodded. "But he's supposed to have died of cancer at San Quentin," I continued, then quickly briefed him on
my conversation with María.

"Ah, yes," Justin said, finally closing his mouth. He
seemed amused, and I realized he'd thought I'd come upon
this information through *extraordinary* means. "This case is a
little twister," Justin finally said. "I talked to Tom Carlson,
that deputy friend of Bob Messinger's."

As we drove past Josie's house on our way to Fresno, we
saw her get in her car and drive away.

"It turns out that Tom Carlson and his team are only
assisting the cops in Monterey," Justin explained. "But Carlson never once mentioned Carlota Navarro as a possible suspect."

"He didn't? I'm confused."

"So am I," Justin agreed, then added, "but that's not all.
To complicate things, Carlson said sometimes Josie claims

that a convict has had something to do with her husband's death. Carlson told me that the cops hadn't found any basis for Josie's allegations." He glimpsed in my direction, then continued, "When I talked to Tom Carlson, I didn't know that Ramón Caballos was at San Quentin. But when I mentioned the *migra* and the Quentin guard, Carlson just smiled and told me to keep digging."

I seemed to have more questions now than when we started out for Fresno. As we passed endless vineyards, artichokes and other crops, I thought of Carlota Navarro and of her painful journey through those same fields covered with pesticides as she rushed from the Stephenses' residence to Josie's home.

"How do you know Josie knows she's being followed?" I asked. "Did she tell you?"

"I didn't ask, but she knows."

"Did she let you in her house this time?"

"No, she didn't let me in," he said. I thought I saw a smile on his face. "But she opened the door just wide enough for me to see her garment bag on the dining room table."

"Do you think she wanted you to see the bag?"

"I don't think anything Josie Baldomar does happens by accident," he said, and paused to think for a moment. "Maybe it was just to confuse matters, to keep me off Carlota's track or hers, or maybe to make it more difficult for the cops to follow her. One smart woman, that one is."

"Her mother is also smart," I said, then corrected myself. "No, she's more than smart, she's wise."

My conversation with María Baldomar had helped us put into perspective the things we knew about this case. In the end, this knowledge turned out to be a few hard facts, some felicitous coincidences, and a number of possibilities.

"We need to consolidate our plan," I continued. "We're faced with too many suspects running around."

"Not too many," he said. "No matter how I look at it, Carlota Navarro stands dead center in this picture." Then he parked the van and walked to a roadside fruit stand. He came back with some apples, a bag of pistachios, and two sodas. "Whenever the cops suspect foul play in a case like this, they always look close to home for the culprit," he said as he offered me a Hansen's soda. I declined. "So, they suspect Josie Baldomar might have done away with her husband," Justin stated.

"But why would Josie do that?" I asked. Without waiting for Justin's answer, I added, "Look. Josie and Phillipe seemed to be having financial problems. Let's face it, her salary as a teacher's aide is probably nothing to brag about. Josie needed Phillipe, now more than ever. Remember? María said that Josie might be pregnant with his child. Besides," I continued, "María told me that Phillipe knew about Josie's relationship with Carlota."

Perplexed, Justin looked at me and asked, "What do you mean by 'Josie's relationship with Carlota'?"

"From what María has told me, I gather that Josie and Carlota have been in love with each other for a long time, and that Phillipe has known about—and accepted—their relationship all along," I answered. "So, you see, I really can't find a reason for either Phillipe's killing himself or Josie's killing him."

"I see." Justin rubbed his forehead. He said, "Then, the other possibility is greed. And you just mentioned the key words—a cash-flow problem. I wonder if Phillipe had any insurance worth being killed for." He tapped his head with his fingers. "I'll have to check into that when we get back."

"Something still bothers me," I said. "Why hasn't his body been found?"

"The body might be tangled in undersea vegetation, or the ocean currents might wash him ashore far from where he actually drowned..."

"Granted. But it could also be that Phillipe is still alive," I suggested. "Still, I fail to understand how all of these events relate to Sonny's death."

"It's hard to say if there's even a connection between Sonny's and Phillipe's apparent suicides. Nevertheless, the coincidence is mind-boggling. But again," Justin said, offering me some pistachios, "unless we know what motive anyone had to kill Sonny, we're really at a disadvantage."

"What about Ramón Caballos?" I said, indicating I didn't care for anything to eat.

Justin took an apple and bit into it. He thought for a moment, then began to explore the possibility of Ramón's involvement. "Ramón Caballos, a *magic* man, is quite capable of killing, and undeniably had a double grudge against everyone in Art's and Sonny's group." He looked at me, and I agreed. "First, they all took Carlota away from Ramón," Justin continued. "Then, they didn't back him up when he blew up the tank. But he might turn out to be another ghost killer if María is right about him dying in prison."

Justin drank one of the sodas and started the engine again, to resume our drive to Fresno. "But suppose that he isn't dead and still in San Quentin," he said. "Then, I wonder who might have carried out the deed for him."

"Is he still in San Quentin, though?" I asked. Justin's eyes twinkled, indicating that he'd asked himself that very same question.

"I'll ask Leo to look into that. Nonetheless," he said, "Carlota Navarro's got to be the key. Judging by the number of people looking for her, including the *migra* and the San Quentin cop. I'd say everyone else agrees on that."

"But, other than María and Josie, we're the only ones who know that Carlota might be staying with Dieguito. By the way" I asked, "any idea where Dieguito lives?"

"In the Valley of the Moon, not too far from Quinta Selena. The town's name is Agua Caliente. A lot of Mexicans, Chicanos, and Native Americans live there. But first we have to look at the photos and the lab reports."

"Any chance that Art is with them?"

"I'm hoping he is."

"He probably knows about Sonny's suicide—death, I mean." Justin heard me correct my slip of the tongue and gave me a quick glance.

What if we were wasting all this investigation on something that didn't happen? What if Sonny really had killed himself? I suddenly realized these two questions had been on the back of my mind all day long as we trekked across the San Joaquín Valley.

"I've had those same doubts," he noted. "I think it's healthy," he reassured me. "It keeps you from fabricating things, from making the investigation an intellectual pursuit."

One thing seemed certain, I realized as Justin spoke, and it was that he and I had managed in less than forty-eight hours to find our way to a point of no return in the maze. I suspected that, now, whether the basic questions were relevant or not, he and I had to push forward trying to find the exit; an attempt to find our way back would take just as much energy.

More than anything, if I didn't see this investigation through to the end, I would end up with many—too many—unanswered questions. For me, never finding the answers would be the same as being wrecked upon infinity. If to none other, I subscribed to this idea of hell.

# Nine
## Twists, Deadly Turns and Dead-ends

Fresno, situated in the heart of the San Joaquín Valley, was flat and laid out as a grid of straight streets and avenues. But, in its wealthiest district we found ourselves driving through meandering, gently sloping country roads that led to houses hidden behind tall eucalyptus trees and oaks. We had the impression that we were in a woodsy, mountain region.

"It's incredible," I said, admiring the ingenuity of the planning engineers. "The terrain is just as flat as anywhere else in this valley. Yet, you get the impression you really are traveling through hillsides."

"Isn't it?" Justin shook his head in amazement. "That's it," he said a moment later as he pointed to a two-story, early California, white stuccoed house with a red tile roof. The dark green, freshly-cut turf caught my eye right away. "That must be the Stephens's house," Justin concluded.

In the house across the street, an elderly woman was hosing down a perfectly designed rose garden surrounded by a picket fence that came up to the packed gravel sidewalk. Some buds were still visibly fresh and moist. In this Shangrila, people seemed to care nothing about the drought or other people's needs, I realized sadly.

No one answered at the Stephens's house. So we walked across the street to talk to the lady with the perfect garden. Before we had a chance to ask her anything, she told us, "You're too late. You should have been here yesterday. They already hired a gardener and a housekeeper."

"Beg your pardon," Justin said in a very polite tone. I'd seen him do that with other people who were rude or made racist assumptions. His attitude usually disarmed them. I stayed out of it, as more and more I had this terrible urge to snap every little rosebud off her plants. No, I thought, let Justin handle this one.

"We're not looking for a job," he said to her. "But we are looking for the Stephens family."

"You're too late. I already told you," the woman said, still assuming that we were looking for domestic employment. "Randolph left yesterday, and she left this morning."

Justin was making little progress. I wondered what he would try next.

A man—in his mid-seventies at least—stuck his head out a window. "Edith," he said, "Hilde made some lemonade for us. Come inside." The man disappeared from our view, but he must have decided to look us over, for a few seconds later he opened the front door. Slender and tall, with a slow but sure stride, he came up to where we stood. He had a transistor radio close to his ear. "Everything okay, Edith?" he said loudly. Pointing at his ear with his finger, he indicated to Justin and me that his wife was hard of hearing. His eyes twinkled and he smiled delightedly.

Justin and I looked at each other and laughed softly. We realized that Edith had never heard us say we were not looking for domestic employment.

"Yes, Oliver," Edith said as she turned towards him. "Turn off that radio. The A's game won't start until five, you told me."

Still smiling, the elderly man came up to the white picket fence around the garden. "Who's going to pitch today?" I asked, then commented, "Stew sure *mowed* them down yesterday."

Justin looked at me and raised his eyebrows, obviously enjoying himself. Edith ignored us and continued watering the rose bushes.

Oliver came closer. "Mike Moore will be pitching. He's very good, too, you know?"

"No doubt. Another shutout, you think?" I sputtered.

"The A's will win today's game, too. The Giants don't stand a chance," Oliver said with animated gestures. Something in his demeanor reminded me of both my father and paternal grandfather, and I found myself enjoying our short exchange.

"Where are you from, young lady?" Oliver asked.

"We're both from Oakland," I said to him, pointing at Justin and myself. "Home of the A's," I chirped, adding, "but we're originally from Argentina." Justin gave me a quick glance, then took his amused gaze away.

"What are you doing here? You and your husband should be home getting ready for the game," Oliver said.

"Don't worry. My *husband* and I will make it home before the game begins," I reassured him. Feeling a little uncomfortable at being deceitful in order to extract information from him, I took my gaze away. But reminding myself of the reason Justin and I were there, I continued probing. "We've been trying to locate the Stephenses. We're visiting, and we had a message for them from some of their friends in L.A."

I wasn't good at improvising, but I must have sounded convincing, for Oliver nodded and said, "Well, young Randolph left yesterday morning. He and his sister had a very good offer, you know? The real estate agent came yesterday to get the place ready. And Remmine left early this morning," Oliver elaborated. "I hope a nice young couple moves in. Like Mark and Eleanor when they first got married." He sighed. "Those were happy times."

"Don't start getting sentimental, Oliver," Edith warned from behind a yellow rose bush. Oliver, Justin, and I smiled as we realized Edith wasn't hearing-impaired, but rather was afflicted with a selectively domineering sense of hearing.

"I thought the sisters owned the house," I remarked. Justin gestured with his hand, cautioning me to slow down.

"Sandy and Remmi decided to give the house to their younger brother," Edith said behind Justin, startling him a bit. Here were two names Justin and I recognized immediately from the tape of Carlota's story. We turned our attention to Edith, who was now saying, "Good girls, those two, always looking after Randy, you know, with their father dying before Randy was even born and their mother passing away when he was fifteen. Simply awful, to grow up without your father and lose your mother at that age."

I looked at the house across the street, at the tall eucalyptus and oaks, and I imagined Carlota hiding that night in their shadows, waiting for Dr. Stephens to return. I wondered if Edith and Oliver had been aware of that night's events. Perhaps in the end no one else found out about the rape. Maybe Mrs. Stephens was able to keep it hushed. Regardless of how she found out about it, Mrs. Stephens had known what her husband had done to Carlota. Why else would she go looking for Carlota later? And what about the two young girls, I wondered. Had they ever learned about the circumstances surrounding their father's death?

"Do you happen to know where Randy is living now?"

"He moved up north to that valley where all those computer geniuses live," Edith said. Silicon Valley, I reasoned. From the look in Justin's eyes, he obviously shared my conclusion.

"Why not?" I asked rhetorically, knowing I was treading muddy waters, hoping I would not slip too soon. "Randy's a computer genius himself," I said as I held my breath in expectation of the fall.

"That he is," Oliver agreed, his enthusiasm obvious. "And after he graduates from Stanford, he'll be able to write his own ticket." He sounded as proud as a grandfather would be of his grandson's talents and accomplishments.

"He should have been a doctor, like his father and his grandfather," Edith interjected. Her remark made me think of my mother-in-law's enthusiasm when Tania announced she was going into medicine. Darío and I had not expected Tania to go into medicine just because her father and grandfather were medical doctors. But, I realized, my mother-in-law had expected Tania to uphold the family tradition.

"I guess it's important to uphold the family tradition and follow the father's footsteps," I said.

"Having *two* doctors in the family is *more* than enough," Oliver commented, disregarding his wife's attitude with a slight shrug.

"Now," Justin said, tapping his lips with his finger. "Is it Sandy or Remmi who is the..."

"Sandy, of course," Edith said, then looked at Justin with a glint of suspicion in her eyes.

"She's at that Navy hospital near San Francisco," Oliver said. "She's a lieutenant."

"Ah, yes," Justin remarked. "She's at Oak Knoll Navy Hospital in Oakland."

"That's it," Oliver said. "Smart girl. It's not easy to become a navy surgeon."

A woman wearing a light yellow uniform and apron stepped out of the house carrying a tray with glasses and a pitcher of lemonade. "Some lemonade?" Oliver offered, pointing at the pitcher. He walked to the gate and opened it, inviting us to join him and his wife in the rose garden.

"Yes, please," I said, to Justin's surprise, for he was getting ready to decline. He looked at me, trying to guess my reason for wanting to stay longer. I had none, other than looking forward to a glass of cold lemonade and Oliver's company. As we all sipped, Oliver and Edith gave us a tour of their garden.

"We must be getting back," I said after a while. And waving my index finger I chirped, "We musn't miss that A's game."

"Enjoy," Justin said to a smiling Oliver.

We walked back to the van, which we had parked a block away.

"A dead end," I said, and checked my watch. I hadn't realized it was three o'clock in the afternoon.

"Maybe," Justin said noncommittally to my comment about the Stephenses. "But we still don't know why the note and scissors that Carlota left by Dr. Stephens's side the night he raped her appeared sixteen years later next to Sonny Mares's body. We'll have to talk to the Stephens children at some point."

"I guess every avenue is still open," I said.

"Uh-huh," he answered. Then he asked, "Hungry?"

"I am."

We stopped at a Japanese restaurant in downtown Fresno. An hour later, when we settled back in the van, Justin picked up the map to figure out the fastest way to the highway back to Oakland.

I glimpsed the title of the article he was reading in the psychiatry review: "Dreams, Imagination, and Existence" by Michel Foucault. *Dream, imagination, and existence*—the words blazed through my consciousness, leaving a trail of doubt and anger. Why was he reading about dreams? Was he trying to figure me out, see if I really had a dark gift as I claimed? "Don't be ridiculous," I told myself, but I didn't sound very convincing.

I realized that ever since Friday, when we were at Sonny's house, and Leo had put me through that let's-see-how-good-you-are session, I had suspected that Justin had told him about my clairvoyance. I now knew frustration had been nagging at me since that evening. But I was angrier at myself for keeping quiet, for not saying anything before. Had I become so complacent? Deep inside me, a voice cautioned that I was making a mistake, that it was the wrong time to get my tongue back. But my mind seemed locked on a track, spinning around doubt and suspicion over and over.

"There's so much I no longer say," I whispered. Justin gave me a questioning look, but asked me neither to repeat nor clarify.

A discomforting feeling began to settle in my stomach, and I looked away. I watched the coppers, ochres, browns, and yellows amidst the light and dark greens of the San Joaquín Valley. And I saw the reflection of my soul in all of them. Perhaps, for me, autumn had also finally arrived.

Justin pushed in a tape and Sarah Vaughan, one of his favorite vocalists, began to sing. "I'll be seeing you, in all the old familiar places..." Her voice rolled, liquid and vital, but I was feeling so tired and frustrated that not even Vaughan's mellifluous cadences seemed to offer a reprieve.

It had been a long day, a day of alternate currents: revelations and illusions. All sorts of contradictory feelings and ideas swirled around in my head. But my mind refused to ponder anymore on the significance of this or that clue, to analyze my feelings or Justin's motive, or to decipher any dream. I turned to face the window and curled up as best I could. Then I closed my eyes and let the engine's drone and Vaughan's cadent lyrics lead me into oblivion.

When I woke up, Sarah Vaughan's singing had been replaced by the voice of a radio sportscaster, and the roar of the baseball fans at the Oakland Coliseum had drowned out the hum of the engine. The A's were winning the second game of the World Series five to one. In the side mirror I saw the western sky ablaze with the light of the setting sun.

"I phoned Sarah Sáenz Owens, Art's landlady," Justin said as I looked around trying to figure out where we were.

"She's expecting us. She says she found the negatives and developed them. We have to pick up the photos at her house."

"Okay," I said, reaching for the Hansen's soda.

"You're not going to like it," he warned. "It's warm."

"I need the sugar," I told him. "I feel groggy."

"Did you have any bad dreams?" Justin asked, looking straight at me.

"No," I uttered with a gurgling sound. "Maybe that's why I feel so weak." I attempted a smile. The sugar in the soda had begun to take effect.

Ten minutes later we were knocking at the Sáenz Owen's house in Piedmont. She was waiting for us, and handed us a large envelope with the three photographs she'd been able to develop.

Sarah suggested we look at them under her reading lamp in the study, and we followed her there. She looked in her drawer and took out two small magnifying glasses. Justin and I looked at the photos, then at each other.

"Have you ever seen this man around here?" I asked her, pointing at Ramón Caballos.

Sarah looked at the photo then shook her head. "But this is the woman who gave Art the bow and arrow," she observed, pointing at Carlota Navarro. "I've given it a great deal of thought since I developed the photo and I am positive." She looked inquisitively at Justin and me. "Do you have any idea where Art might be?"

"We're not sure," Justin replied. "But we think he might be with Dieguito in Agua Caliente. If we have to go to the Sonoma Valley, would it be possible for us to stay at Quinta Selena?"

"By all means," Sarah reassured him. "I'll phone my house manager. When should I tell Robin to expect you?"

"Tomorrow, but we don't know the exact time. I'll phone ahead if you don't mind."

"Not at all. You two might want to stay at either Quinta Selena or at the caretaker's cottage." Sarah turned to me. "We don't have a caretaker, and the cottage is really a guest house," she clarified for me. She turned to Justin again and said, "Let Robin Cardozo, my house manager, know which space you want when you call to confirm your arrival." She put the photos back in the envelope and handed it to Justin.

"Will do," he said as he took the envelope.

A while later, on the way to my house, Justin asked, "Would you mind if we stop by Las Garzas?" His request came as a surprise. When it came to Mexican food, Justin was very particular. He was a nephew of Tito Garro, a great California chef, who had taught him not only to cook authentic Mexican food, but also to pay attention to what he ate. Justin had developed a taste for gourmet Mexican cooking. He was a superb cook, and I had on various occasions enjoyed a delightful meal prepared by him.

And now, he wanted to stop at Las Garzas. "Your uncle Tito is probably turning in his grave," I teased, still not believing that he would want "take-out" from a Mexican restaurant.

"I have to see Leo and Bob Messinger's lab at nine," he explained. "I don't have time to cook. But I'll drop you off first," he added.

Ten minutes later, after we turned from Park Boulevard onto Excelsior and Justin parked the van across the street from my house, we spotted the moon rising slowly from behind the Oakland hills.

I gathered my things and unfastened my seat belt. I then looked at Justin who had turned off the engine. "C'mon," I said, "I'll cook something for both of us. I'm hungry, too."

Justin wasn't moving.

"C'mon," I urged him. "Or you'll be late for your appointment with Leo and Bob."

"I think it's better if I don't," he muttered, and didn't finish the thought.

"Why not?" I looked for his eyes, but he avoided looking at me. "Talk to me, please," I wanted to say. Instead, I restated my question only to realize that I was hyperventilating and my legs felt weak. As I had suspected earlier that day, I knew something was happening that I wasn't sure I wanted to confront.

Justin seemed more distant than ever, then finally turned to look at me. "If I go in there with you," he stressed, pointing a finger at my house. "I..." He hesitated.

For an instant, we were both totally quiet. All I could hear was the wild beating of my heart. I felt only my blood rushing down my torso to my belly, leaving in its wake a tingling, aching want that was at once familiar and new.

"If you went in with me," I finally said, and had to stop to take a breath before I finished the sentence, "you would get a good meal, listen to some good Charlie Parker or Miles Davis, and maybe even take a short nap while I prepare dinner."

Justin agreed with a nod and a half-smile, jumped out of the van, and slammed the door. The sudden gush of air and the noise slapped my ear. I felt an old emptiness begin to spread out in my chest. It's better this way, my reason said. And my body had no other choice but to acquiesce.

Negotiating the steps up to the porch in the semi-darkness, I looked in my purse for my keys, found them, then dropped them. When Justin bent to pick them up, I looked over his shoulder and saw the woman coming out of the shadows, looking directly at me with wild eyes. I took a step back, then was frozen in place.

"Carlota," I whispered to Justin, who had just stood up. I pointed at the woman standing by my car, carrying something I couldn't make out. Disoriented, she took a few steps, stretched her hand to us, then collapsed. Justin jumped over

the side of the stairs while I rushed down the steps to the spot
where, seemingly inert and lifeless in the moonlight, Carlota
Navarro lay next to a box and an old Mexican burlap shopping
bag.

# Ten
## *Foxglove and Old Fears*

Shortly after Víctor Trummer, our family physician and an old friend of Darío's, arrived, a reluctant Justin left for his appointment with Bob and Leo. Although I sensed no danger from the woman lying on the bed in the guest room, so weak she couldn't even talk, Justin had not wanted to leave me alone with Carlota Navarro before Víctor got there. After a brief introduction, Justin left for his meeting.

As soon as Víctor Trummer walked into the bedroom and I introduced him as a doctor, Carlota showed him a number of prescription medicine vials. "I also take digitoxin, but I don't have it with me," she explained.

"Hmm. Digitoxin...Who prescribed that for you?"

"Dr. Damasco did, a long time ago, when he first treated me for the seizures," she said, and threw a glance in my direction.

"Digitoxin. Fascinating," Víctor said, then proceeded to examine Carlota, who followed his every move with her eyes. "Uh-huh. Uh-huh," he kept saying as he checked reflexes and vital signs. Then he felt the swollen lymph glands on her neck.

My having been married to a doctor did not help me understand what these "Uh-huhs"—seemingly uttered by one and all doctors alike, including Darío—ever meant. So, as soon as the stethoscope was off his ears, I asked, "What do you think?"

He patted Carlota's hand while he told her in a reassuring tone, "Rest awhile, Miss Navarro. Mrs. Damasco and I have to talk. We'll be right outside if you need us." Then, he motioned for me to follow him out of the room.

Out in the hall, Víctor asked me, "What do you know about her condition?"

"Apparently—well, recently, I found out that she was Darío's patient at one time through Healing Hands." Víctor nodded to indicate he understood that Carlota had few resources. "She was accidentally exposed to some kind of pesticide when she was fourteen," I explained, trying to be brief and to the point. "I understand, from other people who were with her at the time of her accident, that she was dying, but a specialist in pesticide contamination was able to save her. Carlota, however, was left with some kind of neurological impediment."

I paused, then decided to relate to him what María Baldomar had told me about Carlota's condition. "From this little information, I gather that she has seizures. Mrs. Baldomar— the woman in whose house Carlota lived in Kingsburg—told me that these seizures affect Carlota's memory. She also explained that Carlota goes through periods of depression followed by others of euphoria. Based on what Darío used to tell me about conditions such as hers, I've assumed that Carlota's illness largely resembles manic-depression. Am I wrong?"

"You may be right," Víctor responded. "She could be suffering from a kind of bipolar depression. This would explain why she's taking an anti-depressant. And all of this is the result of pesticide contamination?"

"It would seem so."

"I've read reports in medical journals about the effect of pesticides and herbicides on human beings. Ironically, people still feel it's a problem only for the farm worker," Víctor remarked as he began to write a prescription. "I always tell Irma there is a human price to be paid for the unblemished apple or grape. But that's what we consumers demand." He finished writing the prescription. Handing it to me, he added, "The proverbial poisoned apple. Amazing, isn't it?" He began to write another prescription. "Miss Navarro tells me that Darío prescribed a low dose of digitoxin for her."

"Digitoxin? That's a cardiac stimulant, isn't it?"

"Yes, a cardiac glycoside, extracted from digitalis. I can only guess what Darío had in mind when he prescribed it, but what is important is that it seems to work. Or so Miss Navarro has just told me. She said that she began to feel much better after Darío started her on the digitoxin.

"I won't give you a prescription for the digitalis. But make sure you mention it to the Healing Hands physician. They have her records.

"Well, then," Víctor Trummer said, pointing at another prescription slip he was handing me, "This one is for the antidepressant she told me she's been taking. I suspect that she has probably been off her medication for only a few days. But the seizures, coupled with lack of rest and improper nourishment, have weakened her." He paused, then added, "So she also needs a vitamin and mineral supplement, and three square meals a day. We need to build up her red blood cells. Those swollen lymph glands in her neck worry me." Víctor spoke fast, and I tried not to miss a word. "It might be a good idea to get some nourishment into her, maybe some clear broth at first, chicken and vegetables later if she can tolerate them. I'm also giving you a prescription for a glucose solution to be taken orally. That brain has to be fed, or she might go into convulsions again and she'll start vomiting."

He handed me the third prescription. "I'm sure Healing Hands will reimburse you for the expense. As a matter of fact, it might be a good idea to have their oncologist look her over."

"The oncologist? That's a specialist in tumors," I said, then asked. "Is it because of the swollen glands on her neck?"

"Yes."

I sighed.

Víctor looked at me. "How about you?" he asked. "Are you still having trouble sleeping at night?"

"Not so often, now," I assured him.

"You look a bit flushed." He touched my forehead. "You could use some nourishment and rest yourself," he suggested, then gave me a long look. "Irma tells me you've decided to become an...investigator?"

How does Irma Trummer know? I was about to ask him. Irma and I hadn't seen each other since Darío died eighteen months earlier. I guessed the gossip express had been busy lately. "I'm apprenticing for a private investigator's license," I said.

"I see. Do you like doing that rather than...?" He began to ask, but seemed to change his mind.

Smiling, I completed his question. "Rather than being a doctor's wife or a speech specialist?"

Víctor looked at me and reciprocated with a smile. "You've always been independent and self-sufficient, Gloria. I've always admired that in you." He paused, then let out, "I wish Irma would..."

"Careful what you wish for," I said to Víctor jokingly. Then seriously I asked, "Really. How are you and Irma doing?" Shortly after Darío died, rumor had it that the Trummers were getting a divorce.

"Much better," Víctor answered.

"I'm glad to hear that," I remarked.

He pressed my elbow to indicate that we could go back in the room to talk with Carlota.

"Miss Navarro, you need rest," Víctor told Carlota. "I'm leaving some sleeping pills with Mrs. Damasco. If you can't sleep, take one pill, but no more than two in eight hours. I want you to eat well and take your medication faithfully. All right?"

Carlota, who had propped herself up on pillows, agreed. "Thank you." She reached into her sweater pocket and took out two twenty-dollar bills and offered them to Víctor Trummer. "I'm sorry," she told him, "this is all I have with me."

Víctor folded Carlota's fingers over the bills and said, "This one is for Dr. Damasco. All right?" Carlota looked at Víctor then at me, and she thanked us.

As I opened the front door to let Víctor out, I saw Carlota's burlap bag and box. In my haste to get medical attention for her, I had dropped both items by the door, and I hadn't given her belongings a second thought. Picking up both things, I noticed that the box was a bit heavy, and something inside it made a scratchy noise. Thinking it might contain a pet, I opened the box carefully and took a quick look inside. Instead of an animal, I saw a three-leaf prickly-pear cactus, thrusting out of a plastic bag with soil in it. I knew that kind of cactus had special significance for her. Carlota had said so in her taped story, recalling that Chuchita, her childhood friend, and her mother had given her a similar cactus when she left her village. Although I knew this plant couldn't be the same one she had brought from Mexico, I couldn't help wondering why in heaven Carlota Navarro was now carrying a similar plant with her. As a matter of fact, I thought, why had she come to see me? How had she found out where I lived? Should I be worrying about my safety? Somehow I sensed that I had nothing to fear from her. Until I could get some answers from her, I decided to trust my intuition.

I took the box with the cactus in it and set it down on the back porch where the plant could soak up some sun in the morning.

I walked into the guest room carrying the burlap bag as Carlota opened her eyes. Her eyes brightened when she saw the bag. But I noticed that her neck and face looked flushed.

"I put your cactus on the back porch for now. I hope it's okay," I told her as I put the bag down on the floor next to her.

"Thank you."

I went back downstairs to fix something for her to eat. I made chamomile and mint tea and warmed up some canned chicken broth. I set a basket with crackers and Melba toast and some dishes on a large breakfast tray.

While the broth simmered, I called my mother. I asked her if she could come by in the morning to give me a hand. I offered her no explanation as to why Carlota had come to see me that night—something I was still trying to figure out myself. But I told her that Carlota had been one of Darío's patients and was in need of help.

"I'll be right over," my mother told me.

"There's no need for you to come right now," I said, trying to dissuade her. "I really need you tomorrow. Eight o'clock, all right?"

After twice reassuring her I could manage without her for the time being, I hung up. Pouring the broth into two large mugs, I put them on the tray next to the basket with crackers.

By the time I walked back into the guest room, Carlota had taken out some of the contents from her burlap bag. Wearing a pair of glasses, she sat up in bed reading a sheaf of dog-eared papers. A hardcover edition of Van Den Bosch's *The Pesticide Conspiracy* and a worn-out pocket edition of a study on suicide titled *To Fall Upon One's Own Sword* flanked her legs. *Enjoy Your Dying,* a guide to a peaceful life before death, lay next to the other two books. I set the tray on the bed, then took a cup of soup and another of tea and put them on the night table as I told her, "I haven't had anything to eat since noon. I hope you don't mind if I join you."

"I don't mind," she assured me. Taking some crackers from the basket, she crumbled them and poured them over the soup. I sipped my broth slowly while Carlota spooned hers into her mouth with a shaky hand, spilling some on her clothes. I was tempted to help her. But, although she was much older now, I sensed in her, still, the fierce determination of the adolescent who had survived many journeys through hell, who had refused to delegate her own care to someone else. The woman in front of me was not insane, I was sure, but she suffered from a mentally impairing condition. I searched my subconscious for a reason to fear her. I found none.

"Would it be impo-(...)-sing too m-(...)-uch if I took a shower?" she asked when she finished the soup. I noticed the blank stare that accompanied the speech intervals created by her brain seizure. They were recurring much too often, I thought, and prayed that Justin would return soon so he could get her prescriptions filled.

"Are you sure you're up to taking a shower now?" I inquired. "You could do it in the morning when you feel stronger."

"I've been perspiring, and my skin gets very irritated. I need to keep cool and clean. The itching won't let me rest."

Looking at her skin, I realized that the reddishness I had noticed before was a result of the irritation. "All right," I said. While she finished her tea, I got a clean terry bathrobe and a large bath towel from the linen closet and handed them to her. "Why don't you take your clothes off? I'll put them in the washer and you'll have clean clothes in the morning."

"That's very kind of you. Thank you," Carlota said, then added, "I have a pair of clean underwear and a T-shirt in my bag."

After I started the washer, I went upstairs to turn on the shower, then went back to the bedroom. Carlota was sitting on the bed in the terry cloth robe.

Unexpectedly and directly to the point, she declared, "Someone is trying to frame me for Phillipe's and Sonny's deaths. María said that you could help me." She kept her head

down, but gave me a probing look. I tilted my head and gazed
directly at her. She lowered her eyes again, then explained, "I
talked to María after you (...) left today. That's when I de-(...)-
cided to (...) come to see you. She gave me your address."

That explains it, I thought, as I remembered handing
María a slip of paper with my address and phone number.

I motioned for her to follow me to the bathroom, thinking
all the while that I hadn't said anything to María about
Sonny's death. I had only told her about Art's disappearance.
Perhaps Carlota had also talked to Josie.

I decided to let her tell me only what she wanted me to
know for now, but asked, "Why do you say that someone is
trying to frame you?"

She answered with a question of her own. "I (...) don't
real-(...)-ly know who or why. Do you (...) know?"

"I don't." The lapses were more frequent, and I was afraid
she might faint again, so I again asked, "Are you sure you'll be
all right?"

"I'll be fine...Really."

"All right," I said. Just the same, I didn't stray far from
the bathroom.

After a half-hour, I knocked on the bathroom door.
"Everything okay?" I inquired, and put my ear to the door. I
knocked a second time. Getting no answer, I tried the door
and looked in. Wearing the terry robe, Carlota was sitting on
the edge of the tub, her back pummeled by a now cold shower.
Her wet hair indicated she had gotten into the shower. But
her eyes, wide open, stared into blank space with the fixed
gaze of a blind person. Turning the water off quickly, I tried to
pull her up and help her to her bed. She resisted. I tried
again, this time a little harder.

Suddenly, she was up. Mumbling something that sounded
like, "Don't do this. God's going to punish you!" She pushed
me and leaped over me. I reeled back, bumping my cheek on

the sink, but managed to grab her robe and used her energy to rise to my feet. Pushing me again, she ran into the guest room. I was hardly out the bathroom door when I heard the clinking of glass against glass as Carlota swept with her hand a glass jewelry case, a vase, and some other empty perfume bottles I kept on that dresser. They came crashing down, but none broke. She seemed suddenly possessed of extraordinary strength, and I tried uselessly to wrestle her down to the carpet. Holding on to the bed, she was able to stand up again as I tugged on her. All the time she kept repeating the same warning: "God's going to punish you!"

Pulling off the bedcovers, she tumbled back onto the carpet. I grabbed the flat bed sheet, jerked it off the mattress, and, wrapping it lengthwise around her hands, I managed to immobilize her enough to then tangle the sheet around her feet.

Panting and exhausted, I hung on to the two ends of the bed sheet and sat next to her, trying to regain my normal breathing. I released the make-shift straitjacket a little, just enough not to cut her circulation for too long. But she was quiet, hardly resisting anymore.

In the struggle, Carlota's burlap bag had fallen, and its contents were strewn over the carpet. The first thing that caught my attention was a large Ziploc plastic bag filled with clothes. A smaller bag contained a tube of toothpaste and a toothbrush. Other miscellaneous items lay around, including her reading glasses and the papers she had pored over earlier. Under the glasses, I saw a small bundle of dry herbs tied with a black ribbon. Seeing the bundle, I remembered that Sonny had told Leo about finding on his doorstep a sheaf of herbs tied with a snakeskin coil. Was this the same bundle? If not, where had Carlota gotten her herb bundle? Why were her herbs tied with a black ribbon and not with the snakeskin?

Noticing that Carlota had stopped struggling, I let go a little. During the violent episode, I had been concerned about Carlota's as well as my safety, but I hadn't been afraid of her. How could I fear someone so vulnerable, I asked myself. But my subconscious warned me to be careful. The memory of Luisa, lying lifeless as Carlota seemingly lay now, her eyes staring upon infinity, fixed and totally inscrutable, was playing upon my emotions.

I couldn't bear to see Carlota's eyes open like that, so I slid her lids shut with my fingers. Only the pulsating hollow at the base of her neck indicated to me that she had won another reprieve from death.

# Eleven
## Soldados *and Moonshadows*

An hour after her seizure, Carlota came to and looked around in confusion. By then Justin had returned from his meeting with Leo and Bob Messinger. Due to the urgency of the situation, he had immediately gone out again to get Carlota's medicine. This time he had come back just before she awoke. The relay of events had given us little opportunity to talk about what had occurred at my house while he was gone, or his conversation with Bob and Leo.

"Do you know where you are?" I said, as I offered Carlota a glass of water and her medication. She didn't respond right away, but I could see in her eyes that she recognized me. She took the medication and drank all the water. Indicating she wanted more water, she stretched out her arm and I poured more water into her glass. She looked around as she sipped it.

"Did you carry me from the bathroom to the bed? It must have been difficult." When I didn't make any allusions to what had happened, she inquired, "How bad was it?"

"I have nothing to compare it with, but I think it was very bad," I told her. "I hope I wasn't too rough on you." I uncapped the bottle of glucose solution and poured some into her glass. "Dr. Trummer wants you to drink this, too. 'Nourishment for your brain,' he said."

"I'm sor-(...)-ry to be such trouble," she apologized. "I hope I didn't break anything." Her speech had become a bit slurred and her accent heavier on the r's, which now resembled the Spanish rolled r's.

"Don't you remember anything that happens during a seizure?" Justin asked, then looked me over to make sure I was all right. He shook his head when he noticed the bruise on my cheek, not in disapproval of me but of himself for having left me alone with Carlota. I gave him a reassuring glance.

"I don't. I usually can't remember anything afterwards." Carlota finished the glucose solution in one gulp and shivered as she handed me the glass. Holding it by the rim with his fingers, Justin took the glass from me and set it on his palm.

I sat on the bed, facing her. "Don't you think it's better if you tell us all you know about this mess?" I suggested.

She lowered her eyes. "Someone is trying to frame me."

"You told me that before, but I don't think you told me everything you know." In a stern voice, I added, "We can't help you if you don't level with us."

"I really don't know who's responsible," she said, and sighed. "I wish I could tell you why, but I don't know that either."

"Do you know that an immigration officer and a prison guard are also looking for you?" Justin asked.

"It doesn't surprise me that the *migra* is looking for me. Josie probably called immigration, but I don't know anything about a prison guard."

I was going to tell her that Josie hadn't reported her to immigration, but I decided instead to pry into her relationship with Ramón Caballos, so I asked, "Do you know where Ramón Caballos is now?"

Carlota looked at me as if I had just mentioned the name of someone she had just met and couldn't remember.

"Do you remember who Ramón Caballos is?" I asked.

"Yes," Carlota finally replied. "I know who he is. The last time I heard anyone talk about him was two years ago, when María told me he was dying—of cancer." She paused, then added, "I assume he is dead by now." She seemed suddenly lost in thought, slumping down on the pillow. "Cancer is a terrible disease, everyone says. Horrible pain... No one deserves

to die that way. Not him, or me..." She looked up. I didn't have
to make use of my extrasensory awareness or intuition to see
the terror in her eyes. Straightening up when she saw me
observing her, Carlota cleared her throat, then added, "No
human being deserves that kind of punishment."

Justin and I looked at each other but said nothing. "But
you don't know for sure that he's dead, do you?" Justin broke
the silence.

Carlota looked at both of us, then lowered her eyes and
said, "No. I guess I don't. I visited him in prison long ago. But
he told me never to go back. And I never went back to see him.
I believed María when she told me..."

"Do you know of anyone who could tell us if Ramón is
really dead?" Justin asked. "Someone we can contact to make
sure?"

"I just don't understand any of this," she stated. "But,
why would Ramón wish me ill?" she disputed instead of
answering Justin's question. I motioned for Justin to keep
quiet. "He always tried to protect me. He loved me," she continued. "I couldn't be wrong about that."

"Perhaps he loved you, but prison has a way of turning
love into suspicion and hatred," I told her.

"No. You don't understand," Carlota affirmed. "He was a
man of convictions. He believed in what he was doing." She
pressed on with great intensity. "And he was willing to pay
with his life for it, if necessary. But Ramón also believed
Sonny and Art when they agreed to help him blow up the tank
of pesticide." Her tone was becoming a bit shrill and her
accent heavier. Looking at me, then at Justin, she asked, "Do
you have any idea what I'm talking about?"

Carlota was aware of the look that passed between Justin
and me, and taking that as a "yes," she continued. "Sonny and
Art had both agreed to help Ramón blow up the pes-(...)-ticide
tanks on several farms. Sonny and Art had been drinking, and

Josie says they really didn't intend to do what Ramón said, but Ramón wasn't drunk and he was dead serious. The next day, Sonny and Art, once sober, re-(...)-considered what they were about to do. Josie told me that partly they were afraid, but also they didn't want to do anything that would upset what César Chávez and the Farm Workers Union were trying to accomplish through peaceful means."

"Were Josie and Phillipe also involved?" I asked.

"Only because Josie and Phillipe had joined the picket lines in support of the farm workers during those days in the Coachella Valley, and because Sonny and Art talked to them about Ramón's plans. They tried to dissuade him, but Ramón got furious with them. Then, they went to the farm Ramón said he was going to sabotage first, thinking that they could still talk him out of it. But they were too late. When Ramón was arrested, they all testified against him. They hadn't wanted to do that, but they had to make sure that the Farm Workers Union wasn't blamed."

I was afraid that she would have another seizure, so I put my arm around her and she hushed up. After a while, she said, "Anyway, there is this man, Soldado *de la paz,* who used to know Ramón because they shared the same cell at Folsom. Soldado came to see me in Kingsburg once, a long time ago, after he was released."

"What was this Soldado guy in for?" I asked, sure that the name had to be a nickname—"Soldier for Peace," a contradiction in terms, to say the least.

"He'd killed another guy in self-defense, but he got sent to the penitentiary anyway," Carlota explained. "He got himself a better attorney and appealed. He had a retrial and was found guilty of manslaughter. Since he had already done the five years at Folsom, they let him out on good behavior."

"He brought me a bow Ramón had made for me in prison," Carlota continued. "No one had ever made anything for me. The bow was beautiful. Because in-(...)-mates are not allowed to handle knives, Ramón had used a small rock to carve the bow, Soldado told me. It had taken him a long time, and his hands had bled all the time he was making it. Soldado made a few arrows for me and taught me how to use the bow."

"Did you give Art the bow and arrows?" I asked. Carlota nodded.

Before I had a chance to ask Carlota if she had recently taken the bow from Art's house, Justin inquired, "Where does Soldado live?"

"He lives here in Oakland," Carlota told us. "I stayed with him when I first came here. His buddies are Native American and Chicano Vietnam vets, with the exception of a couple of African Americans."

"What do they do?" I inquired.

"They see themselves as a group of urban warriors for peace. They help other Vietnam vets like themselves to regain their self-respect. Soldado says that they need to empower themselves through the 'old Amerindian ways.'"

"Do they all live together like in a commune?" Justin asked.

"Yes, they do. They support themselves by refurbishing campers and painting them in bright colors. Some of them make wood carvings which seem to be popular. They sell quite a few of those. So far they've done well. They own a large lot near the embar-(...)-cadero where they live and work. Soldado and his urban warriors are a tight-knit group."

On occasions, I'd passed their camp—a huge lot located near the railroad tracks and the embarcadero. I'd seen the urban warriors' mobile homes lined up in back of a large building, which comprised the woodshop and the carving area. I had also noticed that some of the campers Soldado and his urban warriors refurbished were painted and decorated in psychedelic colors. Perhaps for that reason they seemed quite

appealing to the "Deadheads," the old hippies who flocked into
Oakland every time the Jerry García Band—the former
Grateful Dead—played at the Calvin Simmons Auditorium. I
was sure Justin had also seen the urban warriors compound.

"What is Soldado's given name?" I asked.

"I don't think anyone really knows."

"Do you think he knows where Ramón is?"

"He might." Carlota seemed tired. Her eyes seemed fever-
ishly brilliant, perhaps the effect of all that glucose in her
brain. I went to the bathroom and brought the sample envelope containing the sleeping pills Víctor Trummer had left for
her. I offered her one, and some water, which she took.

"One last question." Justin spoke, hesitantly at first, then
continued. "You called my service asking for Art the day
Sonny was found dead in his apartment." Justin waited for
Carlota's acknowledgement, and when she nodded, he went
ahead. "Did you know Sonny was dead when you called me
looking for Art?"

Carlota took her gaze away from both Justin and me. I
caught a glimpse of her trembling hands just before she hid
them under the bed sheet. Taking her time, she finally said,
"No. I just...didn't know where else to go when Josie began to
blame me for Phillipe's disap-(...)-pearance. She thought I had
convinced him to go away, I guess." She finally looked at both
of us, then added, "Art has al-(...)-ways helped me."

"Do you know where Art is now?" Justin asked.

"No, I don't. But I know he's all right be-(...)-cause Dieguito has spoken to him. I think both of them are very scared.
I am, too, for Josie and for myself."

"Scared of what?" I asked.

"Phillipe has disappeared. Sonny is dead." Carlota
seemed scared, yet her eyes started to close as the narcotic
began to take effect.

Justin had been holding the glass that Carlota had drunk from. I suspected that he was going to give it to Bob Messinger and have him lift Carlota's fingerprints from it. He took the glass with him when he left the room.

"One last question," I whispered, and Carlota opened her eyes wide, trying to focus on me. "Do you know if Josie or Phillipe visited Ramón Caballos in prison before he died?"

She shook her head, but I was not sure she had understood my question. I tucked the blanket around her, just as she was trying to tell me about her falling out with Josie. "But she doesn't want me...around, anyway. She doesn't understand...I won't be here to take...care of...the baby..."

Carlota finally went to sleep. I went into my bedroom. Taking my travel alarm clock from my dresser drawer and a blanket from the rattan chest at the foot of my bed, I turned off the light.

As usual, for no apparent logical reason, I was drawn to the window and looked out. I sensed the presence of someone hiding in the shadows. The image of the rattlesnake flashed briefly in my consciousness, making me a bit lightheaded.

Before going downstairs, I made sure every upstairs window was secured. For the first time since Tania had mentioned it, I considered the possibility of getting a gun. As if I had suddenly taken in a breath of nitrous oxide, the mere possibility of owning that kind of power over life made me feel giddy, and my skin crawled with fear.

# Twelve
## Muerte y Angel

For weeks after Darío died, I couldn't sleep in our bed. I used to walk around the house in the dark. I would end up in the living room and sit on a corner of the love seat to look at the Oakland hills. Then, I would listen to the language of memory that filled the darkness and my solitude. Grief, I discovered, has its own distinct, organic rhythms, and giving in to them seemed to be the only way to wholeness again. From that time on, whenever I felt troubled and restless, I took my place on the love seat and let my heart speak to me. Tonight, prompted by my presentiment of danger upstairs, I had intended to wrap myself in a blanket and sit on my favorite corner of the seat to keep watch.

I went downstairs thinking that Justin was getting ready to leave. But I found him instead sitting in an easy chair. Since his eyes were closed and he was so still, I concluded he had fallen asleep. Turning the light dimmer to off, I covered him with the blanket I had brought down with me.

One of us had to be rested for the next day, which in all likelihood would be another long and perhaps dangerous journey. Events were unfolding quickly now and a resolution seemed near.

I was walking out of the living room to get a *ruana* I kept in Darío's office when, out of the corner of my eye, I saw a shadow move swiftly across the kitchen door to my left. I turned to look, just in case, knowing in advance no human was there. This was one shadow I knew well. When I asked him, my ophthalmologist had said that the peripheral shadow was probably produced by a dislodged, floating speck of mat-

ter in my eye's vitreous fluid. But I preferred to believe
instead Mami Julia's explanation to us, her grandchildren.
Each one of us walked around with our *muerte* beside us, she
would tell us, just at arm's length on our left, and with our
*ángel,* who never became visible, on our right.

As long as you see *muerte's* shadow on your left, everything is all right," my grandmother explained. "But," she
warned, "Beware when *muerte* and *ángel* decide to change
places."

I wrapped myself in the *ruana.*

Justin's voice startled me out of my reverie as I walked
back into the living room. "Don't trust her," he warned. At
first I thought he was talking in his sleep, but I turned around
anyway. He shifted positions in his chair, then added, "*Se
aprovecha de ti*—She's preying on your emotions."

"Carlota?" I leaned on the doorframe. "She's not preying
on my emotions. I'm doing that all by myself." I heard Justin's
soft laughter. "Seriously," I continued, "she needed help, and I
gave it. I knew all the time what I was doing, and she *is*
gravely ill."

I seriously doubted that Carlota was telling us the whole
truth. That consideration had, nonetheless, nothing to do with
my procuring the medical care she needed. Interested in the
reasons behind Justin's distrust of her, I asked him, "What
makes you not trust Carlota?"

"Leo told me earlier this evening that when he canvassed
the neighborhood on Saturday, one of the neighbors—the man
who owns the plumbing warehouse at the corner—told him he
saw a woman fitting Carlota's description staggering out of
Sonny's building on Friday afternoon. She was acting very
strangely," Justin replied. Sitting up, he elaborated further.
"She was seen leaving Sonny's apartment two hours before
Leo arrived at Sonny's place. The coroner says Sonny died
between one and two p.m. Leo discovered Sonny was dead at

about four-thirty. That puts Carlota around the scene close to
the time of death. But when I asked her upstairs if she'd seen
Sonny on Friday, she said she hadn't," he reminded me. "As I
said, I don't trust her. I bet the prints on that glass and those
found in Sonny's place will match."

I could hear in his tone that he was already distancing
himself from the woman upstairs. He was relegating his com-
passion for the woman who suffered from a fatal condition,
which I sensed would claim her life all too soon, to a corner of
his conscience. Perhaps this was the only way private and
homicide investigators could or should function, given the
misery and tragedy they constantly witnessed. At that
moment, I seriously considered whether I was truly cut out to
be a professional detective, as I couldn't even begin to remove
myself enough to see things from a perspective other than
Carlota's.

"What would you do in her case?" I said. "Suppose you've
been stalked, raped, persecuted, and treated like a criminal
all your life," I let out, trying to keep my tone down and the
edge off my voice, but not succeeding. "And you have no immigration papers. C'mon, wouldn't you also deny having seen a
man who's found dead two hours after you visited him?" It
suddenly occurred to me that Carlota might have found Sonny
dead when she arrived, that she had panicked and left. But
she might also have seen who did it.

"Granted," Justin replied, also trying to keep his voice
down. "But judging by that bruise on your cheek and your
banged up jewelry case, I'd say she loses it in a bad way sometimes, and when she does, there's no telling what she might
do. She wouldn't remember what she did anyway."

"That doesn't mean that she's a killer. If she were, she
would have killed Dr. Stephens, and she didn't," I protested.

"She's still holding out on us," Justin reminded me, and I
agreed with a nod.

"Anyone else seen walking out of the building besides her?"

"A slew of people, but none other fit her description," he answered.

"Were only two sets of fingerprints found in Sonny's apartment besides his?" I asked, knowing that the only way to find out whose fingerprints any of those were was to compare them to others on file. As far as the government was concerned, Carlota didn't exist, so her fingerprints would not be found anywhere, except on that glass Justin had taken earlier.

"Yes." He got up as he added, "Would you mind if I make some coffee?"

"Not at all. I'll join you." We walked into the kitchen. I opened the refrigerator and took out a bag of ground Colombian Supremo and handed it to him. He looked in the bag, then at me. "It's fresh," I said. "I ground it this morning." Justin was as picky about coffee as he was about food. "So," I wondered, redirecting our conversation to Sonny's death, "what about the cause of death? What did Leo tell you about that?"

"His heart stopped," Justin stated. He must have seen my look of incredulity, so he restated for my benefit, "Sonny's heart stopped."

"I see. We were chasing windmills after all. It wasn't suicide or homicide, just plain natural causes. Why didn't you tell me before?" I sighed, thinking how easily our theoretical construct had been brought down. I couldn't help laughing, but I noticed Justin wasn't amused. I looked at him and raised my eyebrows. "What's the matter? You seem disappointed."

"Sonny might not have killed himself, but he might not have died of natural causes either," Justin announced, as he filled the coffee holder then poured water into the well and turned on the coffee maker.

"What!" I exclaimed, totally taken by surprise, but trying to keep my voice low. "I'm not good at conundrums. Would you mind telling me in straight English what that means?"

"Sonny had high blood pressure. No one—not even Leo— knew about his condition." He opened the cupboard to get two mugs out, and I got a can of condensed milk and opened it. "He was taking medication for his hypertension. The coroner found a small amount of beta blockers, which help stabilize blood pressure, still in his blood."

"Sonny could still have ingested the medicine himself. A much larger dose that slowed his heart down to a complete stop," I rebutted.

"That's true. And that's what everyone thought when they found a half-empty vial of high-blood-pressure pills and a half-consumed glass of whiskey and soda. The prescription was refilled five days before he died. He normally wouldn't have taken such an extraordinary amount of medication, but Sonny apparently did."

The coffee was ready, and I poured two cups and continued listening to him. "But that was only a contributing factor," he cautioned. "The real culprit was good old foxglove." He sipped his coffee.

"Digitalis?" I poured some milk into my cup and sat at the table, speechless. I remembered Víctor Trummer had mentioned Darío's prescription of a small dose of digitoxin for Carlota to control the seizures. Dr. Trummer hadn't wanted to prescribe it until Carlota saw the specialist at Healing Hands. She had told him she had none with her.

"*Pues sí*," Justin remarked. "Good old digitalis." He got up and paced up to the sink and back to his seat, but didn't sit down.

"The coroner says it was probably mixed in the menudo Sonny had for lunch since there were no traces of it in his drink." He thought for a minute, then asked, "When we were at Sonny's, did you see any menudo anywhere?"

"No," I replied. "I didn't see any, but I did see a styrofoam container in the dish rack. Maybe his visitor brought it with her," I said, and reminded Justin that a woman had been with Sonny the day he died.

"If she put the digitalis in it, then she would have had to wash the container." Justin nodded and added, "Clever."

"Was it patent digitoxin, or a leaf extract or powder?"

"I don't think anyone said which kind. Why?"

"I think that lots of other people close to this case know about medicinal plants. Ramón is a shaman; he has studied the herbs," I reminded Justin. "So has María Baldomar, for that matter. And Josie had access to that knowledge through her mother."

"Yes, but none of them was seen at the scene. Carlota was," Justin emphasized.

I didn't respond to his last comment. Instead, I asked, "What about the grapes? No lethal substance in them?"

"Not in the bunch we found in Sonny's refrigerator," he assured me. "As a matter of fact, those grapes were just *uvas*, with only a trace of sulphur, nothing more." He finished his coffee and poured himself another cup. "But Bob Messinger found alcohol and jimsonweed extract in the grapes we found at Art's house." Justin looked up at the ceiling, then at me. "We're dealing with someone who's quite deranged," he warned. "Or someone who doesn't really know about poisons."

"How peculiar." I got up, rinsed my empty cup, and put it in the sink. "It almost sounds as if..."

"Someone is trying to confuse matters?" Justin completed my thought, and added, "Or as if we're dealing with two random acts that might truly be coincidental."

"I suppose coincidences do happen." I turned to look at him. "For all we know at this point, Carlota might be right when she says that someone is trying to frame her." Justin didn't answer, so I asked him, "Is the Oakland Police Department going to conduct an investigation after all?"

"They're still not sure. Leo told me that Frank Madrigal will look into it. I doubt they'll be able to find out more than we have. So Leo still wants us to go ahead and dig some more. I asked Leo to call San Quentin and find out what really happened to Ramón Caballos. In the meantime, we should talk to Soldado tomorrow. We'll see where that leads—hopefully to Ramón's whereabouts, if he's still alive."

I agreed, but requested, "Please don't tell Leo where to find Carlota. For now, anyway."

After a brief hesitation, Justin bowed his head twice, acquiescing, but his eyes betrayed his reluctance to go along with my request. "I think it's better if I stick around for a while. Just to be sure you'll have help if you need it."

Justin looked at me, and I nodded my approval. So he went back to the living room while I put Carlota's clothes in the dryer and set it. I locked the back door, leaving the key in the latch, and turned off the lights on my way out. Tania had left her bat on the counter, and I removed it, leaning it instead against the wall next to the door.

Before closing the mini-blinds in the kitchen, I looked out the window. Mist had moved inland from the ocean, making the lights on the hills quiver like Christmas tree lights underneath a veil of angel hair.

I turned to my right quickly, trying to catch *ángel* unaware as I used to do when I was very young. I saw neither her nor *muerte,* for which I was grateful. At least for tonight I felt safe. I knew that although death was now invisible, she still walked on my left.

# Thirteen
## *The Small Gift*

I thought about Carlota upstairs. She was trying to find ways to enjoy her own death, to keep from grieving for herself. Could someone who valued life so much disregard someone else's life? I wondered as I curled up on the love seat and pulled my *ruana* over me. For a while, there in the darkness, my mind struggled to understand Carlota's possible motives while my conscience wrestled with notions of order and punishment. My heart, on the other hand, pleaded only for her life. For an instant, I felt as if I had inadvertently entered some other consciousness—still a woman's consciousness but greater and far more knowing than mine. My heart skipped a beat. "God," I said under my breath. A different, deeper feeling of well-being spread over my heart and mind, and I began to fall asleep.

An instant later, it seemed, although I had been sleeping for hours, my eyes shot open. A slight tremor, a thump followed by a click woke me. I held my breath while I listened and began to uncurl slowly, extending my aching arms and legs gradually and rubbing them to get the circulation going. But my heart was already beating fast against my breastbone. Dropping the *ruana*, I sat on the edge of the love seat, peering into the darkness, trying to discern Justin's shape on the sofa. I cleared my throat lightly, then called softly, "Justin?" but got no answer.

Making sure he really wasn't there, I moved carefully towards the stairs. Upstairs, Carlota seemed fast asleep and nothing looked disturbed. From my bedroom window, I checked the street and turned suddenly when I felt as if some-

one brushed against me in the dark. No one was there. I
checked every room and realized that Justin was probably in
the guest bathroom, as I saw light underneath its door.

"Justin," I called softly, rapping at the door. "I think
someone is trying to break in."

"I'll be right there," he said.

Confident that Justin would be backing me up, I started
downstairs again. Blood rushed to my temples as I heard
scratching and creaking noises coming from the kitchen. A
soft buzzing filled my ears, and the skin around my chin felt
itchy as I moved closer to the kitchen door. I couldn't be sure,
but I thought I heard Justin coming out of the bathroom.

Trying not to dwell on my daughter's more drastic suggestions for my self-protection, I got Tania's baseball bat and
walked slowly towards the door. My legs were shaking lightly,
and I began to breathe through my mouth. The ache on both
sides of my jaw made me realize I had been clenching my
teeth the entire time.

I steadied myself on the counter and took a couple of deep
breaths. I was sure now that someone was just outside the
door. Trusting that Justin would come to my aid right away, I
placed the small end of the bat under my arm and held its
wide end with my hand like a lance. Fortunately, the door
opened to my left, so I turned the key on the deadbolt quickly
and pulled it open.

"Where are you?" I heard Justin call out to me.

"Here," I answered as I saw the intruder, clad in black
and wearing a ski mask and gloves, standing in front of me.

I had expected to see someone there, but my night visitor
hadn't expected to be discovered and froze in place. I used the
element of surprise to my advantage. Holding the bat with
both hands now, I bent forward and charged ahead. The
prowler stepped to the side, seemed to stumble on something,
and reeled backwards with a grunt. I swiftly turned and

charged again out the kitchen door. This time, I rammed the bat into flesh. Despite my efforts to keep my balance, I fell to one knee as I heard Justin call out again. I answered him immediately and, using the bat as support, was quickly on my feet.

The intruder had also gotten up and was now holding a knife; its surface caught a glimmer of moonlight. I could sense Justin behind me, sizing up the situation, but I didn't dare look at him. Attentive to the shining blade, I twisted slightly to my left and brought my bat up. Aiming in the dark for the hand that held the knife, I swung and struck, but the prowler was already charging at me. I felt the knife point puncture and rip sweatshirt and skin. An instant later, the cold air came in contact with the cut in my upper right arm, close to my shoulder, making me cry out in pain.

As I slumped to the ground, I saw Justin lunging out of the kitchen and tackling the prowler, who managed to get lose and ran towards the side of the house and the street. Justin followed swiftly. I managed to get up.

Putting pressure on my bicep with my left hand, I ran back into the kitchen and down the hall to the front door. I opened it and saw Justin wrestle the prowler to the ground. Grabbing the assailant by the collar of his coat, Justin pulled him up to his feet. But the prowler wiggled out of his jacket and took off. He jumped into a car with a running engine parked only a few feet away and sped out of sight. Justin glanced at me and threw the jacket in my direction. He ran to his van, backed out of my driveway, and took off in pursuit of the assailant's car.

With fear and anger rushing through me and threatening to overload my heart, in the dead calm of early morn I was suddenly standing alone in the middle of the street. After I examined the prowler's pea jacket briefly, I folded it over my arm to take it inside. Something pricked my skin. I reached for the spot and pulled out a slightly bruised, fleshy cactus leaf that had become stuck to the garment.

Sadly, I noticed that not one of my neighbors of fifteen years peeked out to check on the action in my backyard or on the street. Our neighbors in Jingletown, the Oakland neighborhood where I was born and raised, would have been out in a flash, armed with rakes and pots and pans to help another neighbor in distress. Perhaps in the upper San Antonio District where I now lived, we had gotten used to sleeping soundly in spite of the never-ending hum of the MacArthur Freeway and the frequent wailing of police and ambulance sirens on their way to the emergency room of the Highland County Hospital, which was nearby.

Carefully unhooking the prickly leaf from the pea jacket, I walked back into my house and turned on the lights in the hall and the kitchen. Before I secured the back door again, I put all the cactus leaves and soil back in the box. I placed the box under the sink so Carlota wouldn't see the damage. I hoped that cactus, like its owner, was a survivor, as I would not be able to tend to it until the following day.

I took a look at the pea jacket, which was the type worn by sailors or people in the Navy, and noticed that the buttons were on the left. It was a size L, but without a doubt, it was a woman's jacket. Inside one of the pockets there was a paper with a phone number—an Oakland number—written on it. I called the number, but there was no answer. Instead I heard two beeps. I realized that the number I had dialed was a pager's number, so I immediately punched in my phone number and hung up. I put the paper back in my pocket. I was walking out of the kitchen when the phone rang.

"This is Dr. Stephens," a woman's voice at the other end of the line said. "What seems to be the trouble?"

My heart skipped a beat. "Dr. Stephens!" I exclaimed, partly out of surprise and partly our of elation at such felici-

tous coincidence. I quickly added, "I'm terribly sorry. I must
have dialed your number by mistake." Justin had a surprise
coming, too! I prayed he was all right.

Upstairs, after checking on Carlota, who seemed to have
slept through the commotion, I went into the bathroom and
took off my sweatshirt. As far as I could tell, the cut in my
arm was superficial, but needed dressing nonetheless. Wash-
ing the cut with warm water and plenty of soap, I patted it
dry, then opened the medicine chest and took out some tubes
of antiseptic and antibiotic ointments and a box of bandages.
When I closed the chest, I saw Carlota's reflection in the mirror, watching me. I turned around, ready to reassure her that
everything was all right, but she looked at me quite confi-
dently. "I'll do that for you," she told me. She took the medicines and bandages from me. Lowering the toilet-seat lid, she
motioned for me to sit down. I did as I was told. Then she
washed and dried her hands.

"Were you awake during all that hullabaloo?" I asked,
trying to ignore the smarting in my upper arm and the aching
muscles in my legs and back. Even more so, I tried to ignore
the questions still buzzing around in my head.

"Awake enough to know something was very wrong," Carlota said as she applied the antiseptic and antibiotic ointment
as gently as she could. "Tranquilizers and sleeping pills don't
work so well on me sometimes." I squirmed and closed my
eyes to hold back the tears. They trickled out, regardless, and
Carlota handed me a tissue to wipe them off." Just in case you
and Mr. Escobar were the losers, I crawled under the bed,"
she confessed as she began to look in the box for a bandage big
enough to cover the cut. "Then I decided to go downs-(...)-tairs
to see if I could help you, but I was feeling very weak. Probably the effect of the sleeping pill. All I could do was to sit on
the stairs, shaking and praying. Just then, you dashed back in
the house and went out the front door. I thanked God you

were safe. When I finally felt strong enough, I walked out on
the porch and saw Mr. Escobar leaving. I watched you stand-
(...)-ing there in the middle of the street; you were holding a
coat and picking something off it that resembled my *nopalito*.
Then, you looked around and headed back to the house. Not
knowing what your reaction would be at seeing me out there, I
went back upstairs and crawled into bed."

"You know what I was thinking all that time I was in the
middle of the street?" I wiped a tear and laughed softly.

"That you were not afraid to die," she offered, and when I
shook my head, she asked, "What then?"

"I was thinking: How am I going to explain to Carlota
about her broken-up cactus?"

"You weren't!" She laughed for the first time since she
had entered my house—a roaring crystalline laughter.

"May I ask you something personal?"

"Sure!" Carlota answered, without any hesitation.

"I'm sure the potted cactus you brought is of special
importance to you," I said, prefacing my next question. "But
do you always carry it with you?"

"I know it must seem silly or odd to you. It's the first time
I took this plant with me. María planted it for me a few
months ago because she said I would need it for a journey I
would take soon after." She paused. "That journey began two
weeks ago. Anyway, María grew this one from the cactus at
her house. I brought that cactus from Mexico. It had only
three small leaves at the time."

"I knew that this plant couldn't be the same cactus you
brought from Mexico," I stated. Carlota gave me an inquisitive
look and I realized she had no idea that I was familiar with
her story. "I have been taking care of Luisa's writings and
publications and I came across the tape with your story in it."

"I see," Carlota said, then was quiet for a while. As she finished dressing my wound, she added, "You and Luisa were like sisters, no?"

"We *were* sisters."

"You must miss her very much," she remarked. I said nothing. "You would probably give anything in the world to change what happened that night in the Napa Valley," she added, then asked, "Wouldn't you?" She pushed the shower curtain aside and sat on the edge of the tub. "People don't understand what it is to owe someone your life, to always be aware of what they did for you." She looked at me and seemed so much older than I had figured at first. "I feel that way about Ramón," she continued. "He gave up his life for me and others like me." Her voice echoed my feelings, and the old familiar guilt began to wrap around my heart.

For an instant we were both silent. I handed her the mending tape Darío always used on minor cuts while they healed. "What about Josie? She also seems like someone who loves you," I offered.

Busy with the mending, Carlota was quiet for a while, then said, "I love Josie very much. I'll always be in love with Josie. You're right, she loves me as much as she can love anyone. She is funny and generous, and hard working—something a lot of people don't give her credit for," Carlota said, echoing Myra's praise for Sonny the day before. She placed another piece of mending tape on my cut as she added, "But..." She paused and looked at me, then decided to finish the thought. "But she has always wanted—needed—so much more than what Phillipe and I could give her.

"I have small gifts and simple needs," she continued. "For three years after my exposure to the pesticide, I stayed with Josie and Phillipe. During that time, I realized that the important things for me would always be love, loyalty, companionship. What I wanted most was the love of someone I could trust. Josie was that someone.

"When I discovered my feelings for Josie, I decided to move out. Living with Phillipe and her just didn't seem right. María found out that I was looking for an apartment and asked me to consider moving in with her, and I did. I really had few other options. Shortly after that, I came to the Bay Area. Then one day I was at Sanborn Park on Fruitvale Avenue. I was looking for cans and bottles to sell. As I walked in front of the Latin American Library, I saw Art coming out of the building. He hadn't changed much since the time I'd met him at María's house, back in 1973. At the time, he and Sonny had taken me to see a woman doctor who treated me for the pesticide contamination. I didn't think he would recognize me, but I waved at him anyway. He smiled at me, as though we had just seen each other the day before. He came up to me, kissed me on both cheeks, and invited me to his house. There, he fed me while we talked for a long time, then took me back to Soldado's camper compound, where I had been staying. As I mentioned to you last night, I had met Soldado when Ramón asked him to visit me in Kingsburg. When I first came to the Bay Area, I went to see Soldado and he took me in. I did the cooking and cleaning in exchange for room and board.

"Art came looking for me often. He introduced me to Luisa and took me to Healing Hands where I met your husband," Carlota concluded her tale. "A wonderful coincidence, isn't it?" She smiled.

"And one day, you decided to go back to Kingsburg," I said, and she nodded. "In the story you taped for Luisa, you described Josie almost as a devil-may-care person. But the Josie I met today—rather yesterday morning—was far from being that way. What changed her?"

"The change is quite recent—actually, I think it's caused by Phillipe's death. Josie is willful and used to having her way in everything, but she is unhappy now. Phillipe is not there to pamper her, and she believes she's pregnant. María tells me that Phillipe left very little money. With the exception of the house and its contents, and her car, there is nothing else left, not even life insurance. Since they haven't found the body, she can't even claim his Social Security pension. I think she's taking this very, very hard, mostly because she feels that Phillipe's leaving her in such a precarious situation is proof that he didn't really love her," she explained. "She's never had to handle so many problems at once, and seems to be going off the deep end."

I noticed that all the time she had been talking, she hadn't once paused in the middle of a word—the sign that she was not having any seizures now. She was quiet for a while, then said, "I know people have a hard time understanding women like Josie, but I really believe that she has loved me as much as she has loved Phillipe. People's sexual needs always complicate things."

Carlota had spoken slowly, in her slightly breathy voice, without an ounce of malice, I sensed, nor with any hint of desire to hurt or judge. She intrigued me, and despite Justin's warning I realized that not only did I like her but I also trusted her.

"I hate to tell you this, but you are in a heap of trouble," I warned her. "And we have only until tomorrow—this afternoon—to get you out of it." She looked down at her feet. "Now, be honest with me and answer my questions, were you at Sonny's the day he died?"

Carlota looked directly into my eyes, then said, "I went there, but I never went in." As if guessing my next question, she added, "Because there was someone with him, a woman. I didn't see her face, but I did get a glimpse of her back when

Sonny first opened the door. A brunette, taller than him and
rather plump, she seemed. I don't know if there was something wrong with her back, but she seemed quite rigid. That's
all I can remember. I had a seizure after I left Sonny's place.
When I came to, I was walking down Fruitvale Avenue. As I
said, I only had a brief look at that woman. Then the next day
I learned about Sonny's death, and I realized I'd be in trouble
if anyone had seen me there. That's when I first phoned Art,
to ask for his help, but I was unable to reach him. Art had
always talked about his good friend, the private eye, so I
phoned Mr. Escobar when I couldn't get in touch with Art."

She sighed. Then she looked at me and asked, "Does it
happen to you sometimes that you can't remember faces of
people you knew very well?" When I responded with an "Uh-
huh," she went on. "I remember Chuchita, my childhood
friend, and her mother. I will never forget Mark Stephens's
face. But for the love of God I can't remember Ramón's face.
And yet, he was so important to me," she said, folding her
arms over her chest. "At times I forget what Josie looks like.
It's as though a praying mantis were eating away at my memory." She rocked herself lightly. "I sometimes go to sleep
repeating my name again and again. I'm afraid that I'll wake
up and not know who I am." She laughed softly and looked at
me briefly. "I'm sorry. It's just that every-(...)-thing seems so
hopeless."

"Justin and I will do whatever we can to clear you of any
charges," I promised her.

"Thank you," she said, and smiled. When Carlota had
first walked into my house, she seemed older. Then, as she lay
in bed asleep, she seemed very young. Out of curiosity, I
asked, "Just how old are you?"

"I am thirty-four."

In her *memoir noir,* Carlota had mentioned that the
woman seer in her Mexican village had predicted her life

would be difficult, but that she would finally obtain complete happiness when she reached thirty-five. I had intended to remind her of that. Instead, I ended up announcing to her, "Dr. Trummer is afraid you may die if you don't get medical care soon." And I realized that I had finally articulated what I had been afraid to express to Justin earlier when we had talked about Carlota.

"I know that, but it's too late," Carlota stated, and not even a hint of negativity or complaint was detectable in her voice or her eyes. "Two months ago, I saw the specialist at Healing Hands." I must have looked distraught because Carlota patted my hand. "Don't worry yourself about it. María has taken care of everything for me. I have the herbs she gave me, and I'm ready."

I realized she was talking about the bundle of herbs I had seen fall out of her bag during her seizure earlier. A death bundle, I concluded. "You might not have to use them. You can fight and win over this one, too," I said, trying to encourage her.

"I'm done with the fighting and the crying," Carlota told me. "But I'd like to leave behind a clean name. That's all I have left." We were both quiet for a while.

"I think it's better if you go back to bed," I advised.

"Yes. I'm tired," she said.

Since Carlota was about my daughter's size but thinner, I took out an old pair of Tania's jeans, which she hadn't worn in a long time. I matched the pants with a clean shirt and a green, oversized, cotton sweater from my closet. I handed her the clothes.

Before I went downstairs to wait for Justin, I took an anti-inflammatory, pain-killing pill. Twenty minutes later, while I was getting Carlota's clean clothes from the dryer, the phone rang. It was Justin asking how we were and saying that he had pursued the prowler down the MacArthur Freeway but had lost him somewhere around the Oakland Zoo Area.

"Leo is coming to help," he mentioned.

"Did you tell Leo about Carlota?"

"No, I didn't. I'm keeping my promise to you," he reassured me. "Besides," he added, "I'm beginning to believe her, but I still have unanswered questions. So I reserve the right..."

"Of course."

After I got the paper with the number of Dr. Stephens's beeper, I read it to Justin on the phone and explained what had happened. "Do you remember that Oliver and Edith told us that Sandy Stephens was a doctor in the U.S. Navy? Also," I emphasized, "you lost our night prowler somewhere around the Oakland Zoo, which is just around the corner from the Navy's Oak Knoll Hospital."

"Where Dr. Stephens works. Of course!" Justin sounded excited. "I'll check her out. I'll come by your house at eight."

"All right. I'll see you in the morning, then."

Lying in the dark, I thought about how some people grow to a ripe old age without ever having anyone close to them die. And here I was, forty-two years old, and already I had found a child who had been murdered and known a young man who was also murdered. I had seen the two murderers killed. And within two years, I had lost my father, my husband, and my best friend, three of the most important people in my life.

Now, Carlota was lying upstairs losing an ounce of her life in every breath she exhaled. And the only thing I could do for her was to make certain that she didn't spend her last days on earth in jail. It seemed like such a small gift, a minor compensation for a woman who had fought so hard to survive.

# Fourteen
## *Death's Metaphors*

"Good morning, *m'ija*," my mother said, then proceeded to inform me that quite a few of her neighbors' pets in Jingletown were missing. "And in this neighborhood," she reported, "I counted at least ten reward posters for lost cats and dogs." I knew better than to interrupt my mother's soliloquies; she would come to the point eventually. "It's so hot and the birds are acting strange, too," my mother continued. Going out to the yard, she stood there pointing at the cirrocumulus clouds gathering in the southernmost sky, then she said, "The heavenly flocks—that's what Mami Julia used to call a mackerel sky like this one. And you know what your grandmother used to say about all these signs when they came together." By reading the *signs,* I remember Mami Julia had been able to predict two minor earthquakes in her lifetime—hardly a record on which to base this prediction. Obviously, my mother believed that she could also foretell the time and day of seismic activity.

Out of the corner of my eye, I caught sight of Carlota leaning on the banister of the stairs across from the kitchen door. She looked exhausted.

My mother came back in and cautioned, "We're going to have an earthquake. We'd better make preparations." Trying to ignore the slight tremors I had felt just before the intruder tried to break into the house, I quoted family statistics to reassure her that we had nothing to fear. My mother was getting ready to refute my arguments when a cheery though shaky Carlota walked gingerly into the kitchen.

*"Buenos días,"* she greeted both of us and leaned on the back of a chair for support. I felt slightly apprehensive, as I wasn't sure how my mother was going to relate to her. But Carlota turned to my mother and said, "María Baldomar, my second mother, also believes that animals go into hiding when there's going to be a disaster."

After giving me a "you-see-I'm-not-crazy" look, my mother poured some orange juice into a glass for Carlota and asked her, "Would you like some breakfast?"

"Yes," Carlota answered. Then, turning to me, she inquired, "Would it be all right if I make myself some chilaquiles?"

"No, no," my mother admonished her. "You're in no condition to be cooking. Sit here and I'll fix them for you." Carlota did as told.

Seeing that the two of them were going to get along famously, I relaxed and finished my coffee.

The bell rang. "That's probably Justin," I said. My mother poured a cup of coffee and handed it to me with a smile.

"What's this?" I asked, and she gestured indicating it was for Justin.

She glanced at Carlota, who was also grinning. The conspiratorial look that passed between them didn't go unnoticed, but I chose to ignore it. Taking the cup, I picked up the pea jacket, then, pointing at the chalkboard above the phone in the kitchen, I said to my mother, "Those are Justin's numbers, and the other is Leo Mares's number at the police department. Carlota will explain to you what happened last night." I kissed my mother and rushed out before she had a chance to question me.

Forty-two years old and still trying to keep things from my mother—I marveled at the irony. I headed for the door, opened it, and handed Justin the coffee. "Compliments of my mother."

"Just what I need for this splitting headache." Clean-shaven and bathed, but red-eyed, Justin immediately took a large draught and sighed. "Thanks, Pita," he called out to the kitchen.

My mother answered with an "Uh-huh."

"Bring it with you," I suggested to him and began to walk out of the house. The injured muscles in my arm pulled and smarted, but the pain wasn't as bad as I had feared.

I saw Justin wave at a man in a car parked about twenty feet from my house. "I asked my cousin Rafael to keep an eye on Pita and Carlota while we're gone," he explained before I had a chance to inquire. "I hope you don't mind." When I shook my head, he asked, pointing with his cup at my arm, "How do you feel?"

"It's just a superficial wound. It hurts, as expected, but it's not too bad. I've been taking Ibuprofen and the swelling is going down," I said, then asked, "We're going to Soldado's camp on East Eleventh, right?"

"Before we go there, I'd like to stop by Bob Messinger's lab," he said. "He's expecting the glass with Carlota's prints. He already has the copy of the other fingerprints that Leo faxxed to him for comparison." I looked at him but didn't say anything. Seeing my hesitation, he continued, "I doubt he'll have a positive match, and it might clear Carlota once and for all."

Once outside, I offered to drive so he could relax a little, and Justin handed me the keys to his van without hesitation. I gave him the jacket in exchange. We fastened our seat belts. "Did you talk to Dr. Stephens?" I asked. I started the engine and drove up the street.

"Yes," Justin answered, placing the mug in the cup holder. He examined the jacket. "But she has an alibi. They had an emergency at Oak Knoll, and she was there all night. That's why she called you back immediately." He held the jacket by the shoulders. "It's a woman's jacket, all right, but I'm sure it isn't Sandy Stephens's. She's only five feet four and as slender as you. Our night visitor might have been a woman, but much heftier and taller than Sandy." Justin took a sip of his coffee. "She seemed a bit apprehensive when I mentioned that we were investigating the homicide death of Sonny Mares. But she didn't say anything."

I spotted Soldado's trailer camp. I drove past it, made a U-turn at the corner, and pulled up at the first available parking spot across the street. Some of the urban warriors' mobile homes were partly visible, parked in a wide circle behind the large woodshop. A few of the men were working on camping trailers, covering them with wood shingles. A Cyclone fence surrounded the entire camp. Up front, a chain and padlock barred unwelcome visitors from walking freely into the camp through the main gate. It looked peaceful enough.

As soon as we got out of the van, we saw a smaller gate with a deadbolt lock and walked towards it. A large wood shingle hung beside a cord and bell, warning guests nor to even bother ringing if they were "packing" or were under the influence of either drugs or alcohol. We rang the bell. A woman peeked from behind one of the trailers. A large African American man wearing a folded bandanna around his head, a narrow-brimmed hat and cowboy boots approached the gate with an unhurried stride. A large ring with keys of every conceivable size hung from his concho belt and clinked every time he took a step.

Justin took a couple of steps back, then stated in a matter-of-fact tone, "We're looking for Soldado."

"What's your business with him?" the gatekeeper asked, wiping the sweat around his neck and mouth with a red handkerchief.

"We have a message from his friend, Carlota Navarro," Justin indicated to him. "It's *privado*—personal, you understand?"

The gatekeeper acquiesced with a nod and a half-grin. "He ain't here," the man informed us. "He's at the park on East Fourteenth and Seventh Avenue."

"How will we recognize him?" I asked.

"If you know what Soldado means," the gatekeeper snorted, "you'll know him."

"Gotcha. Thanks, man," Justin said, and we walked to the van. I was ready to start up the street, but Justin pressed my hand to have me wait. He wanted to see what reaction our visit unchained. While we waited, I turned my attention to a leaflet on the traffic sign pole. "$20 Reward" was written above a picture of an Angora cat. For an instant, I considered seriously my mother's seismological theory. Now she has me looking at posters of missing pets, I thought and smiled.

Justin caught my amusement and looked at me inquisitively. I told him about my earlier conversation with my mother concerning earthquakes. "My grandmother used to say the same thing about those kinds of clouds," Justin commented with a grin and threw a glance towards the camp, which remained as peaceful as before. "Let's go," he told me after a short while.

Justin looked at his watch. It was eight o'clock in the morning and he had scheduled a meeting with Leo Mares and Frank Madrigal at the OPD at nine-thirty, he told me. Hoping to locate Soldado quickly, we walked into the small park through its northwest corner and began to walk across it. A building stood on the southeast corner of the park, and we headed towards it.

Although this part of Oakland was an extension of downtown's Chinatown, the area marked a boundary to what was commonly known as East Oakland. Clinton Park, like most parks in East Oakland, was a square block of contradictions. I watched elementary school children—some accompanied by their parents, others alone—walk to school or stop for a swing or a quick thrill down a slide, while homeless children, bag ladies, and gruffy-looking transients competed with bathing birds and squirrels for a turn at the water fountains. Justin pointed at the old Chinese couples doing their Tai-chi morning routines.

An older Yemeni woman held out a slip of paper and asked Justin something in Arabic. He smiled and said, "Sorry, no Arabic. Spanish." The older woman giggled and walked on. People often mistook Justin's nationality.

When she first met him, my mother thought that he was Greek. With his black, curly hair and almond-shaped brown eyes circled by long, curly dark lashes, Justin had what could be described as a Mediterranean look. Although he had never found a direct line to an Arab or Greek ancestor, he was sure someone on either side of his family was from that part of the world.

We caught sight of a group of men and women sitting under two magnolia trees. They were a diverse bunch in age and ethnicity whose common bond was the bagged jumbo beer bottle they passed around. We headed towards them, hoping to locate Soldado, but he wasn't among them.

"Morning, man," Justin said to a brawny, African American man who sat by himself, watching the action on the two benches next to his. Judging by the overalls, the landscaping tools, and the thermos and lunch box next to him, he was a Parks and Recreation worker. "You know Soldado?" The man nodded. "Seen him?"

"Gettat'f here, man," said a belligerent, staggering, blonde woman, who had overheard Justin's question. "We don' wanna see that dude." She took a swig out of the Colt 45 bottle. "Wanna haf some, honey?" she offered, looking at me. But a short, stocky red-haired man snapped the bottle from her and shoved her to the ground.

I was getting ready to say something to the redhead when he himself, apologizing, helped her up. "Let's go see Soldado, sweets," he said to her, but she shook her head.

"Check the Pasca Plasma Center. I think I saw the 'urban warrior' go in there a while ago," the African American man Justin had first addressed said in a sarcastic but sober tone. "Can't see it from here, but's just 'cross that school," he told us, pointing at the park's southeast corner.

As we got near, I realized that the small, graffiti-splashed, mural-decorated building was a public school for adults of diverse nationalities who wanted to learn English.

A couple walked out of the plasma center across the street. I watched them as they counted the money they had been paid for their blood. Then they got in an old, beat-up Chevy Nova. In it, two children waited for them. The Nova chugged along East Fourteenth Street. If there was ever a metaphor for a decadent capitalist system, that plasma center was it, I concluded as I spotted a man who could be Soldado. He was a dark-skinned man in his mid-fifties, muscular but of average height, wearing an olive green T-shirt, fatigues, and camp boots. His hair was cropped to a half-inch of his scalp. He was trying to break up a scuffle between an African American man and a tight-fisted Chinese young man whose books and notebooks lay strewn around him. Justin and I approached cautiously.

"He's Chinese, and too young anyway to have been a VC, man," Soldado was telling the African American man, who had just taken a swig from a beer bottle another man had offered him. "Can't you see, bro?" Soldado was saying. "This Asian brother is not your problem. *That* is," the urban warrior said, and drove the point home by tapping the beer bottle with his index finger. Then he emphasized further, "Booze, man.

That's what's keeping you from getting the job you say this here brother's stealing from you." He picked up the books and notebooks and handed them to the young Chinese man, who headed towards the school door. The African American made an obscene gesture and walked away.

The conflict in Indochina had ended nearly fifteen years ago, but many still found it hard to own up to the shame and tragedy it caused. I realized those feelings would die only when all of us who had lived through that period of our history died. At least Soldado and his "urban warriors" were trying to do something about it.

"Soldado," Justin called out, and the urban warrior turned to face us.

"What can I do for you, bro?"

"Do you remember Carlota Navarro?" I asked as we got closer.

"Carlota? Sure I remember her," he answered, and gave me a piercing look. "Are you a friend of hers, li'l brown sis'?"

"I am," I said. "She's been sick and needs your help."

"Name it," he said, then motioned us to a bench where we could sit and talk.

"Actually," Justin said, concluding, I supposed, that he could trust Soldado, "someone is trying to hang the murder of a Chicano on her."

Since I had no idea he had changed his mind about Carlota, I was as surprised as Soldado at Justin's explanation, but I didn't jump to my feet as the urban warrior did. "Who is trying to hang the murder on her? Who?"

"We don't exactly know," I said, tapping the bench with my hand. It was an unconscious gesture, but Soldado understood I was telling him to sit down, and he sat again. "But Carlota thinks," I explained, "that Ramón Caballos might know something that might help us find out who's doing this to her, and why."

"Last I heard," Soldado said, "Horseman—I mean Ramón—fled Quentin. Finally."

"Had he tried to escape before?"

"Sure. Twice from Folsom. After that he was sent to maximum security at Quentin." He shook his head. "This last time, I hear he made it, but almost took out one of the Quentin guards. That guard was a bad dude, too. I hear he wants Horseman bad."

Justin looked furtively at me, and I nodded, indicating I remembered that both the *migra* officer and the San Quentin guard were also looking for Carlota. "We heard Ramón had cancer and was dying," Justin said, trying to see whether the information we had was correct.

"That *vato es de acero*—he beat the cancer, as far as I know," he replied, and slapped his leg. "He has powers, you know, and a spirit that won't quit. I'm free now, and I've stayed clean and dry 'cause of him. I owe him. A lot of us at the camp owe him." He turned serious as he informed us, "But he would do anything to protect Carlota. I guess I don't have to tell you he'd do anything for her."

"Do you know if he held a grudge against Sonny Mares and Art Bello?" I asked.

"*Pos sí,*" Soldado confirmed. "Of course he blamed those *vatos* for telling him they would help him blow up the tanks and not doing it. Instead, they squealed to the pigs on him. But I don't think he would do anything to them, as long as they were helping Carlota. And he knew they were."

"How did Ramón know so much? Did he ever get any visitors while he was in the pen?" Justin asked.

"Nah. One visitor only, but he didn't come very often."

"Who was that?" Justin asked.

"Don't know his name. A tall, lean, blond man with hazel eyes," Soldado told us. "Ramón would always come back laughing after this dude's visits and tell me, 'If you're patient,

what you want comes to you with the next turn.' Horseman
never explained who the man was, but I guessed the dude had
something to do with Ramón in the past and wanted something from him."

"When were you at Quentin?" Justin asked.

"I got out five years ago, but I went back often to see
Horseman."

"Do you know if he was ever in touch with a Josie Baldomar?" I asked.

Soldado shifted positions. I wasn't sure if his restlessness
had anything to do with my question. "I know Josie," he said
after a while. "Horseman never talked to her. But Josie came
to see me about a month ago. Beautiful woman," the urban
warrior exclaimed, and, winking at both of us, smacked his
lips and emphasized, "just beautiful."

Justin and I exchanged glances, then he asked, "Did she
know Ramón had escaped?"

"I'm not sure. We did talk about Ramón, but mostly we
talked about Carlota. She wanted to know if I'd seen her." Soldado frowned and wrinkled his mouth, then, waving his index
finger, said, "There was someone who used to write to Horseman." Soldado had a restless streak and he stood up and
started stretching his arms and legs. "A broad—a *gabacha*—
used to write to him often. If I remember correctly, she even
went to Quentin to see him."

"How recently?" I asked.

"Even two months ago—last time I talked to Horseman
before he broke loose—he was getting letters from her." Soldado laughed. "You know? Now I remember he told me then
that he was going to join her soon. I'd bet my *chante*-on-
wheels he is where she is."

"Do you happen to know her name or address?" I inquired
anxiously.

"Horseman always called her the 'high-class kid' and I once saw the initials RH on an envelope, but I never knew her real name. She lived somewhere around Santa Rosa, or one of those towns in Sonoma County, I think." Soldado looked away.

Justin and I threw a glance at each other. Then, I followed Soldado's gaze to the blonde woman and red-haired man walking unsteadily up the path and waving at him. "Sorry," he told Justin and me as he pointed with his chin towards the tottering couple. "I think I'm finally getting through to these two love birds."

"Hey, *ése*," Justin yelled after Soldado, who was already walking away. "We haven't talked, all right?"

"Sure, man. *No hay pedo,*" Soldado replied and waved goodbye.

As I drove around the block on our way to the police department, I looked in the rear view mirror and saw the "love birds" and Soldado cross the street in the direction of the trailer camp while a white Cadillac pulled up at the curb in front of the plasma center. The hand of a man who had just walked out of the center stretched out while another from inside the car reached out. Both hands exchanged death wishes, neatly tucked inside a cigarette pack.

# Fifteen
## *Tamale Blues*

After parking the van in a two-hour meter zone outside the Oakland Police Department, Justin and I got out and began to walk towards the building.

It was only eight forty-five in the morning and the temperature was already sixty degrees. By noon it would reach the eighty-four degree mark that weathermen had predicted. For folks in the San Francisco Bay Area who were used to misty, cool, breezy days, this Monday was going to be a scorcher. There was hardly a breeze, but the little there was carried the aroma of fresh-steamed tamales. It most likely emanated from Mi Rancho, the Mexican market across from the police department. As it reached my nostrils, my Mexican mouth salivated while my American arteries constricted at the thought of all that lard.

Subconsciously, Justin sniffed the air. He caught me watching him amusedly and smiled but didn't turn to face me. Gourmand or tortilla-chile-and-bean eaters, we hungered for a greasy *tamal* just the same. Luisa once cleverly referred to this passion as a block in our cultural DNA. I laughed to myself, partly at the memory and partly due to my nervousness as we walked into the police building. Not even the thought of savoring a *tamal* could ease my apprehension about our meeting with the two cops.

What if they asked me about Carlota? If Leo—not to mention the other homicide cop—was as smart as Justin said he was, he would soon begin to question why an intruder had tried to get into my house. Then he would probe. And when he did, he would suspect that I was keeping something from him.

He would surely come after Justin for harboring a murder suspect, and for his being disloyal and unethical since Leo was Justin's friend and his client.

Where did my loyalties rest? If I had to choose, whom would I save? Whom would I sacrifice? At what cost? During my involvement in the Chicano Civil Rights Movement in the 1970s, I had often lived with these kinds of ethical dilemmas. I hoped that this time I would not have to face such a quandary.

I glanced at Justin. Maybe he was so tired that he didn't realize he should be concerned. Or perhaps, he simply waited to see what transpired before deciding on the course that his conscience would dictate. Either way, he didn't seem to be concerned about our meeting with the police.

We checked at reception, then took the elevator upstairs. Leo was waiting for us. Frank Madrigal would not be joining us, Leo announced, as the homicide detective's wife had been taken to Alta Bates Hospital's maternity ward in Berkeley. Most likely he would not be back at work for at least the rest of the day.

"So," Leo suggested, "let's get down to business. I checked DMV records, and the department has a brand new Volvo registered under Sandy Stephens's name. That 1980 Buick—the car that you say the prowler at Gloria's house was driving last night? Sandy Stephens doesn't own a 1980 Buick. But I asked the Department of Motor Vehicles to check on that partial registration you gave me," Leo continued. "It'll take DMV a few hours to get those records."

When Leo saw the prowler's jacket Justin was carrying, he reached for it. "I'll take that to the lab." He then turned to me and asked, "Did you touch the slip where the phone number was written?"

"I don't think so," I answered. "I tried to be careful when I handled it. Anyway, you have my fingerprints on file should you need to check them."

"I have a question for you, Gloria," the policeman warned and looked me in the eye. As soon as he mentioned the word "question," I knew that in a second or two I'd be facing up to my worst fears. But I held his gaze. "Why would the owner of this pea jacket be interested in breaking into your house?"

So many possible answers buzzed around in my head at once that I ended up holding on to none. Gaping, and knowing Justin could not help me, I didn't even look at him. "Carlota Navarro is staying at my house," I stated. Leo looked at Justin, then at me.

"Did Justin tell you that we're looking for her?" Leo's voice went up a decibel on every word. He rose to his feet. "Did he tell you that she's become the prime suspect in Sonny's murder?" As if we had intentionally agreed, we both turned to look at Justin, who only raised his eyebrows. It was obvious at that point that Justin was staying out of the argument. I was on my own.

"Look," I answered, trying to remain in control in spite of my blood furiously lapping up my temples. "Carlota Navarro is very sick. She's not going anywhere," I assured him. Then, trying to be as logically persuasive as possible, I said, "Besides, if, as you say, she's guilty—which I don't for a second believe— why is someone trying to eliminate her? Have you considered the possibility that she might have been an unknowing witness? That she can actually identify the murderer? That someone is trying very hard to make her appear guilty?"

Leo sat on the edge of his desk and gave me a hard look. "You have some evidence to back up these...these allegations, I suppose?"

Considering at that point that anything I said would seem lame, I simply stated, "None other than my intuition. But," I added, without giving him a chance to rebut, "you don't have much in the way of proof either. Someone places Carlota outside Sonny's building. It's true that she can't account for that particular hour of her time because she had a seizure. But she can call to her defense a number of physicians who have treated her over the years and who will testify that she's suffered from this disease since she was fifteen and has never killed anyone. Besides, even if the D.A. agreed to charge her, a good lawyer will tear your flimsy case to shreds."

"She's right," Justin finally said.

"Did you know that Carlota Navarro was at her house?" Leo asked Justin.

"Yes, I knew. I also knew that Carlota was very sick and was going nowhere," Justin explained. "Gloria and I had planned to tell you about her today. You just beat us to it." He paused, looked at me, then at Leo. "I tend to agree with Gloria," he continued. "Think about it. Suddenly, someone is trying to get into Gloria's house. To do what? To rob her? Then," he added, "I follow this frustrated would-be burglar to the vicinity of Oak Knoll Hospital while Gloria finds that number in the pocket of the burglar's jacket, tying him or her to Dr. Sandy Stephens. Too many coincidences again, but this time I tend to believe that Carlota has had nothing to do with it."

Being as succinct as possible, and asking me to clarify details as needed, Justin reviewed for Leo everything we had been able to uncover, down to our conversation with Soldado.

Justin stood up. "Look, Leo, I wouldn't say this if I thought Carlota was guilty. I think she's the key to what's happening, one way or another. But we—Gloria and I—still don't know how the pieces fit together. I agree with you on one thing, though. If we really want to find out who killed Sonny and find Art before he's also killed, we have to hang on to Carlota."

"You think whoever murdered Sonny will go after Art and make another attempt on her life?" Leo asked, looking at Justin, then at me.

"I do," Justin said, and I backed him up with an "Uh-huh."

Leo was pensive for a while. Justin and I glanced at each other and waited. "Tell you what. Since Madrigal is not due back today, and since Carlota right now is only wanted for questioning, I won't mention any of what you told me to anyone else. That'll give you until this evening to come up with some hard evidence that will clear her. Otherwise, if I know Madrigal, a warrant for her arrest will go out first thing in the morning." He pointed a finger at Justin. "*¿Hecho, carnal?*" Leo asked, making sure the conditions were agreeable.

"*Derecho, carnal. Gracias,*" Justin said, accepting the terms.

"May I ask *you* a question now?" I inquired. When Leo nodded, I asked, "Won't you be in trouble with the department? I mean, after all, Frank Madrigal is supposed to be conducting the investigation."

"Not if you deliver. If you don't," Leo cautioned, "I won't be the only one in trouble. You better make sure nothing happens to Carlota." I must have looked quite distraught because he smiled at me, then told me, "You would have made a good lawyer, Gloria Damasco."

Accepting the compliment with a half-smile, I stood up.

"Any idea when Sonny's funeral will be?" Justin asked, also getting ready to go.

"The wake is in four days, on Thursday, October 19th, in the evening, at the Cooper Mortuary on Fruitvale Avenue. The funeral procession will start from there at eleven the next morning."

"How are your mother and sisters holding up?" I inquired.

"They're doing all right, but I haven't told them that Sonny might have been murdered. If that's the case, I'll tell them after the funeral," he said, and stood up.

Justin and I began to walk towards the door.

"I'll keep you posted," Justin reassured his friend. They gave each other their customary handshake and patted each other vigorously on the shoulder.

A few minutes later, Justin and I were walking out of the police department. "I don't know about you," I said, "but I'm going to Mi Rancho and I'm going to take home the greasiest *tamales* I can get my hands on. C'mon," I added, trying to entice him, "I'll treat you to a brunch of bad cholesterol and *café con leche caliente.*"

"Sounds good, better than going to the sauna to sweat this headache out, which I can't do anyway," he said in a surprisingly cheerful tone, given the state of his head.

"You seem pretty happy all of a sudden."

"All in all, we got off quite unscathed, don't you think?"

I knew Justin was alluding to our meeting with Leo. I looked him in the eye. "I had no idea you were so apprehensive about this meeting."

"I would have been a fool not to have been."

We walked into the delicatessen and ordered the tamales.

"Why do you think Leo is letting us do this?" I asked. "Doesn't he trust the OPD's detectives, Frank Madrigal, to be more precise?"

"Leo knows that, in most cases, if a murder is not solved within seventy-two hours, there's a good chance the murderer won't be caught. Sometimes a suspect is apprehended by coincidence, in connection with another offense, for example. I think Leo trusts OPD, but they might not get to it on time. Oakland cops are already carrying pretty heavy loads."

I paid for the tamales and we began to walk back to the van. "So Leo is afraid that Sonny's murderer might not be caught soon," I guessed, and Justin confirmed my assumption with a nod. "Why didn't you go to work for OPD?" I asked.

"I had a chance, but I took the job in San Jose instead."

"Why San Jose?"

He stopped walking and looked at me through enlarged pupils that quickly narrowed down to the size of a pin's head. In the brief interval, the tiredness in his eyes was replaced by the sullen anger I had seen in them Saturday night, the first time we listened to Carlota's story. At that time, he had shut his anger in and raised a wall between us.

"Who was she?" I asked. I waited for a warning to go off inside me and, when it didn't, I asked the questions I had meant to ask since Saturday night. "What did she do to you? Why are you so angry?"

Justin didn't answer, but he didn't look away either. He let out a long sigh that rushed out of his mouth as if he had been containing his breath for some time. I felt it against my cheek. "She was killed," he finally said. "Raped and killed."

"Oh, my God! Please forgive me. I didn't mean to pry..."

"It's all right," he said in a reassuring tone. "I want to tell you about it."

"Did it happen here in Oakland?" I asked, and he confirmed with a nod. "The summer your parents died?" I put my hand on his upper arm and felt the slight trembling of his muscles under my fingertips. Without thinking, I leaned my head on his arm and said, "I'm so sorry. To have to endure losing three of the most important people in your life. What was her name?"

"Carmen was her name," Justin said. "She was going to school and rooming with Elena, my sister. They were both in their first year at San Francisco State University. I was already a graduate student at Berkeley."

"How did it happen?"

Justin took in a mouthful of air, exhaled slowly, then said, "The day it happened, I was supposed to meet Carmen at her college library. I had taken my father to the hospital, and he had been given radiation therapy. My mother wasn't feeling well. Before I could meet Carmen at the campus, I had to fix dinner for Patti, my baby sister. She was only about ten at the time.

"Anyway," Justin said. He'd been speaking fast and paused to catch his breath. "I borrowed my father's car, but there was an accident on the Bay Bridge, and I was late getting to the campus. Carmen had already left. I went mad trying to find her. I checked every possible way she could have walked home."

Justin's voice faltered, and his breath quickened. He put his hand on his chest, right over his heart, and took a couple of deep breaths. "Two days later, they found her body," he continued. "But the police had no clues as to who'd done it." He paused briefly. "I went without sleep for three days, trying to piece things together and to find out what'd happened to her. I talked to every one of her friends. But no one had a clue about who the killer could be or why he'd done what he did." Justin stopped. Closing his eyes, he rubbed his forehead, then pressed his right temple with his fingertips.

Wiping the moisture that had collected around the corner of his eyes, he continued, "My father died a few days later, and within the next six weeks my mother also fell ill and passed away. I concentrated on taking care of Patti and on finishing my M.A. thesis. Then my uncle Tito offered to take Patti to live with him and his wife Mirna in Monterey. My uncle encouraged me to attend the police academy." Justin was lost in thought for an instant. Then he glanced at me. I was glad to see a softer look in his eyes.

"Did they ever catch Carmen's murderer?" I asked after a while.

"Years later," Justin replied. He took in a deep breath, then added, "They caught the man. His name was Sid Holmes. By the time the police arrested him, he had raped and killed five young women in other parts of California. His sixth victim survived and identified him."

Justin frowned and swallowed hard, trying to hold back the tears. Then he said, "Justice was served." I put my hand on his shoulder and he brushed his cheek against my fingers. "Thanks for asking."

I smiled.

We reached the van and Justin walked around to open the passenger side for me. Getting in, he turned the key in the ignition, and we headed back to my house.

Once we decided on the details regarding our trip to the Sonoma Valley, he called Sarah Sáenz Owens to tell her that we would be arriving at Quinta Selena by mid-afternoon at the latest.

"That's great!" Justin exclaimed to some news Sarah had given him. He then asked, "When did he call you?" His excitement was evident, and I prayed the good news was about Art. He asked a third question, "Where had he been?" After a brief listening interval, he jotted down something on a pad. The rest of the conversation was an intermittent series of comments. "Yes, it's good news. Thanks... No, we don't mind staying at the main house... Sure... Yes, either Gloria or I will call you right away. Ciao."

"Was that about Art?" I asked. My heart picked up a faster pace. After Justin acknowledged my question with a yes, I blurted out, "Where is he? Is he all right?"

"He's with Dieguito now. Art's been doing some investigating of his own and he wants me—us—to meet him and Dieguito today. There's something about this address near Quinta Selena which Sarah couldn't quite explain," Justin spoke fast and smiled most of the time he was talking. He handed me the paper on which he had written an address in the town of Glen Ellen, near the city of Sonoma. "Art told Sarah that he decided to be brave again, and 'die on his feet, facing the enemy.' ¡Ese carnal!"

"Just like him," I added.

Justin began to hum along with Dexter Gordon's sax interpretation of "I'm a Fool To Want You," now playing on the jazz station. "Without blues, jazz would have no soul at all," he said in an animated voice.

During Gordon's lyrical interlude, I watched the waning moon suddenly become visible. And now, translucent, like a thin slice of nibbled ice, it drifted on in the mackerel sky. I fought hard not to let the images in my vision surface. Letting relief, hope and Gordon's music take over, I concentrated on the good news we had just received, and I prayed that Justin's *muerte* and *ángel* remained in their respective places long after the first light of the next dawn.

# Sixteen
## *In Love's Shadow*

Reassuring my mother that, disaster or not, everything would be all right, I waited outside until her car cleared the yellow traffic light and turned left at the corner.

Justin had already made preparations for our trip to the Valley of the Moon. After informing his answering service of his whereabouts, he called Bob Messinger to find out if Carlota's fingerprints matched those found at Sonny's place.

Carlota and I went upstairs to get ready. Her cheeks were flushed, and she spoke faster than she had before. Remembering that María Baldomar had mentioned that Carlota underwent various changes when she was on her medication, I realized that the medicines Víctor Trummer had prescribed were finally taking effect.

She seemed possessed of inexhaustible energy. Although her incessant conversation got a bit on my nerves, her speech was clearer. Her voice lost its breathiness, and her comments became incisive. Judging by these signs, I surmised that she had entered the manic phase of her condition. But I wasn't quite prepared for her emotional frailty during this stage. In the time it took us to get ready, she had already burst into tears once. And, she had accused me of looking down on her when I casually suggested that she look in Tania's closet for some extra clothes in case she needed them.

An hour later, when she saw me re-dress the flesh wound in my upper arm, which she herself had helped me clean and bandage the night before, she told me in quiet desperation, "You don't care what happens to me, or you wouldn't have let anything happen to yourself." After her emotional outbursts, which passed quickly, she tended towards euphoria.

I was packing a pair of hiking boots, two *ruanas*, along with some warm clothing when Carlota came to sit on my bed and sheepishly apologized for her behavior.

"Can we take your Walkman player and some cassettes with us?" she asked in the next breath. Before I had a chance to answer, however, she left the room and went downstairs. I soon heard her rummaging through the music tapes.

Other than a few visual artists and poets, including Luisa, whose sulky and passionate behavior every so often took me on short emotional roller coaster rides, I had never been around a person who could suddenly become as unstable as Carlota could, or who truly suffered from manic-depression.

"*Calma. Ten calma,*" I reminded myself. I reached in a drawer for a flashlight and a compass that Darío had given me during our first family camping trip. I slid the compass into my back jeans pocket and put the flashlight into a small sports bag.

I reached in the medicine chest for the two other sleeping pills Víctor had given me. Hoping that Carlota wouldn't need them, I also put them in the sports bag, together with my antibiotic cream and painkillers.

When I finally made it downstairs, Carlota was lying on the sofa listening to a Paco de Lucía tape, seemingly in a peaceful mood. Seeing her so calm and relaxed after the unnerving episode upstairs, I agreed with Mami Julia who'd often said that music would tame the wildest heart.

"I love this music," she commented, taking the headphones off when she heard me putting the tapes she had selected in a box. She was adding them to the rest of our traveling gear when Justin arrived.

As soon as we got our bags and other things in the van, we were on our way to the Valley of the Moon. We had just merged into I-80 when Justin's phone buzzed. "Yes, Bob," he said, then he listened mostly, muttering an occasional "I see." He turned to look at the back seat where, I thought, Carlota was comfortably resting, listening to the tapes on the Walkman. Justin kept quiet, nonetheless.

We rode in silence for a while, but a short time later Carlota tapped on my shoulder. She was pale and seemed distressed as she said, "Sorry to bother you, Gloria, but I get carsick. I wonder if you have any Dramamine I can take."

"No, I'm sorry. If you'd told me before we left the house, I would have..."

"How about the sleeping pills. Did you bring them?"

"We don't have that long to travel..." I started to say, but Justin gestured to indicate that I should give Carlota half the pill. I handed it to her. She took it and drank up the water.

When I was sure Carlota was asleep, I asked Justin about his earlier conversation with Bob Messinger.

"The good news is that Carlota's fingerprints do not match the ones found in Sonny's apartment. Leo told Bob to let me know that there's only one 1980 white Buick matching the partial plate number. It's registered to a Felix Hunter. Guess," Justin said, looking at me on the sly, "where this Hunter guy lives."

"In the city of Glen Ellen!" I blurted out, then asked, "Is it the same address Art gave Sarah?"

"That's right," he confirmed, then asked, "What do you suggest we do with *her* when we get to Sonoma?"

"I don't think we should leave her alone," I told him. "I don't know much about clinical depression, but just observing her in the last couple of hours I can see how fragile and vulnerable she is. Also," I added, "we shouldn't let her out of our sight. We're in enough trouble with the police. And I'm still afraid for her."

"All right," Justin said. "Let's see how it goes. Maybe someone at the house can watch her."

We were quiet for a while. The radio was off. I was enjoying the tranquility and, without realizing it, I began to fall into a semi-conscious sleep, filled with disjointed images and loud sounds.

When I woke up, we were entering the city of Sonoma.

We drove up towards the main plaza. In its midst stood city hall and the visitors bureau, surrounded by picnic tables and trees. I lowered the window to feel the fresh air. As we cruised around it, I saw the old adobes that had once been the houses of General Mariano Vallejo and his brother, Salvador Vallejo, on Spain Street.

I had never before been in Sonoma, the heart of the wine country and the site of historical events that changed the fate of Mexicans in California forever. Forgetting the urgent reasons that had brought us to the Valley of the Moon, I let my excitement at being there grow for a moment. Doing research at the Oakland History Room to uncover the lives of the Peraltas, an old Oakland Californio family, I had also discovered the Vallejo family, friends of the Peraltas.

I saw the Mission of San Francisco Solano, which stood kitty-corner to us and the Bear Flag Revolt Monument. The monument had been erected in honor of those who fought against the Mexican Army to take control of California. The building across from the mission and the monument had been the Mexican barracks. I knew they had been occupied by the Bear Flag rebels after the Mexican Army, led by General Vallejo, laid down their arms. A short time after Vallejo's surrender, California became a U.S. territory and every gold-digger's rainbow's end.

Carlota stirred behind us, and I turned to see if she was awake. She seemed a bit disoriented as she unfastened the seat belt and sat up, but she quickly got her bearings. Letting out a long breath, she said, "*¿Ya llegamos a la cuna de la traición?*"

"The cradle of treason? Is that what you call Sonoma?" I asked, guessing that Carlota's comment had something to do with the city's historical past.

Pouring coffee into a plastic tumbler, I offered it to her. She took it and drank it in large draughts. "Well," she asked, "wasn't Vallejo our first *vendido*? I mean—the man sold out to the highest bidder," she emphasized. "And he traded California for a post in the new state government."

"I hadn't thought about it that way," I answered. "But I suppose his actions were somewhat opportunistic."

"Do you always have to be so non-committal? When did you abandon your political commitment? Next you'll be calling yourself *Hispanic*," Carlota snapped. I repressed my anger and hurt at her words as I realized that her short, narcotic-induced nap had only exacerbated her emotional instability.

Justin, who seemed to be reaching emotional saturation, started to say something, but I pressed his arm to ask him not to interfere.

"I'm going to the visitors' bureau to get a map or directions to that Madrone Lane in Glen Ellen," Justin announced, stepped out, and closed the door gently. "I'll look for you in front of the mission."

Shortly after her sharp reproach, Carlota tapped me on the shoulder. "I don't know what comes over me. I'm sorry. The last thing in the world I want to do is to hurt you or Justin," she offered as apology.

"It's all right," I tried to reassure her without being condescending. "You're absolutely right. I myself have been thinking that I am growing politically apathetic and quite selfish," I told her. "And when this is over, I know I have to do a lot of mental and emotional housekeeping. I just don't think I'm ready to do anything about my political complacency in the middle of this mess."

Carlota's laughter rose up as unexpectedly as her temper had flared up a moment before.

I opened the door and stepped out to stretch my legs and regain some of my good mood. The day was beautiful, one to be enjoyed outdoors. So I suggested to Carlota that we walk to the mission and wait for Justin there. Agreeing, she immediately stepped out and began to walk away, giving me little time to secure the van and catch up with her.

"Look," she commanded, pointing with both index fingers in opposite directions. "One flyer about a missing cat over here. There's another about a missing cocker spaniel over there." She walked around as she talked.

When we reached the mission's front garden, she seemed cheerful and energetic again. "Wow," she exclaimed as we reached the Mission grounds. "Look at this cactus." She stretched her arms out as if to embrace the thorny giant, which still showed tender plum-colored blossoms and pears. With a red tinge now spreading over her cheeks, she seemed magically transformed.

My interest in this plant sprang from a different source as I searched my subconscious for confirmation that this was the same cactus I'd seen in my dream. I sensed it wasn't. "It must be ancient. It's so big," I said.

"They're like that around here," Carlota said as she gently but purposely pressed her hand against a leaf until the prickles pierced her skin. She looked at the cluster of red dots on her palm and the blood dribbling from an unexpected breaking in her wrist. Automatically, she put the spot to her mouth and licked the blood with her tongue.

Reaching in my bag for a tissue, I handed it to her. Unconsciously, I took a few steps backwards and found myself almost at the curb. With my eyes open this time, I saw the

flaming arrow zoom across my memory. The woman tied to
the old cactus in my vision raised her head, and her doleful
countenance came into full view. I scanned the corner, expecting to see someone there watching us. Fear began to work its
way up my spine, but I saw no one.

"Let's get out of here," I heard Justin prompt behind me,
then I felt his hand on the nape of my neck. My skin crawled
with excitement mixed in with my anxiety and fear, and I
pulled gently away. I called to Carlota as I turned around to
look at Justin. He seemed oblivious to the feelings I was expe-
riencing. I handed him the key to the van.

Carlota was humming a tune and swaying gently around
the ancient cactus, her arms still stretched out and her eyes
closed. "We'd better be going. Quickly," Justin whispered in
my ear, adding, "Josie Baldomar is here."

"Do you think Josie's seen us?" I asked in a low voice, and
Justin raised his eyebrows and shrugged his shoulders. "Are
the *migra* and the Quentin guard still following her?"

"Didn't look like they were," he murmured while he kept
an eye on the traffic around the plaza. "I'm going to get the
van. I want you and Carlota to go into La Casa, that Mexican
restaurant across the street."

"That one?" I asked pointing discreetly at a restaurant
immediately across Spain street.

"Yes," Justin confirmed. "Behind the bar there's a door to
an outside patio that connects to an alley in back of the
restaurant. Go right as you exit and follow it to the street.
Keep out of sight and wait for me there."

"Time to go," I said to Carlota. She opened her eyes and
gave us a dazed glance at first. But grasping the gravity of the
situation, she rushed to join us. "I hope no one followed you," I
remarked as she approached. I was already wary of having to
play hide-and-seek or race around with Carlota in her weak
condition.

"What if someone (...) is following us?" Carlota asked, her eyes staring into empty space. She was now standing right next to me. Although she had obviously heard only my last remark, it had been enough to trigger her anxiety. Justin signaled me to cross the street and the three of us jay-walked to the other side. Carlota and I went up the steps of the restaurant.

"Here," Justin told me as he handed me a tourist map of the area with its wineries and historical sites. He pointed at a spot with the legend *Lachryma Montis*, and instructed us even as he walked away, "Wait about ten minutes. If I am not back by then, go to this place and wait for me."

"I know where that is," Carlota spurted. "It's General Vallejo's last home. It's not too far from here. We can walk there."

Carlota and I rushed through the restaurant. On our way to the patio we saw a woman raise a small bunch of grapes above her mouth. Then, she began to pick the grapes one by one from the bunch with her tongue and teeth before chewing them. Stopping at the woman's table, Carlota suddenly snatched the bunch of grapes from the woman's hand. She threw them on the floor and crushed them with her shoe. All the time, she fired questions at the dumbfounded lady. "Don't you care that farm workers are poisoned and die of cancer every year? That babies are born with birth defects? That people go crazy from the pesticides used on those grapes? Don't you know that you should (...) boycott table grapes?"

The woman, who was by then in a total state of shock, could only stare at us.

Carlota hadn't been yelling, but she had spoken in a loud enough voice to get the attention of a waitress and the bartender. The last thing in the world we needed right now was to be caught in a fracas.

"Let's go," I urged Carlota, tugging on her arm.

Surprisingly, she didn't resist me. "It's important people know (...) we're still boycotting grapes and why," she said, still in an excited voice. The pauses in speech were coming closer to one another. I was afraid that the recurrence of such speech patterns might precede one of Carlota's seizures.

"I agree, but this isn't the time or the way to do it. We'll come back—when this is over—and we'll talk to the restaurant's manager or form a picket line outside," I reassured her as I kept pushing her ahead. We quickly moved through the main dining room to the patio. Carlota picked up a handful of tortilla chips from a basket on an unoccupied table and handed me some of them. I was hungry, but the idea of eating at that point made my stomach turn, so I gave them back to her. As if she had no care in the world now, Carlota leaned on the wall and slid down until she was crouching. She ate her chips while we waited.

"Do you really think (...) I'm afraid of dying? Why do you take such good (...) care of me?" Carlota hurled these seemingly unrelated questions at me, but her tone was no longer defiant or angry.

Although I tried not to make much of her repeated speech lapses, I knew we had to get her to Quinta Selena very soon. Checking my watch, I glanced at her briefly, then told her, "I know you're not afraid to die. But as long as you're in my care, I'll do everything to protect you. I promised María to take care of you, too."

"Would you take a bullet for me (...) like Luisa did for you?" Carlota asked as she searched my face. "But then, why would you tra-(...)-de your life for mine when I'm going (...) to die soon anyway?"

The muscles in my throat contracted and I took my eyes away from Carlota's blank stare. I tried to say something but words seemed to be buried deep underneath many contradictory feelings. I couldn't have answered Carlota's question

right away even if I'd wanted to. I expected Carlota, in her
manic condition, to press on with the subject as she had done
earlier at my house. But this time she didn't.

"Did you take your medication?" I asked her. She nodded,
but her head was moving slowly and the vacant look in her
eyes made me nervous.

I was checking my watch again and getting ready to walk
to *Lachryma Montis* when I saw Justin's van pulling up. I
asked Carlota to keep low as we ran to the van and got in.
Once we were inside, Justin kept going for a few blocks. Then
he parked the vehicle, checking around to make sure no one
was following us.

I looked up at the hills and the higher mountains behind
them. I could see the upper story and rooftop of a huge house
rising above orchards, vineyards and forests. I assumed it was
Sarah Sáenz Owens' mansion.

When Justin was sure we were not being followed, he
headed towards Quinta Selena, the next stop on the way to
our final destination.

# Seventeen
## *Fear's Fetishes*

Half an hour later, we passed through the Quinta's portals. Justin drove a short distance up the road to the caretaker's cottage, where Art and Dieguito waited for us. I glanced briefly at the mansion, which towered above the oaks and the pines and was even more imposing than I had imagined.

As soon as they heard the van drive up, Art and Dieguito looked out the window then came out to greet us. For a few seconds we were a cheerful group, hugging and enjoying our long-awaited reunion.

Wearing an old Pendleton and the stubble of at least five days on his face, Art seemed to have aged years in the two weeks since I had last seen him. The circles around his large, light-brown eyes were darker than usual, making his usually youthful countenance look troubled and depressed. He seemed happy to see me especially, and hugged me for a long time. Then, with his help I took down the basket of food and the container with soup that I had brought with me. We scurried into the cottage.

Justin introduced me to Dieguito. After his excitement at seeing his friends safe, Justin asked Art and Dieguito, "So, who's this guy who owns the white Buick? Felix Hunter is his name, Leo Mares told us. How did you get his address?"

"We don't really know who he is—I mean, we haven't seen him. We only know his name," Dieguito explained. "But Ted, my neighbor, saw him and a woman nosing around my house very early this morning. I wasn't at home because I was up at Lake Tahoe with Art."

"So," Justin said, "how do you know who this man and the woman nosing around your house really are?"

"Well," Dieguito said, "they told my neighbor that they were looking for someone who had hit their car, and that they'd been told that person lived at my address."

"They were looking for a reckless driver at five o'clock in the morning?" I blurted out.

"That's exactly what my neighbor said to them. So this alleged Felix Hunter pushed Ted out of the way. Then he and the woman got into a Buick and left. Ted got the license plate number though, and he asked his sister, who works for California Auto and Home Insurance, to see if she could check it out. And she got the dude's name and address for us. Quickly, too."

Dieguito's gray eyes sparkled, and he grinned, proud of himself. With an automatic gesture, he swiftly ran his fingers down his left braid to straighten it, though it didn't need any attention.

"When was the last time you heard from Sonny?" Justin asked Dieguito as he threw a quick glance in Art's direction. Art had been unusually quiet, taking in everything that was being said, but unable or unwilling to say anything.

"Sonny called me the day before he died," Dieguito answered. "He told me that someone had left a bowl of grapes at his door every day for a week. Then, he'd found a bundle of herbs tied with a skin coil on his doorstep. Sonny wanted to know about the herbs. From his description I'd say it was jimsonweed."

Art caught the look that passed between Justin and me when we heard about the herb bundle tied with a skin coil. Bob Messinger had told Justin that the grapes we'd found in Art's refrigerator in Piedmont contained jimsonweed extract, a potent hallucinogenic.

Justin and I turned our attention back to Dieguito, who was saying, "The following day, Sonny found a stuffed rattlesnake in his garden. Two days later, he found an anonymous note on his work table. It said, 'Remember the summer of 1973? Time to pay for what you did!' In addition to the note, Sonny also said that he was hearing strange noises at night but never could find who or what was making them. One time, he heard a humming and when he went to check, the VCR and TV were on, but he didn't remember leaving them on. He was spooked."

"I'd be scared, too, if that happened to me," Carlota said, addressing her comment to Art, who was standing next to her.

"Getting back to the couple who tried to get into your house," Justin said, "Did your neighbor describe them for you?"

Dieguito thought for a moment, then said, "Ted said the dude—Felix Hunter—was about six-feet tall, approximately one-hundred ninety pounds, long hair tied in a tail. It was too dark, and Ted couldn't really see the man's face."

"A pretty generic description. It'd fit a lot of men around here," I offered, and everyone agreed with an "Uh-huh," except Carlota who didn't say anything, but headed for the sofa and sat down. I checked my watch and realized that she was probably hungry and I looked for the container with the soup I'd brought for her.

Dieguito looked at Carlota. "You look pale. Are you all right?" He touched her cheeks with the back of his fingers. Carlota softly whispered a "Yes."

Justin began to get the utensils and the rest of the food out of the basket. I poured some hot soup for Carlota into a mug and took it to her. They all began to help themselves, except Art, who sat next to Carlota on the sofa.

"What's that swimming in your soup? A chicken or a vulture's neck?" Art joked, trying to make Carlota laugh.

"Stop be-(...)-ing silly," Carlota playfully reprimanded Art, who looked in my direction, expecting, I assumed, reassurance about Carlota's condition. Shaking my head, I confirmed his worst fears. He looked down at the floor.

Hearing about the vulture's neck made me think immediately of Ramón Caballos and Art's film, which Sonny seemed to have been watching the day he died.

"Did you—or Sonny—have any idea who might have left all those fetishes outside his apartment?" I asked Art.

Although his eyes showed hesitation, after a brief pause, he said, "No idea." Then he added, "I can't tell you guys how scared I was when I got the snakeskin. That, too, was the first fetish Sonny got, about a week before he died."

"When did you get the grapes?" I asked.

"Grapes?"

Justin looked at me, then at Art. We had assumed that Art had been aware of the bunch of grapes someone had left in his refrigerator. And that he was still in Piedmont when it had happened. Looking at Art's puzzled eyes, we realized that the grapes had been put there by someone after Art had left town, maybe even on the same day we went to his apartment.

"Why didn't you call me when you began to get all those...deadly presents?" Justin asked, reproach evident in his voice. "I would have helped."

"I know that now, but... Well, first I laughed the whole thing off. Then I was scared shitless. My only thought was to put distance between whoever was doing this and myself," Art said, and laughed for the first time since we first saw him. "When Sonny told me about the stuffed rattlesnake, I panicked. I packed my bag, told Sarah I was going to Quinta Selena in case anyone came looking for me, and headed up the sierra to Lake Tahoe. I thought of calling you, but I suspected that what was happening to Sonny and me had to do with deeds past. If that was the case, you shouldn't have to pay for them."

"Did you think it was Ramón Caballos who was doing this?" I asked.

Art looked puzzled again, yet he answered my question, simply saying, "Yes."

I explained that we had viewed his film at Sonny's flat in Jingletown, that it had shown Ramón Caballos leaving the scene of an exploding tank of pesticide. I briefly recounted my visit with María Baldomar, who had told me that Ramón Caballos had apparently been convicted of that crime.

"I didn't know Sonny had a copy of that film on video tape," Art said. "I thought that he had destroyed the only copy he had. My copy was used as evidence during Ramón Caballos' trial. And the police never returned it to me. Just to have a backup, I gave the third and last copy to Phillipe and Josie Hazlitt for safekeeping before the trial. Years later, Josie told Sonny that the film had been damaged when a pipe burst and flooded their basement. In time, I forgot about the film. Sonny and I tried very hard to forget about that chapter of our life," Art said, breathing in the last few words. He looked at Carlota, who was placidly lying on the sofa listening to a tape. "There isn't anything Ramón wouldn't have done for *her*," Art said, pointing in Carlota's direction with his chin. "I understood his outrage. I just didn't think it was the right course of action—blowing up the tank, I mean. Killing the guard."

"I understand you and Sonny had to testify against Ramón at his trial," I said.

"Why didn't you ever talk about all of that?" Justin asked. Without giving Art a chance to respond, he went on, "Leo and I remember hearing you and Sonny talk in riddles whenever you talked about that time in your lives. And we ended up making up all sorts of stories about you, obviously none of them true."

Art looked directly at me first, then at Justin. "You have to remember that Chicanos in the civil rights movement viewed any collaboration with the police as treason. For Sonny and me, the situation was even more complicated. Giving testimony in a court of law against a Native American *carnal* was cultural and political heresy. But if Sonny and I hadn't told the police what we knew and let them have the film, we would have seriously compromised the integrity of the farm workers' movement." Art had been speaking fast, and he paused to catch his breath.

"So, we were witnesses for the prosecution and collaborated with the enemy," Art continued. "Luckily, once the Sheriff's Office found out they couldn't use Ramón's sabotaging of the pesticide and the death of the guard against the farm workers, they kept everything hushed up. Very few people were in court when Sonny and I gave our testimony. Nonetheless, we still stayed in the valley for a few weeks, then we came back to the Bay Area. Sonny and I never made it back to Fresno. I kept in touch with Carlota, María and Dieguito. Sonny... Well, he saw Josie once in a while. As far as we were concerned, that chapter of Sonny's life and mine had ended."

"Until Sonny told you about the objects left on his doorstep?" Justin asked.

"Of course," Art replied. "I immediately thought of Ramón. But we'd been told that he'd died in prison." Art paused, then added, "I've never been much of a believer in ghosts. But the way Sonny was talking, I began to believe...I don't know what..." He chuckled, then sighed.

"He's not dead, and he recently escaped from San Quentin," I informed him. "Soldado, an old friend and ex-cellmate of Ramón, says that Ramón's apparently been keeping company with a young woman who used to write to him at San Quentin. She lives in Sonoma County."

"Around here," Dieguito said.

Everyone was lost in thought for a moment. "I think that we should pay a visit to this Felix Hunter, don't you?" Justin said, looking at Dieguito and Art, then at me.

"I don't want to stay here by myself," Carlota exclaimed, getting excited. "I want to go with you all."

"I want to go, too," Art said, mimicking Carlota. They both laughed like silly children. "Seriously," Art said. "I think it's better if we don't all go," he directed his comments first to Justin, then to me.

Justin looked at me. I agreed with Art's suggestion and offered to stay with Carlota.

"I'll stay with them, too. I'm tired of playing hero," Art said with a glitter in his eyes.

"Would you and Dieguito mind unloading the van? I'd like to talk with Gloria," Justin told his friends as he signaled for me to follow him to the kitchen. Carlota was resting comfortably on the sofa. Art and Dieguito went outside and began to unload the van and put the stuff in the trunk of Art's car. He had offered to take Carlota and me up to the main house later.

"I have the feeling that things are going to start moving fast, and I might not have another chance to give you this," Justin said, taking out a small holster. Visible in it was the handle of a gun. Taking the weapon out of the holster, he removed the magazine. I saw a slim copper and bronze bullet under which, I was sure, others lay. He held the gun on the palm of his hand. "I want you to keep this with you at all times, even when you're with me."

He put the gun in my right hand. It was a small gun, not heavy, and I was amazed at how much it felt like a toy in my hand. How could anyone kill with such a small thing, I wondered. But of course people killed others with guns as small as the one Justin had just handed me, and with bullets no bigger than a pinky's knuckle.

"I don't want it," I exclaimed, already feeling short of breath at the mere idea of using it or of someone else using it against me.

Ignoring my protests, Justin went on to explain, "It's a light, small gun, a .25 caliber, but effective up to about fifty feet. The action is not too hard." He took the gun from me and pointed at a small button on the left side of the handle while he said, "Push up to release the safety and down to lock it. Fix your eye on this small projection on the tip of the barrel, but keep your finger off the trigger until you're ready to fire. After you fire, the recoil is going to be hard on your hands, so don't ease up."

"I don't think I am going to remember,..." I said, but stopped when I felt Justin's hand on my shoulder.

He wrapped his arm loosely around me. "You'll do just fine," he reassured me when he saw me wiping the sweat off my forehead and upper lip. "If I...when this is all over..." He stopped in mid-sentence.

I turned to face him. He tightened his arm around me, and I felt him tremble. My heart began to race. I hadn't known how much I had wanted to feel his touch until the instant my mouth searched for his, and I felt him responding with a kiss as anxious as mine.

Feeling a bit embarrassed, I gently pulled away from him. He brushed my cheek with the back of his fingers. Then, without looking back, he walked out of the kitchen.

I held on to the kitchen sink to steady myself. "Gloria," I heard Carlota call out from the living room. I took a step back. The bulk of the gun pressed against my muscles, sending such a great rush of fear and excitement up my spine that for a moment I felt giddy. I reached back for the gun but didn't pull it out. From that place in my subconscious where caution becomes the calibrator of instinct, the question slowly emerged: If the occasion arose, would I be capable of pulling the trigger?

# Eighteen
## Hansel's Feather/Gretel's Yellow Band

Art drove us up to Quinta Selena where Robin Cardozo, Sarah's house manager, was already waiting for us. Carlota and I were given a bedroom on the second floor, facing east, with a spectacular view of the Valley of the Moon.

Carlota looked tired yet quite restless. Thinking that she would be unable to sleep, I offered her the other half of the sleeping pill, but she didn't want it. Taking off her shoes and removing the yellow band from her hair, she got in bed. I wanted to talk to Art, but first I sat on a chair by the window to wait until Carlota dozed off. The bulk of the gun and the compass in each of my back pockets made my belt press tighter against my diaphragm. So I loosened my belt.

Carlota's breathing was now taking on the rhythm of deep sleep. Grabbing my light cotton jacket, my *ruana*, and the flashlight, I started to join Art downstairs when I heard the steady, repetitive sound of tapping on a tree outside. "Woodpeckers," I said under my breath. I stuck my head out but I couldn't see the bird that was making all that racket. I gave a sweeping look to make sure no person was making that noise either.

It had not rained at all since the previous winter, and the surrounding hills and mountains were still covered by golden grass. Over the brow of the hill, I watched a plume of smoke rise. Since the sun had already begun its descent and the temperature had started to drop, I assumed the smoke came from the fireplace of a house hidden from view.

I took out the compass and pointed it in the direction of the smoke. Since I knew that part of the house faced east, I

was not surprised when the compass indicated that north was
to my left. I surmised, then, that the plume of smoke was rising from a house northeast of Quinta Selena.

Although I was almost certain I would not see it, I scanned
the sky above for the moon. It would rise soon enough, I said to
myself as I locked the windows. Then I went downstairs to
speak with Art.

I found him in the sunroom, reading the papers. "The
drought is driving everything and everyone crazy," he commented, showing me the paper and pointing at the headline
that warned, "Look Down Before You Take That Next Step." A
sub-heading cautioned the reader further: "An Unusual Number of Rattlesnakes Found on Lower Elevations."

I took a mouthful of air in and let it out slowly, then asked
Art, "Do you believe in premonitions?"

Art smiled. He seemed much more cheerful than he'd been
when we first arrived at the cottage. "I keep an open mind.
What's on yours? You seem quite preoccupied."

"I am," I said, then began to tell him about my visions,
especially about the rattlesnake and the woman tied to a cactus. "I also have this terrible feeling that Justin's going to get
hurt," I concluded.

"Have you told him about your...premonition?"

"I tried to tell him earlier, but...I'm a coward," I said. "I
just can't bring myself to do it."

"It's unders...." Art left the sentence hanging in midair,
but not on purpose, I realized. I watched him cock his head as
if to listen better.

I heard a couple of creaking sounds, then nothing. The
house was made of stone, but it had enough wooden floors and
paneling in it to be noisy.

"There it is again," Art said. The noise he was talking
about sounded as if someone were chopping wood or pounding
on a wooden board. "While I was upstairs, I heard a similar

noise, but I thought it was made by a woodpecker," I suggested as I sat down. Art sat on the arm of the chair he had occupied a while before. The noise stopped, and he relaxed.

"I guess I'm on edge," he remarked.

"We all are," I said. "For good reasons."

We were quiet for a while. Art was the first to break the silence. "It's fascinating."

"What's fascinating?" I asked.

"I don't know how to explain it—I feel as if a cycle that started back in 1973 is coming to a close. I just hope this cycle doesn't end with my own demise." Without waiting for my response, he added, "Maybe I'm just being morbid." He laughed softly. "For the cycle to end like it began, those of us who were involved in the action of sixteen years ago would have to be here at the same time. Aren't cycles supposed to work that way?"

"I'm not sure how cycles work. But, obviously, Sonny and Phillipe are no longer here, and if they need to be physically present, then you indeed have a problem," I commented. "However, Justin saw Josie Baldomar drive into Sonoma earlier today. It won't be long before she gets here."

Art gave me a puzzled look, then asked, "Where is Phillipe? What's happened to him?"

"I'm sorry. I thought you knew," I said. "Phillipe Hazlitt has been reported missing, probably drowned. All of his belongings were found on a beach in Monterey. The police are looking into his death."

"Another suicide? That's so strange. Why would Phillipe kill himself?" Then, looking directly at me, Art said, "It makes no sense."

"Suicide—if that's what it was—never makes sense, except perhaps in cases of terminal illness."

"Do you think he was murdered? Is that what you're saying?" Art asked.

"There's something strange about his...disappearance," I said. "María Baldomar told me she believes that Josie thinks Carlota had something to do with Phillipe's taking his own life."

"I see," Art remarked. After a brief pause, he added, "Does María think that Phillipe took his own life because of Josie's relationship with Carlota?" Giving me little chance to respond, Art clarified, "The relationship has been going on for years. And Phillipe knew about it all along. I was sure María suspected it—if she didn't actually know about it. Carlota and Phillipe weren't the only ones in Josie's life," he said, but didn't complete the thought.

"I know Josie had other lovers. Carlota implied that last night."

"Yes. And Phillipe knew about all of them." Art tapped his chin with his finger. "But I think he understood Josie better than anyone else. He accepted Josie's extramarital affairs as long as she stayed with him. Deep inside, I think he realized that Josie's infidelities had more to do with her need to be constantly and unconditionally admired. Worshiped, actually."

"There's no denying she's quite beautiful. And I'm sure she can be quite charming."

"Josie loved Carlota as much as she loved Phillipe," Art commented further. "Carlota, more than anyone else, would do anything for Josie."

"Not quite, it seems," I said. Art gave me an inquisitive look. "Carlota wants to be left alone now. I'm guessing, but I'd say she wants to go away, and Josie insists on going away with her. I'm not sure, but I think Josie's pregnant and wants Carlota and herself to raise the baby together."

"Then that might account for Phillipe wanting to kill himself," Art suggested.

"Maybe not. Phillipe knew that Carlota is terminally ill. He was also aware that she was going away without Josie.

Apparently, Josie did follow Carlota to Oakland, judging by what Soldado told Justin and me. Did you see either Carlota or Josie while they were in Oakland recently?" I asked.

"No," Art said, rubbing the back of his neck. "I had no idea they were in Oakland." He then gave me a curious look. "Do you think Carlota...?"

"Of course she didn't kill Sonny," I reassured him, and was quite surprised at how sure I was about Carlota's innocence. "But she was seen leaving Sonny's place earlier," I explained. "That's why Leo thinks Carlota was involved. I, personally, think Carlota witnessed something there she's not telling anyone about."

"I'm not sure what to think..." Art said. Then he put his index finger on his lips and pointed at his ear, urging me to listen. I heard a distant, intermittent tapping, followed by a grating noise. "There it is again. Do you hear it?" Art jumped to his feet.

"Robin, the house manager, might be fixing something to eat," I suggested as I reached for the flashlight. I slowly rose.

"That's no cook," Art rebutted. We both listened attentively.

Carefully, we began to check each room in the house and look out every window to locate the source of the noise. Robin Cardozo, the manager, came out when she heard us moving swiftly through the house. Although she looked at us with curiosity, she whispered, "Anything I can do for you?"

"How many doors to the outside are there?" I asked, trying to keep a calm attitude to offset the seriousness of my question.

"Four," Robin answered. "One in Mrs. Owens' bedroom; it opens onto the summer terrace, but it remains locked at all times when she's not here. Three doors down here, one in the kitchen, another in the dining room, the third in the living room," she said as she pointed to the general location of each entryway.

"There is also one downstairs in the cellar, right?" Art reminded Robin.

"Yes," she confirmed, then asked, "Is there something wrong?"

"I don't know how much Sarah told you..." I said slowly, giving myself time to explain as best I could the urgency of the situation.

"Enough to know that Art here and your friend upstairs are in danger," Robin stated. "So tell me, how can I help?"

"Brava!" Art interjected and clapped his hands, applauding her courage. She welcomed the compliment with a smile and a head bow.

"Let's secure every window and door to the outside," I suggested. Following Robin's directions, she and I checked the ground floor while Art went downstairs to make sure that the outside door to the basement and wine cellar was locked.

Robin was about to say something when we heard Art cry out. We both rushed to the basement and found him kneeling down, rubbing his right wrist. Robin rushed to help him while I went up the steps leading out of the cellar. I carefully stuck my head out the door, which was now open. There wasn't a soul in sight. I inspected the cellar door and noticed that the latch that secured the padlock had been pried open.

The grove of madrone trees on that side of the Quinta had apparently been watered earlier. The ground was still wet, and shoe prints were visible on it. The individual who had broken into the basement had run into the madrone grove. Judging by the prints, the intruder was either a woman or a small man.

"What happened?" I asked Art when I went back inside. "Did you see who it was?"

"A woman, I think, pushed me. It's dark in here. I couldn't really see who it was." Art had barely finished the sentence when we heard a door slam upstairs and the footfalls of at least two people going down the kitchen steps. One of the people running was Carlota, I assumed. But who was the other?

"Call Justin," I said to Art while I went out the cellar door and ran to the back of the house, followed by Robin.

Through the trees I could see only the black-jeaned legs of someone running downhill. I recognized the green sweater Carlota had been wearing. For some reason she was wearing her yellow hair band around her arm. Whoever had abducted her hadn't given her enough time to put on her shoes, for I could see that she held them clipped tightly between her fingers and thumb as she ran. "I can't run! I don't feel so good!" I heard her say with a fainting voice. Then, all of a sudden, I heard nothing but the shuffling of leaves, more distant with the abductor's every step.

"I'm going after them," I stated. "Please show Art which way I went," I added, pointing at the spot where we had last seen Carlota and her kidnapper disappear.

"Should I call the police?" Robin asked.

"No. Don't," I commanded. "Carlota is an undocumented person and the police might take her into custody," I explained, then added, "Art will tell you what to do."

As I began to run, I turned back and saw Art running backwards while telling Robin, "I couldn't reach Justin. I left the phone number and the instructions on a slip of paper on the kitchen table. Keep trying, and tell him everything. Tell him to meet us on Alta Vista Road, near the trail to the old ghost dancing place. Dieguito knows where it is."

A few minutes later Art caught up with me, brandishing the flashlight and the *ruana*. "Just in case," he told me.

"Where's that place that Dieguito is supposed to know? How do you know about it?" I asked him. I took out my compass and looked at it.

"It may be a wild goose chase, but Dieguito and I saw something from the caretaker's cottage just before you guys arrived."

"A plume of smoke?" I asked. Then pointing to my left as I looked at the compass, I added, "In that direction?"

"Yes," Art slowed down and looked at me. "How did you know?"

"I saw it, too, from upstairs. It caught my attention because I saw no houses around there." I paused. Taking in short breaths, I tried to steady my respiration. Art began to do the same. I looked at the ground. "Why that place?"

"Before we came up here to meet you and Justin, we saw activity at that old place. For many years after the mission was built, many of the natives gathered at that clearing, a hollow between two hills, to worship their own gods and dance. One night, a group of christianized mission Indians led a raid against the rebel group and killed them all," Art said while we both looked at the ground, trying to find a sign that we were still on the right trail. "Ever since, the spot has been considered 'unholy ground.'

"More recently, beginning about two months ago," he continued, "there was some kind of activity there—fires burning in the night. That kind of thing."

"Do people believe that the Native Americans are doing that?" I asked.

"To tell you the truth, most people Dieguito and I talked to didn't know what to make of it. Except that someone was up to no good. And I'm sure it isn't the Native Americans. Curiously enough, it is Mexican American workers who adamantly refuse to visit the spot. One of those workers, who was brave enough to check out the action, was found the next day, dead from snakebite. Snakes seem to like the old ghost dancing place. I guess because it is warmer there than anywhere around it, even in winter. People who've visited the spot say they hear a rumbling inside the mountain. I have always suspected that, onc of these days, a geyser will break through the mountain wall.

"Today, some of the same grape workers told us that two nights ago—the night of the full moon—they saw the glow of fires. They also heard a man chanting. All of them are so afraid that no one wanted to go and check it out. Dieguito and I went to look the place over. We found bundles of weeds and herbs tied with snake coils. We also saw ashes of copal in a lava-stone burner and a small altar. You can imagine how I felt when I saw all that, especially after what happened to Sonny. But we saw no one around."

Art and I resumed our search for clues down the trail.

"And you think whoever has taken Carlota is now going there?" I said, crouching to inspect a spot we came to a short distance away. Next to the trampled leaves, I had seen small areas that looked as if someone had purposely swept over them. I suspected her abductor had been dragging a reluctant Carlota. But now there was only one set of shoe prints, and not a sign of dragging feet or shoes was visible. I deduced that Carlota was being carried, perhaps unconscious. A very large woman could possibly carry Carlota in her condition, but I tended to believe the prints were those of a male with very wide feet, someone who either wore sandals or went barefoot.

"If I'm not mistaken, the kidnapper carrying Carlota is heading northeast," I informed Art after checking the compass again. "You might be right and he might be going to the old ghost dancing place. The smoke I saw was in that general direction, too."

I set out down the path I suspected Carlota's abductor was following. Art, who had stayed behind, caught up with me. "Look at this," he said, showing me the yellow band Carlota had been wearing on her hair. "I found it on a raspberry vine back there."

A few feet down the trail, we found a strange-looking feather resting on a bunch of weeds held together with a black ribbon. Her death bundle, I thought, as I remembered that it was the same assortment of herbs I had seen in Carlota's bag back in my house.

"Either we're about to meet Hansel and Gretel or we're being set up," Art said.

I agreed.

We both knew, nonetheless, that we had no choice but to follow that trail. I hadn't counted, however, on the trail splitting into two others a short distance away. Each of the paths showed the signs of someone treading on it recently.

"I know all the hiking trails around here," Art said. "I know these two trails wind downhill and end up below on Alta Vista Road below. Why don't we split up and meet down on that road again?" Searching his pockets, he took out a piece of paper and a pen and quickly drew a map of the trails winding down to the road, then across it to the old ghost dancing place. Seeing no other possibility, we reluctantly agreed to separate.

Sunset was fast approaching as I made it down the hill and waited for Art. When he didn't show up, following his directions, I walked along the road and looked for the trail on the map he'd drawn for me. Just past a bend on the road, I saw Justin's van parked a short distance ahead of the trail I was searching for. I rushed to the van, but neither Justin nor Dieguito—or Art, for that matter—was in it. Assuming that Art was with them and that all three had already gone up to the old ghost dancing place, I put my *ruana* on and hastened my pace.

I wasn't sure where the trail I chose would take me, but I had no doubts now I would recognize the place by the cluster of cacti, the sound of the rattlers, and the red energy of a murderer walking away in the moonlight.

# Nineteen
## *Dreamshadows and Rattlers*

By the time I climbed up closer to the old ghost dancing place, all that remained of the sun was an ochre afterglow on my left. In the east, the waning moon rose slowly. Its amber light illuminated the vineyards on the slope of a nearby hill as well as the cluster of prickly-pear cacti near me. Seeing something shiny down the path, I went to see what it was. I recognized one of the barrettes that Carlota had worn the evening she came to my house in Oakland.

Certain that I had followed the right path, I turned off the flashlight and stopped a moment to rest and get my bearings. As I looked back up the path I'd just traversed, I saw a light scan the semi-darkness in my direction. Although I was too far away for someone to spot me, I stepped off the path for a minute.

Scanning the terrain, trying to find another way to the hollow between the hills below, I heard what sounded like a snake's rattle, soft at first, then a bit louder. A minute later, farther away, another followed, as if the second rattler were acknowledging the former's warning. My stomach turned and my heart began to beat faster. I had just walked into my recurring vision.

About to turn on the flashlight, I remembered my father's warnings. He had often told us that light attracted snakes, that they moved towards it instinctively, and that some of them actually lunged forward when a gun was fired and got a bullet between the eyes all on their own. I wasn't about to attempt proving or disproving my father's theory nor risk having someone more lethal than a snake hear the shot and come after me. Although intellectually I knew having a gun offered an illusory sense of protection, I reached back into my pocket to make sure the .25 was still there.

As I was raising my head to check on the stranger's progress, out of the corner of my eye I caught sight of the rattler about four feet away from me. As if to test the distance between us from its half-coiled position, the snake thrust its head forward a couple of times. Nothing could stop my heart from racing then. "Don't move, Gloria," I commanded myself, sucking in air. With fear rushing through my veins, I couldn't have moved even if I wanted to. Although breathing through my nose was becoming difficult, I tried to keep my mouth shut, for I was afraid that if I opened it, I would no longer be able to contain my scream.

Only a fast-dimming twilight remained now. The moon had begun to move behind a higher hill. Menacing shadows and rattlers surrounded me. Instinctively, I began to rotate, slowly scrutinizing the darkness for the avenue of escape I knew was there. Then I started to retreat, an inch at a time, until I felt the sharp cactus needles press against my back.

I felt the presence of a third person, red and glowing like a flame, somewhere behind me. I knew it couldn't be Justin, Dieguito or Art. But I didn't dare look back at that moment, for I heard the rattler in front of me shake its rattle again, poised for the deadly strike.

I backed away another inch and felt the sharp pain on my leg and on my injured arm shoot up to my neck, making my tears begin to flow. I clenched my teeth to contain my crying. I was sure the prickles from the cactus had drawn blood from the wound on my upper arm again.

The moon began to clear the second hill, and I saw the opening in the cactus cluster. The rattler and I recoiled, each in opposite directions. The rattler sprang towards me, I

towards the clearing in the cluster. As in my vision, I jumped
out of the way and through the opening.

Protecting my face and eyes with my arms, I pushed
through the cacti. For a second time, I sensed the presence of
a third person, this time as a fading, reddish energy.

A few feet away I made out the shape of the large, slumping cactus. Knowing what lay under it, I considered for an
instant not going around it, not confronting the gruesome
scene that awaited me. But as if they had an energy all their
own, my legs kept on walking until I reached the other side.

At that moment the moon cleared the hill and again came
fully into view, giving a yellow glow to everything it gazed
upon—the vineyard, the cluster, and my shaking hands as I
reached down to raise the drooping, agonizing figure of a
young woman clad in nothing but moonlight and fresh blood,
bearing a fleshy cactus cross on her back.

I untied her hands and feet, and her inanimate, cool body
slumped into my arms, bringing both of us down. The cactus
rose gradually to full height as I laid her down on her side and
felt her neck for her jugular vein. At first, I thought I sensed a
light throb on the tips of my very cold fingers. But when I put
my ear to her chest, her heart answered with silence. I had
inadvertently put my hand on her belly, and I was surprised
when I felt a small fluttering on the side of my hand. With my
fingers, I checked her bulging belly and let my hand rest on it.
A thrill ran up my arm to my heart when I felt the fetus growing inside her respond to the pressure and warmth of my
hand. But I immediately recoiled as horror gripped my heart.
Even if the fetus were still alive, if the mother was dead, there
might be nothing that I—or anyone else—could do to keep its
tiny heart from slipping irretrievably into silence. I took off
my *ruana* and covered her with it. She was too big for me to
carry her all the way back to Justin's van. I could go for help,
but that would take time.

Perhaps it was useless, but I couldn't just stand there and do nothing, I thought. I began to rub her hands and feet vigorously to get her circulation going, then started CPR—grateful to Darío, who had insisted I learn the technique. Her mouth had a foul, musty smell, like that produced by the rotting stems of mums in stagnant water.

I had broken into a sweat, and I wiped my forehead as I stared hopelessly at her abdomen, certain the woman's baby would never see the light of day. A wisp of breath or a light heartbeat would have kept me going, but there was none. I covered her with the *ruana* again. I shuddered. And I was suddenly aware of every ache and itch left on my arms and legs by the cactus prickles. I felt the smarting around my arm wound. Just below my ears, I also felt the painful tightness caused by the grinding of my teeth as I tried to put just the right pressure on the woman's chest.

This wasn't the time or the place to lick my wounds. I was more aware than ever that someone far more dangerous than the snakes and the cactus prickles was still at large. And that Carlota was, perhaps, still his prisoner.

I stood up and was about to start walking back to the road when I heard murmuring voices and footfalls coming closer. I crouched again, then risked a swift look at the intruders—three shadows walking by. I saw Justin's silhouette and gait, unmistakable even in the moonlight, and I released the breath I had held back. Lighting the way, Dieguito preceded him, followed by Art. "Over here, Justin," I called out, trying to keep my voice down and my teeth from chattering. A minute later, they were standing beside me. The moon had begun to move behind another hill.

"Are you all right?" Justin asked, reaching for me in the dark. I huddled against him to get warm. "You're shivering," he said, and he held me closer. He took off the *ruana* he was wearing and wrapped me in it.

"We've been worried about you," Art said, rubbing my lower arm. "And about Carlota. Did you find her?"

"No. I didn't find Carlota. But I found this other woman," I said, and directed the beam from my flashlight down to the body on the ground.

"Who is she?" Dieguito asked as he scanned her face with the beam from his flashlight. For an instant, I thought I had seen the woman's eyes move under the lids. I threw light on her face and watched again for some eye movement. When I saw none, I surmised that light and shadow had played a trick on me.

Justin, Art and Dieguito gasped when they looked at the young woman's badly cropped hair and the nicks and cuts around her forehead. Blood from her scalp wounds had run down her cheeks. Some of it had collected around the corners of her eyes and had mixed with her tears. Then, tears and blood had trickled down again towards her slightly gaping mouth.

"For a moment I thought she was Carlota," Art said after looking closely at the woman's face. "Thank God, she isn't."

"Who is this person, then? Is she dead?" Dieguito asked, and bent over to take the woman's pulse.

I was getting ready to tell him that she was dead when we heard a faint sigh, followed by a moan. Just then, the woman stirred and moved her arm, pushing the ruana off her bare chest.

"She's still alive!" I said aloud, throwing caution to the wind. "Hang in there, baby," I whispered as I knelt down and put my hand on her belly. Dieguito also offered his poncho to cover her. Taking off my jacket, I folded it and placed it under her head.

Out of the pouch Dieguito always wore strapped around his chest, he took a small metal flask and unscrewed the cap. I assumed it contained some kind of liquor or invigorating potion. I raised her head and placed my arm under her neck while Dieguito made her drink from the metal container a couple of times. The young woman said something unintelligible. Instinctively, the four of us bent over to hear her better.

"Did she say Felix?" I asked the others, and they all confirmed hearing that name. She moaned and seemed to get agitated.

"I'm not Felix," Dieguito told her. But the young woman seemed to have lost consciousness again. Then, suddenly, she began tearing at something or someone.

Turning to me, Dieguito said, "She's hallucinating. Did you notice that rotten smell in her breath?" he asked me, and when I nodded, he quickly added, "That's jimsonweed."

"Dear God!" I exclaimed. "What's going to happen to the baby?" All three men looked at me simultaneously.

"So," Art said, "whoever did this to her wanted her dead but didn't want her and the baby to feel their pain. Damn him!" Art got up and kicked the ground.

"Looks that way, doesn't it?" Justin remarked while he searched around with his flashlight, inspecting the scene. Being so caught up in trying to revive the young woman and save the baby, I hadn't yet given a thought to the motives of the person who had brought her there.

"Please, give me some light here," Dieguito told Art. "I have to check her back." Art crouched and pointed the light at the young woman's back. "A couple of deeper wounds. But the rest are superficial cuts and bruises." He started applying some kind of jelly on her back and bathed the deeper wounds with a pungent-smelling liquid. "She probably would have died of hypothermia, more than from the bleeding. It gets mighty cold here." He took out a handkerchief from his pouch and pressed it against her back.

Justin came back. He handed me a pile of clothes. Next he gave me a pair of shoes and the young woman's wallet. "I found these scattered all over. Here's something that might interest you," he said, handing me her wallet. He rested the light on it so I could look at the contents.

The wallet contained the usual assortment of credit cards. Included in the collection were also proof of insurance, library cards, and some slips of paper which turned out to be mostly forgotten shopping lists. I looked at the small black-and-white photo of two teenage girls and a younger boy. In the wallet, there were also about twenty dollars in one-dollar bills, and tucked between two of them was a receipt from the Lucky Market on Fruitvale Avenue in Oakland. It was dated Friday, October 13. Going down the list, the word "grapes" caught my attention.

As I picked up her driver's license, it occurred to me this woman could be the same woman Carlota had seen in Sonny's apartment. Just then, Justin rested the beam of light on her driver's license. I looked at it, then at the young, semi-conscious woman lying on the ground.

"Remmine Marie Hunter," Justin said.

"Remmi Stephens," I whispered as I felt Justin's hand search for mine under the *ruana*.

Dieguito stood up and Art gasped at hearing that name.

The young woman seemed to react to the name, and we heard her say, "Yes?"

"Who did this to you, Remmi?" I inquired. She struggled to say something but couldn't form the words.

"Was it Felix?" I said, and she shook her head violently.

"Was it Carlota Navarro?" Justin asked, and Remmi Stephens's reaction was less violent. This time she merely whispered, "No."

The young woman stirred and tried to turn on her back, but Dieguito and I stopped her. "Felix," she shouted, finally opening her eyes wide as if she were waking from a nightmare. She kept repeating, "Felix. Wife. Felix. Wife." We all looked at each other, trying to figure out what she was saying.

"I think she's not going to tell us anything until the drug wears off," Dieguito said, and added, "Which may take hours."

"I don't know about you," I said. "But I'm afraid for Remmi and for the fetus. I think we should get her to a hospital. And soon." I knelt down to help Remmi into her clothes and shoes. "Would you mind?" I said to the men, motioning them away. "I'm going to put her clothes back on." I took the flashlight and placed it so I could see what I was doing. The men turned around and moved a few feet away.

"I'm more confused than ever," I heard Art say. "I don't know what the hell's going on."

"Goes without saying," Dieguito agreed. "Would you mind explaining it to us?" he asked Justin.

"I'm not sure what is going on either," Justin said, and I could hear the irritation in his voice. This was a turn we hadn't expected. We'd had a faint suspicion of a connection with the Stephens family all along; we even confirmed it when someone had tried to break into my house. But we had never thought someone would make an attempt on Remmi Stephens's life.

Remmi resisted my efforts to put on her pants. "You're safe," I reassured her. She seemed to calm down, but kept calling her husband's name and repeating the word "wife." I realized that something else troubled her but couldn't quite figure what it was.

I began to put the contents back in her wallet. As I look at the photo among them, I realized that the children in it were Sandy, Remmi, and Randolph Stephens. For the first time, I noticed that the paper seemed unusually thick for that kind of photo. I called out to Justin, handed him the photo and asked for his opinion.

He ran his fingers along the edges. Then, handing me the snapshot, he said, "You're right. See if you can slide your nail anywhere in there."

I did as he suggested. "It's two photos stuck together. They're coming apart now," I stated. I wondered if Remmi had other children at home, for the substance making the snaps adhere to each other felt sticky. Little fingers, sticky with candy or honey, had perhaps touched them.

Art and Dieguito joined us at that moment. Dieguito went to check on Remmi. Art looked over my shoulder at the two snaps.

"They were stuck together," I began to explain, but Art cut me off.

"The man in this photo is Phillipe Hazlitt," Art said.

"What!" Justin and I exclaimed in unison. We looked at the photo, then at each other.

Before we had a chance to react to his remark, Art asked, "What's Remmine Stephens doing with a photo of Phillipe Hazlitt?" Then, without waiting for our answer, he asked again, "Felix Hunter is Phillipe Hazlitt? Do you think he's alive? Did he do this to her?" His questions echoed my own doubts. I listened for Justin's reaction, but he remained quiet.

Dieguito gasped next to me and mumbled something about Phillipe being dead, which triggered Remmi's restlessness again.

"Did you find Felix Hunter when you went to his house?" I asked Dieguito.

"Not a sign of him, or the young woman..." Dieguito stopped midtrack. He pointed at Remmi, then said, "*This* young woman is the one we were looking for, isn't she?"

Scratching his head, Art said, "I'm more confused than ever. I hope you and Justin can figure it out."

I knelt down to check on Remmi. I held her hand, and it seemed awfully limp. I felt for the young woman's belly. I got no reaction from her or the fetus.

"I don't like the looks of this," I told Dieguito. "Let's get her to a hospital."

"Let's go then," Dieguito said as he struggled to find a way to lift and carry Remmi without hurting the baby. Art and Justin helped him.

I knew that was the right thing to do, but I couldn't help feeling terrible at the thought that Carlota was still out there, perhaps in grave danger. "I hope Carlota is all right," I told Justin. He patted my hand reassuringly.

Dieguito and Art sensed our predicament. So Dieguito immediately suggested, "Why don't you two go ahead and continue your search for Carlota? Art and I will get Remmi to a hospital."

"Are you sure?" Justin asked.

"We're sure," Art answered. "We're worried about Carlota, too," he said, gently squeezing my hand. I smiled.

Knowing that was the best plan, Justin handed Art one of the flashlights and the key to his van.

A moment later, taking turns to carry Remmi, Dieguito and Art began their painful and slow journey to the van. At a faster pace, Justin and I headed down the winding trail towards the hollow between the mountains, the place where warriors had once danced and died.

# Twenty
## *In the Dancer's Shadow*

The moon had begun its slow crossing from the third to the fourth hill, but the sky was now populated by a herd of small cirrus clouds which the eastern wind shepherded together.

Quite suddenly, Justin and I came upon the clearing. Hidden from view, a small diamond-shaped open structure with only a make-shift Spanish-tile roof lay wedged in the hollow between the two hills. Just outside the structure, a small bonfire burned on each corner. We noticed a rudimentary fireplace with a funnel opening up past the open part of the roof, which seemed to be its only furnishing. A fire burned in the rather narrow hearth, throwing a dim light on the area before it and making the space behind it seemed even darker. The cold eastern wind blew through the structure, teasing the flames and making the wood crackle. Other than the crackling of the fire or the hissing of the wind, no sound came from within or around the structure.

Justin and I crouched behind bushes so dry they seemed to sizzle every time a breath of wind touched them. "I think I see something or someone in there," Justin told me, and I agreed with a muffled "Yes" as I watched the silhouette of a man bow and rise once, then disappear.

"We'll have to get closer," Justin suggested.

Difficult as it was, since the ground was covered with this noisy chaparral, we moved quietly until we were facing the other side and had a clear view of the fireplace. We saw the two bundles, which in no way resembled human shapes. They were visible only when they caught the flicker of light from the fire.

All of a sudden, I had an uneasy feeling that someone was watching us. I even thought I heard a noise behind us, as if someone were stepping on dry brush. Slowly, I turned. But I saw no one.

I threw a brief glance at Justin, but he seemed not to have heard anything. Following a sudden impulse, I slowly reached back under the *ruana* and my sweatshirt for the small gun neatly tucked in my jeans pocket. Realizing what I was doing, I left it in its place. I drew in a mouthful of air and realized I'd been breathing through my mouth all the while. My tongue felt thick and dry.

A shadow wedged between two trees began to recede as the moon moved across the sky. Again I heard that crunching sound and felt the presence of someone behind us. I was about to warn Justin when suddenly he turned around with his gun in his hand.

In a loud but calm voice, Justin said, "I suggest you step out where I can see you, and with your hands up!"

For a seemingly endless interval, all we could hear was the rustling of the wind and the wailing of a siren at a distance. Then, as in a jigsaw puzzle, piece by piece, the full figure of the dancer in my vision came into view. Clad in black pants and shirt, he was of medium height and build. A slim, straight nose and high cheekbones made his piercing eyes seem smaller than they actually were. Clipped to his belt was a wornout leather sheath with a knife in it.

"Ramón?" I whispered. "Ramón Caballos?"

He smiled. Undaunted by the gun pointed at him, he turned slightly, enough not to make Justin nervous, but to let us see the area behind him. Someone else was standing half in his shadow, wrapped in a blanket.

A very weak Carlota greeted me with a smile and a hug, then told me, "I'm so glad to see you." I couldn't begin to tell her how happy I was to see her, too.

Ramón saw Justin looking at his knife. He began to rise his hand slowly towards his waist. Ramón's gesture made Justin tense and he raised his gun. Carlota and I gasped.

"I'll give the knife to Carlota as is, all right?" Ramón said.

"Slowly," Justin cautioned. "Use one hand only."

Ramón smiled as he handed Carlota the knife.

Justin stood to the side, still holding his gun but no longer pointing it at the other man. Saying nothing, Ramón signaled for us to follow him as he began to walk towards the shed. I caught up with him as we reached the hut.

"Why did you take her from Quinta Selena and bring her here?" I reproached Ramón. "It's cold. She needs food and medicine."

Showing me Carlota's bag and another bundle, which I assumed contained his belongings, he indicated that her medication was in it. Then he answered my first question, "She's coming with me. I'm taking her home."

"You must be out of your mind," I scolded him. Then I asked Carlota, "Do you realize what you're in for?" Not waiting for an answer, I pleaded with her, "A fugitive's life. That's what you're in for. What you've never wanted."

"Oh, Gloria," Carlota said, "in the end, that's what I've had—a fugitive's life." She held my hand.

"You knew Ramón was coming for you. Why didn't you tell me?" I asked, more disappointed than angry.

"No, I didn't know he was. For a long time I thought he was dead. Then, Soldado told me that Ramón was alive. Three weeks ago, he called me and said that Ramón would make the journey to my hometown with me whenever I wanted." She looked for my eyes. "I didn't want to lie to you. I just wasn't sure what I was going to do." Carlota explained. "My life has

never been my own. I want to be buried in the place where I
saw the light of day for the first time. Don't you see? Ramón is
taking me there."

I did see. I had no arguments left.

"Do you know who tried to kill Remmi Stephens Hunter?"
Justin asked perfunctorily, but aware of Ramón's every move.

"Maybe the same person who killed Phillipe Hazlitt," he
suggested. "*I* sure didn't kill anyone," he emphasized.

"And *who* do you think might have killed Phillipe
Hazlitt?" Justin said.

"Please, Ramón," I heard Carlota say as she stretched her
hand to the old shaman. "Don't."

Ramón looked at her, then at us.

"It's of no use now," Carlota insisted.

"Maybe," Ramón answered. "They're bound to find out. Or
maybe they already know."

"He's right," Justin told Carlota. "Gloria and I haven't
been able to put all the pieces together, but we already have a
good idea who's behind all this. We found Remmi Stephens
tied to a cactus, half dead. She mentioned Felix's wife. Then
we found out Felix Hunter is really Phillipe Hazlitt.

"We don't know exactly how or why, but we strongly suspect Josie killed Phillipe and tried to kill Remmi. We just
don't know why she would kill Sonny," Justin told Carlota.
"Maybe she's not guilty and you know it. If Josie didn't do
these things, why don't you say so now?"

Carlota was quiet then handed me Ramón's knife, which
she had been holding while we talked. Bending slowly, she
went down on her knees, then sat on the ground. For the first
time, I heard her cry. I set the knife on the ground and sat
next to her. I held her for a while.

"You're right," Ramón said. "I'm not sure how Josie found
out that Phillipe was planning to run away with Remmi or
where he was living. But you can be sure she didn't know

about Remmi until recently."

"How do you know all this?" Justin inquired.

"I saw Remmi yesterday, and she told me the whole story. She and her brother Randolph had been trying to find Art and that other man Dieguito to get their help. Remmi knew Hazlitt was dead. She told me Josie had killed him," Ramón said.

"Was Remmi Stephens the same woman who came to see you in prison?" I asked.

"One and the same," Ramón replied. "How do you know she came to see me in Quentin?"

"Soldado told us," I explained.

"I see," he said. "Yes, a few years ago, Remmi was looking for Carlota. At the time Carlota was living at Soldado's trailer camp in Oakland."

"What made Remmi go looking for Carlota so many years after Mark Stephens's death?" I asked.

"Her grandmother had died not too long before Remmi talked to me at Quentin. Apparently, Remmi helped her mother pack away or dispose of her grandmother's belongings, and among the old woman's things, she found a letter her mother had written to her grandmother. It was dated a week after Dr. Stephens's death. In it *Señora* Stephens said that Josie Baldomar had accused the doctor of raping Carlota. But *la señora* had not been able to talk directly with Carlota."

Ramón paused, then knelt down to check on Carlota who was still sobbing softly. "I think it's better if we dropped the subject," he told Justin and me.

"No," Carlota said, "I want to—No, I badly need to get to the bottom of this mess. Before I run out of...time, I want to know all there is." She wiped her eyes with the back of her fingers. "Please, go on," she told Ramón.

"All right," he said. "Before going to see me at Quentin, Remmi went looking for Josie in Kingsburg. Josie wasn't at

home, but Phillipe was, and he talked to Remmi. For some
reason, he decided to help her locate Carlota, but he himself
didn't know where Carlota was. None of them knew. I knew
where she was only because Soldado told me."

"So Phillipe sent Remmi to you the first time she went to
see you," Justin said. "How long ago did that happen? Do you
remember?"

"Yes. I saw Remmi for the first time back in 1982, two
years after Carlota moved to Oakland."

"Did you feel Remmi was being sincere?" I asked.

"I kind of believed she was being sincere when she told
me that she had felt very close to Carlota. No one had paid
much attention to her as a child until Carlota went to live
with them, she said. Her grandmother and her mother and
father were always fussing over Sandy, who was the oldest
and considered quite talented by her parents and teachers.
Then, Carlota, whom Remmi loved very much, went away
without even saying good-bye. On top of that, her father died
of a heart attack the day after Carlota left. Her grandmother
and mother gave Sandy their total attention. Remmi felt
abandoned by everyone, but particularly by Carlota," Ramón
concluded.

"If you believed Remmi, why didn't you give her Carlota's
address? Justin asked.

"I wasn't quite sure I could trust Remmi. You see, she
offered me money for the information about Carlota's whereabouts. I sent her home and told her not to bother me again.
After her visit, she wrote me many times. I actually began to
like her and to look forward to getting her letters, though I
wouldn't admit to those feelings at the time. I always felt that
she was as lonely as I was. But I think that writing those letters to me about her childhood and her life at the time were
kind of therapeutic." Ramón sighed.

"Did Remmi ever go back to visit you?" I asked.

"Yes. She went back to see me at Quentin after her mother died. She wanted more than ever to talk with Carlota. Remmi seemed quite mixed-up and depressed."

"Did you think she still blamed Carlota for Mark Stephens's death?" I asked.

"Maybe Remmi didn't. But from what she told me, her brother Randolph and her sister Sand sure did," Ramón replied. "Again, I didn't think Carlota needed the aggravation. But just a few weeks ago, Remmi went back to see me. I don't know if it's true, but she told me that Phillipe Hazlitt knew where Carlota was but wouldn't tell her. When I asked why, she confessed that Hazlitt and her were in love. By the time Remmi came to see me that third time, she and Hazlitt had begun to talk about living together. He was going to fake his death and they were going away together."

"Did she tell you that or are you guessing?" I asked.

"Oh, no. I'm not guessing. Isn't it amazing—the things people tell you when you're at *la pinta?* They think you can't tell anyone else because you're in prison."

"It could also be that she doesn't have anyone to confide in, including Phillipe," I pointed out.

Ramón nodded. "Also true," he said, then resumed his story. "At any rate, she told me what Phillipe intended to do. She also said that she was pregnant with his child. I wanted to help her, but I still didn't understand why she wanted to talk with Carlota."

"Did you ask her why it was so important that she talk to Carlota?" I asked.

"Yes, I did," Ramón replied. "She told me that she had been having terrible nightmares. Somehow, she knew that the nightmares have to do with her father and Carlota. Before her mother died, she had told her that she believed her father had raped Carlota." Ramón paused and glanced at Carlota, then continued. "*Señora* Stephens asked Remmi to look for Carlota and to hear her story. *La señora* kept talking about her soul burning in hell for all the wrong she and her husband had done to Carlota. The lady seemed quite out of her mind. Despite what their mother told them, Sandy and Randolph Stephens refused to believe that their father would be capable of harming anyone, let alone raping Carlota." Ramón shook his head.

"Why was Phillipe opposed to her meeting with me? Did she tell you?" Carlota asked, taking Ramón by surprise.

"For selfish reasons, I suppose. I'm assuming he wanted to start a new life with Remmi, to forget about the past. But Remmi knew in her heart, she told me, that what their mother said was right. She wanted to ask for Carlota's forgiveness and to honor her mother's last wishes."

"Did you believe her?"

"I did. I knew Remmi Stephens was telling the truth. *La Pinta* makes you paranoid because the cons at Quentin—all of us—we're into constant denial. We've told so many lies. Still, deep inside, even if we don't admit it, we can still recognize the truth. Simple as that." Ramón paused. "I think Remmi truly wants to make peace with Carlota. Knowing that Carlota is gravely ill and that there may never be another opportunity for her and Remmi to talk, I asked Carlota if she would meet with Remmi. Carlota agreed and I sent word to Remmi to meet us here tonight. That's why we're here, but Remmi didn't show up."

Ramón paused for a while. The wailing of a siren, although still in the distance, was growing louder. I supposed it was the ambulance that Art and Dieguito had called to take Remmi Stephens to the hospital.

"I guess Remmi and Phillipe Hazlitt helped you escape from prison," Justin proposed to Ramón.

The old dancer began to gather his belongings as he answered Justin's question with a flat, "I don't know." Then he crouched to talk to Carlota, who had been quiet all that time. "Time to go, *mi flor de nopal*," he said.

She smiled back and reached out to him.

I picked up Carlota's burlap bag and handed it to Ramón.

"This is the only thing she brought with her from Mexico. The only thing she's taking back," Ramón said.

# Twenty-One
## Fathers and Daughters

As Carlota and Ramón got ready to leave, we kept hearing the wail of the siren. Justin gave all the cash he had in his wallet to Ramón, who promised to pay him back as soon as he got a job in Mexico.

"*Vámonos, mi florecita de nopal.*" Ramón extended his hand to Carlota. Just then we heard the crunching of dry brush outside the shed. Justin raised his gun and pointed the weapon towards the spot. An instant later, something hit the ground near us, shattering on impact. Broken glass was strewn around us. I glimpsed at the two photographs, still in their frames, which were now lying at Ramón's feet.

"This is one of Art's pictures," Carlota whispered as she pointed at one of the photos.

We looked at each other, trying to make sense of the events. Just then, out of the corner of my eye, I saw a man's silhouette as he stepped out of the shadows. An instant later, limping and clutching his bleeding arm, Dieguito came into full view. Josie Baldomar followed behind him, pointing a knife at him. At that point, I realized that Josie was the person who had broken into Art's house in Piedmont. She had taken the same photos that now lay on the floor beside us. Although I didn't see the bow and the United Farm Workers' flag, I surmised she had also taken those objects.

As I looked for Ramón's knife, which I had set down on the ground, I caught sight of Carlota hiding it under her blanket. Feeling the pressure of the small gun in the back pocket of my jeans, I slowly rose to my feet.

Looking at Justin, who still had his gun in his hand, Josie commanded, "Put the gun down on the floor and push it with your foot towards me." She pressed the knife against Dieguito's back.

Justin hesitated. Seeing that Dieguito was in his line of fire and being unwilling to get him or anyone else injured, Justin reluctantly put his gun down. Then, he stood up and kicked the weapon towards Josie.

Not taking her eyes off Justin or Ramón, who were standing side by side, Josie moved closer to the spot where Justin's gun lay. She nonetheless, pressed the knife against Dieguito's lower back as she went down slowly. With a swift motion, she dropped the knife and picked up the gun.

Pointing the gun at Dieguito, she told Justin, "Now, hand the flashlight to Dieguito." Against his will, Justin obeyed her.

"Put it down on the ground," she told Dieguito.

Justin looked in my direction. Seeing him gesture lightly with his head, I surmised that he wanted me to move closer to him. I guessed that he wanted access to the gun in my back pocket—possibly our only defense now.

Just then, Josie turned to Ramón and commanded, "Move closer to Gloria."

Although he moved deliberately slow, Ramón nonetheless did as he was told.

No one made a sound. My lungs felt as if they were ready to explode, and I exhaled slowly. Carlota's cold, trembling hand on my arm made me shiver.

"Move over there with them," Josie then told Dieguito. He joined Carlota and me. As if to make room for Dieguito, I took a short step towards Justin. Josie seemed oblivious to my actions, so I risked another step.

"I have to get up," Carlota said to Josie. "Please, let Gloria help me." Even before Josie signaled her approval, Carlota began to stand up, leaning on my arm with one hand. As she rose, I felt the tip of Ramon's sheathed knife brush against my leg. I looked at Josie, and I was sure she wasn't aware Carlota had the weapon under her blanket. In the distance, the howling of the siren stopped.

Josie cocked her head slightly. Then, she looked at me. "You," she commanded, "help Carlota get over here. And no tricks. Bring her stuff."

"No," Carlota stated with a sure voice. "Give it up, Josie," she urged. "Why hurt them? They haven't done anything to you."

"He has," Josie said, pointing the gun at Ramón. Turning to Carlota again, she added, "He's trying to take you away from me."

"Please," Carlota said. "Why are you doing this? Why are you so bitter?"

"I don't have your endurance, or your faith," Josie wheezed, looking in Carlota's direction. She straightened herself up. "I didn't have a father like yours, either."

"What has that got to do with what you're doing now?" Carlota asked.

Ignoring Carlota's remarks, Josie said, "My father made me and my mother work since I was young. He took my mother's and my pay and blew it." She paused for an instant, then went on with her story. We all kept quiet. Oblivious to anything but the sound of her voice, Josie continued, "One day, when I was about fourteen, my father—drunk—told one of his drinking buddies he could have me. My own father!" Josie blustered. "If my mother hadn't come home early from the cannery, who knows what would have happened to me..."

"So you've had a rough life," Carlota told Josie, "but this is not the way to get even with your father. You have to own up to what you're doing before it's too late."

"This isn't about my father," Josie said, looking at Carlota. At first Josie seemed hurt, but an instant later she said in a reproachful tone, "Don't *you* go passing judgment on me. Not you. Phillipe did that and..." She stopped in mid-sentence then began to wave the gun around, making my heart skip a beat. Directing her remarks to Carlota, Josie continued, "First Phillipe abandoned me. Now you're going away with this...witch doctor!"

Ramón made a move towards Josie, and she aimed the gun at him. He quickly backed off.

"Phillipe is dead. So, in that sense, I suppose you could say that he abandoned you, but..." Carlota paused and looked intently at Josie, who shifted her attention to her. "That's not what you mean, is it?" Carlota was equally intent as she asked, "Why would Phillipe leave you now? He knew I would never come between you two. He knew I was going back to Mexico."

"I love you," Josie whispered to Carlota, Then, she added in a clear voice, "But I loved Phillipe more than anyone in the world. I thought he knew that, but he didn't."

"I know you loved him more than you love me," Carlota stated under her breath.

Oblivious to Carlota's remark, and in an angry tone, Josie continued. "Phillipe betrayed me. He left me. Me! The woman he promised to love always. He promised..."

"I'm so sorry." Carlota trembled and seemed to be ready to go to Josie. I held her back.

Being as unobtrusive as possible, I took another short step, trying to get closer to Justin. To get her off guard, I asked, "When did you begin to suspect Phillipe was going to leave you?"

Josie gave me an absent look. She seemed tired all of a sudden and was quiet for a brief time. Then she said, "I'm not sure *when* I began to suspect that something was wrong. But when I did, I went through every one of Phillipe's papers at home and at the office—his bank receipts and correspondence.

Everything. And I discovered Phillipe had been regularly making large deposits into other accounts." Josie paused. "Two of the account holders were Remmine and Randolph Stephens in Monterey. A third account was in the name of a Felix Hunter in a bank in Sonoma. In a desk drawer, inside a large jiffy bag, I found a video cassette marked 'Summer, 1973,' together with an enlarged photo of Phillipe. In the photo, he was crouching next to a woman and holding a young boy in his arms.

"I see," Carlota remarked. "You began to get suspicious."

"You bet I did," Josie said. "I began to wonder if there might be other reasons for Phillipe's frequent business trips to Monterey, for his claim that he had been losing clients. He had been warning me that we could be facing bankruptcy. When he next announced he had to go to Monterey, I made up my mind then to get to the bottom of this business. Phillipe thought he had been very thorough, hiding stuff from me, but I outsmarted him.

"You know how banks ask you for your mother's maiden name and social security number before they give you any information about your account?" Josie inquired in an excited tone. Without waiting for a response, she continued, "Well, I asked my cousin Jerry to phone the bank pretending to be Felix Hunter and to ask for his account balance. Jerry gave the bank officer Phillipe's mother's name. And guess what? Felix Hunter and Phillipe had the same mother and social security number. They were one and the same. The bastard!"

"Is that when you decided to kill him?" I asked.

Josie glared at me, but said nothing. Then, in a rather meek voice, she said, "Yes." She hesitated. Then she finally said, "Two months ago, on a Friday, Phillipe left for Monterey. One of his usual business trips. He was supposed to come back the same day. But he didn't. I knew then that he had left me. For days, I waited for him to return. All that time, I didn't sleep. I couldn't. I couldn't eat either. I drank. Anything I could find. Whisky, brandy, tequila. But nothing worked. Nothing cured my insomnia. Soon I began to feel as though I were covered by a second, heavier skin, by a layer of heat that pressed against my chest, suffocating me. All I could think of was finding Phillipe, having him come back to me."

"How did you finally find out where he was?" Justin asked.

"I did what you—any P.I.—would have done," she told Justin. "I knew that Phillipe had been making large deposits into Remmie's and Randolph's accounts. So, first I parked outside the bank in Monterey where Remmine and her brother had their accounts. But no one that I recognized showed up. Then, I went to Sonoma and watched the bank where Felix Hunter had his account. Phillipe showed up there two days later. He got in his car and I followed him out of town, then south, down the coast to Big Sur. The bastard went wind surfing. Imagine!"

"What did you do then?" Dieguito asked.

Josie seemed to be lost in thought and didn't say anything for a while. Then, as if she were talking to herself, she said, "I hid behind the rocks at the top of the cliff and waited for Phillipe. By a great coincidence, he climbed up to the edge of the cliff where I was."

"He must have been surprised to see you," I interjected, beginning to realize that Justin and Dieguito were trying to distract Josie by making her switch her attention from one to the other. Slowly, I moved closer to Justin.

"He certainly was," Josie responded. Then, turning to Carlota, she remarked, "It's funny, but when I finally was face to face with him, all I wanted was to have sex with him, have him tell me he loved me." Pausing, she looked at Carlota and exclaimed, "But he wouldn't have me. That infuriated me. I got angrier when he told me he had put up with my relationship with you and with 'all the others' for too long. He had now found true love," Josie cried out, repeating several times, "True love. True love." A sob betrayed her unhappiness.

"Remmi Stephens?" Carlota asked.

"Yes," Josie answered as she straightened up to regain her composure. When she spoke again, her voice was cold. "Phillipe refused to go back home with me. So I told him I was pregnant to see if that would make him stay with me. But he again refused." Josie started to speak faster and to wave the gun around. "He told me it was too late for us. He wanted a divorce. Remmi Stephens, he told me, was going to have his baby. She was pregnant with my husband's child!" Josie's voice rose a decibel. "I was very upset, and I called her his *'puta.'*

Phillipe started coming at me, telling me that Remmine wasn't a whore, that I was *la gran puta*—the worst of whores. Calling me *puta* over and over, he began to shove me around. He seemed possessed as he began to slap me and punch me!" Josie's eyes fixed blankly on Carlota. "He was standing on the edge of the cliff. And...I...I just pushed Phillipe back," she added. She swallowed the tears that trickled down to her mouth. "I saw Phillipe go over the cliff. I reached out to him... I did! But it was too late," she continued. "He was gone. He didn't even scream. He just looked confused...like he couldn't believe I'd been capable of pushing him. I couldn't believe I'd done it myself."

"What did you do? Did you try to go down and help him?" Carlota asked. "He could have been just hurt."

"Yes. I tumbled down the steep path to the beach," Josie said, and sniffled. "I found him down there, sprawled on the sand."

"Was he dead?"

"Yes, he was dead. I held him in my arms for the longest time."

"And no one saw you?"

"No one came. It was already dark when I finally mustered up enough energy to get up. I realized I couldn't stay there any longer. So, I rolled Phillipe's body over to the water and let the sea take him."

Carlota gasped.

"He was gone," Josie repeated. Then she was quiet. No one else seemed willing to break the silence.

"Why did you want to kill Remmi, too?" Carlota finally asked. "She didn't betray you. Phillipe did."

"I wasn't going to kill her. I just wanted to scare her so she'd sign a letter authorizing me to withdraw funds from the account in her name." Josie paused. "She had no right to Phillipe's money. I worked hard for it, too." Her hands jerked.

"From what they've told me," Carlota said, turning to look at Justin and me, "you drugged her, you took off her clothes, and you left her naked to freeze to death." She was nearly out of breath when she finished, and she leaned on Ramón and me.

"But I did go back for her just a short while ago. On my way there, I found Dieguito. He told me that the woman had been taken to the hospital. I truly didn't want her to die, but your friends here, they had already gotten to her."

Josie began to wave the gun around as she talked. Carlota and I froze in place. Out of the corner of one eye I saw Dieguito and Justin watch Josie's every gesture, ready to disarm her at the first opportunity. Yet, for the moment, none of us made a move.

"Please, Josie, put the gun down," Carlota pleaded again. "I'll..." she began to say but stopped in mid-sentence.

"Stay with me?" Josie said, guessing the rest of Carlota's statement. "You know you won't. Not now," she whispered.

An instant later, in a suddenly quiet, collected manner, she aimed the gun at Ramón while talking to him in the third person. "That man—he instigated all of this. He wanted his revenge on me for taking you away from him."

"So you decided to frame me," Ramón said to Josie. She answered him with a monosyllable.

"That was clever of you," Ramón continued, taking a short step forward. "You went to Soldado and told him Carlota was dying. You knew Soldado would tell me, and that I would try to escape. You hired those guys who sprang me and nearly wasted Jack Rodder, the Quentin guard. Now, everything makes sense. An escaped con who tried to kill a prison guard? No one would believe I hadn't done any of those things. You could blame me for killing your husband and Sonny and anyone you dreamed up." Ramón paused. "Very clever." Ramón clapped his hands a few times. He took another step towards Josie. This time, she noticed what he was doing and wrapped her finger around the trigger.

"So, you're the one who planted all those herbs tied with snakeskin and left the anonymous threat on Sonny's work table. After reading the note, you knew he would jump to the conclusion that Ramón was coming after him; then he'd warn Art about Ramón, too. Did you also leave the grapes full of jimsonweed in Art's refrigerator?" Dieguito asked.

"Yes. But I knew Art wouldn't touch the grapes. So he was never in any danger," Josie answered.

"I guess sending Sonny the film Art made in the summer of 1973 was the final touch," I told Josie. "More than anything else, that film must have confirmed Sonny's suspicions that Ramón was out to get him and Art."

Josie gave me an inquisitive glance. Although her lips parted as if she were getting ready to answer my question, she didn't say anything. Not knowing what to do next, I looked at Justin.

He also looked in my direction and discreetly pointed at his back pocket. He seemed to be telling me that I should take the gun out and use it. But knowing I would not be able to shoot straight, even if I had the courage to take the weapon out, I felt I had to find a way to get it to him. Since he was only a few feet away, I waited for the opportunity.

"What about Sonny Mares?" Justin said.

"What about him? We spent that morning together in..." She looked at Carlota and decided not to finish her statement.

"You had forgotten your medication," she said, addressing Carlota. "I knew you always looked for Sonny or Art when you were in the Bay Area. So, I told my mother that I was going to Oakland and that I would leave your digitoxin with Sonny. Although she refused to tell me where you were, I was sure that she would let you know where to pick it up. I got there early so I wouldn't miss you. I wanted to give you your medication, but I also wanted to talk to you. I waited for a long time, but you didn't show up. So... Well...Sonny always knew how to turn me on...."

"Please!" Carlota exclaimed, obviously pained by Josie's comments. "And then you killed him? Why?"

"What? You think that I killed Sonny?" Josie took a step back. "You're wrong about that!"

Before any of us had a chance to ask her what she knew about Sonny's death, Josie blurted out, "I'm getting tired. If you don't really want anything to happen to any of *your friends* here," she warned Carlota, "you better get over here." Waving the gun, she motioned for Carlota to move closer to her.

"Please, help me up, Gloria," Carlota asked of me. "And don't try to dissuade me," she implored, anticipating my objection. I put my arm around her waist, and she leaned hard on me, pushing me back a few steps. Josie was watching our every move. Out of the corner of my eye, I saw Justin also take a few steps towards Carlota and me as if he wanted to help us. My back was now at arm's length from him. He quickly reached under my *ruana*. I felt him pull out the small gun from my jeans' pocket.

Josie seemed to suspect something was going on, and raising her gun, she seemed quite prepared to shoot. Carlota stopped in her tracks and I did, too.

Ramón took a step towards her. Josie aimed at him, then took turns pointing the gun at each of us, unsure of her target. She again aimed at Ramón, who, convinced that she was going to shoot, tried to get out of the way. He stumbled and bumped against Justin who dropped the small pistol he had just taken out of my pocket. As I heard the weapon hit the ground in front of me, Carlota threw her blanket off. I saw her take Ramón's knife out of its sheath. She held the knife by the handle as she got ready to throw it at Josie. Unable to sustain the effort, however, she began to shake and lowered her arm.

"C'mon, my sweet. Do it," I heard Josie say when she saw Carlota holding the knife. "I don't want to go to prison," she coaxed. I dropped to my knees and began to feel for Justin's gun in the dark. I found it and fumbled with the safety until I could push the button up. With a shaking hand, I aimed at Josie. But before I could muster up enough courage to fire, I watched the knife zoom through the air like an arrow. As it swiftly pierced the darkness, its blade reflected the fire and looked like a shooting star.

The knife hit Josie's arm.

I watched the sparks coming from her gun as she accidentally triggered it. Then she tumbled. Almost simultaneously, I saw Justin fall to his knees, clutching his stomach. Dieguito dropped to the ground close to Justin.

As I looked up, I could see that Josie was getting ready to shoot again. Although I felt as if the ground were moving under me, I managed to point the gun at Josie. Aiming at the arm that held the gun, I fired twice.

Josie dropped her weapon and stretched her hands towards Carlota. Her mouth moved, forming words I could only guess, for the report of the gun had caused me to lose my hearing momentarily. Then Josie reeled back and fell.

The hard recoil of the pistol had burned my skin and cut through my left thumb. It began to bleed, but I was oblivious to the pain. For an instant my mind went blank. Suddenly and incongruously, the memory of my daughter Tania, a short time after her birth, flashed through my consciousness. I dropped to my knees and put the pistol down on the ground.

# Twenty-Two
## *Moonlit Shadows on a Hill*

I felt someone pressing my elbow as if to help me up, but I resisted. A hand reached down and took the small pistol in front of me.

"Are you all right?" Justin asked me an instant later.

"I killed her, didn't I?"

"No. You didn't kill her. She's not really hurt. Carlota didn't wound her either," he assured me. Then he gently turned me around so I could see Josie. Ramón was pointing the beam of the flashlight at her shoulder while Dieguito tended to her wound. Josie's head was resting on Carlota's knees.

"Nothing serious," Dieguito said.

"It would have been better if you'd killed me," Josie said, directing her remark at me. "You better teach her how to shoot straight," she told Justin.

Justin didn't answer. For the first time since the shooting, I turned to look at him. He was standing next to me. Clutching his stomach, he offered me his other hand. I took it and got up. Then, I noticed the blood staining his shirt. Pushing his hand away, I gasped as I glanced at the bleeding gash just below his rib cage.

"Just a flesh wound," Justin assured me. "Really."

I tried to take a deep breath but couldn't. My tongue and throat felt as if they were covered by a deep layer of moss. I swallowed hard, then managed to talk again. "There is so much blood. Are you sure it's a superficial wound?" I asked. I removed his hand from his wound. I saw that the blood around the gash had started to coagulate. Still, the light was too dim for me to really see the extent of his injury. "I'm sorry," I said. "I knew you were going to get hurt. I should have warned you. Even if...it wouldn't have made a difference."

"You did the right thing," Justin said, brushing my cheek with the back of his fingers. "Knowing that I'm going to get hurt might make things worse. It might even get me killed." He kissed me gently and I responded to his caress. Josie cried out as Dieguito applied some kind of solution to her shoulder, and Justin and I turned our attention to her.

Glancing at Dieguito, then at Justin and me, Josie pleaded, "Let Carlota and Ramón go. Forget that they were ever here. Let's tell the police that I came looking for Carlota and forced Dieguito to come with me, but I only found you two here. Would you agree to that? Carlota deserves a break. And she can't make it without Ramón."

"Are you going to tell the police what you told us about Phillipe's death?" I asked Josie.

"Do I have a choice now?" she answered and attempted a smile.   Justin, Dieguito, and I looked at one another then agreed that Ramón and Carlota should leave before we contacted the police.

Josie turned to Carlota and said, "You and Ramón had better get going." Then, taking her car keys out of her jacket pocket, she handed them to Ramón. "Go back up the hill to Alta Vista Road," she told him, pointing at the path Justin and I had traversed to come down to the old ghost dancing place. "My car is parked on Alta Vista. Take it and get out of town quickly. Then ditch it someplace." Josie spoke quickly. She was obviously in pain. "Take good care of her," she said, smiling at Ramón, who acknowledged her gesture with a nod of his head. Then, she turned to Carlota and said, "Go quickly, my sweet. Please!"

Carlota bent forward and softly kissed Josie. In Spanish, she told her, "I'll be thinking of you every minute of every day."

"Go," Josie repeated, gently pushing Carlota away.

"Yes," Dieguito interjected. "You and Carlota should be leaving immediately. Art's intention was to phone the Sheriff's Office as soon as he got Remmi to the hospital. I'm sure this place will be swarming with cops soon enough."

"Don't be too hard on yourself, Gloria Damasco," Carlota said to me as she kissed my cheek. "Promise?" she asked, and I acquiesced with a nod as I, too, reached out to her.

"Thanks," Ramón whispered in my ear. He helped Carlota put on his poncho, then picked up her burlap bag and his own bundle of clothes. A few minutes later, Ramón and Carlota were rushing across the clearing towards the path Justin and I had previously taken to the old ghost dancing place.

All kinds of contradictory feelings swam around in my chest and head, making my heart heavy and my head light. "It'll be all right," Justin whispered. I felt his fingers around my eyes as he dried the moisture beginning to collect on my cheeks. I kissed the pulsating hollow below his Adam's apple, but said nothing.

We heard faint voices in the distance. "The Texas Rangers?" Josie asked jokingly.

Dieguito chuckled. "They'll be here soon enough," he warned.

"Before they get here," Justin said to Josie, "Would you mind telling me what you know about Sonny's death?"

"A sad business. An accident, I think," Josie began to explain.

"Why do you say that? I don't understand."

"I have the feeling that he intended to kill himself, that putting the digitoxin in his menudo wasn't an accident," Josie began to explain.

"Did he do that?" I asked.

"Why do you say that?" Dieguito questioned at the same time.

Josie looked at all of us, then stated, "Maybe it's better if I start at the beginning."

"Please do," Justin responded.

"I was with Sonny in the morning. He seemed to be all right. Then he started to drink pretty steadily. First, he started acting very strangely, talking about how he hadn't written anything in a long time, how he couldn't write anymore. 'I just don't have it in me,' he said."

"Sonny told me the same thing," Dieguito said, corroborating Josie's statement.

"Out of the blue, it seemed, Sonny began to talk about old times, about the United Farm Workers' strike in particular. 'She's bringing that film in a while,' Sonny emphasized the 'she.' I didn't understand what he was talking about. I actually thought that he and this woman he was expecting were going to watch a porno film. So just to tease him, I said, 'Haven't you had enough? And who's this mysterious woman anyway?' He laughed.

"Sonny said something that sounded like, 'Why don't you stay and watch the movie with us?' By that time, he'd gotten pretty saucy, and his speech was slurred. I wasn't interested in either watching a porno flick or being involved in a threesome. And I didn't really like being around Sonny when he drank. So I put Carlota's digitoxin on the kitchen counter and went out.

"I was getting in my car when I saw a woman and a man drive up. They parked across from Sonny's apartment building. I took a second look at them. Suddenly, I realized the woman in the car was the same one I had seen with Phillipe and a boy in a photo. I was looking at Remmine Stephens, my husband's lover! I thanked my lucky stars, because I had been

looking for her and her brother ever since I found out Phillipe
had deposited large amounts of money in their accounts. So I
decided to stick around to see what they intended to do. Remmine got out of her car and went into Sonny's apartment
building. Her brother Randolph—I assumed—stayed in the
car. I noticed that she was carrying a medium-sized grocery
sack and a jiffy bag."

"Did they see you?" Justin asked.

"I don't think so," Josie answered, then added, "I wanted
to find out what she was up to. Her being there made it that
much easier for me, because I didn't have to locate her anymore. With the brother there, however, I didn't dare confront
her. But I did manage to sneak into the garden without being
noticed." Josie paused to shift positions. Stretching her hands
out, she indicated to Dieguito and Justin that she wanted to
get up.

"I thought that Sonny kept the outside gate locked at all
times. How did you manage to get into the patio and chalk
garden?" Justin asked.

"A long time ago, when he and I used to spend at least
one weekend a month together, he gave me his set of spare
keys. Since Sonny never asked that I give the keys back to
him, I still have them," Josie explained. "Every time I've gone
to see him, I've let myself in through the garden gate, as he
told me to do a long time ago to avoid being seen by anyone. If
you've been there, you know that looking in through the large
window facing the garden, one can actually watch the action
anywhere in Sonny's flat. Sonny wanted to keep his living
spaces open, but he also liked having his privacy. That's why
he had walls built only around the sleeping area, and he built
the tall fence around the patio and garden."

"That's right," I said, as I took the flashlight Justin was
handing me so he could help Josie stand up.

"From my place in the garden, I had a command view of the goings-on in Sonny's flat. When I saw him talking with Remmine, I realized that she was the woman Sonny had been expecting. I regretted not having asked him why she was coming to see him. By then, it was too late. Since I couldn't hear a word they were saying, I could only watch their gesturing as they talked." Josie paused to catch her breath. "Suddenly, I saw Sonny pull Remmine towards him. She fought him. Then Sonny looked in the direction of the door. He let Remmine go, went to the door, and opened it."

"Was there someone at the door? Who?" Justin asked as he helped Josie walk towards the fireplace.

"I don't know. The door itself blocked Sonny's visitor from my view."

"What happened then?"

"His other visitor went away," Josie explained. "Then Remmine decided to leave. From the bag she had left on the counter, Sonny took out a black, flat box which turned out to be a video tape. He went to the VCR and put the tape in, then turned on the TV and lowered the volume."

"Was it a video tape about the farm workers' strike which took place in 1973?" I inquired.

"It's possible.... Yes, I think it was."

"Do you have any idea where Remmine got that video tape?"

"From Phillipe, I assume," Josie replied.

"Why do you think Remmine was taking it to Sonny?"

"I haven't the faintest idea, but I do remember that Sonny didn't seem in the least interested. He went back into the kitchen area. Perhaps he was hungry and wanted something to eat while he watched the tape. I don't know." Josie sighed. "Sonny took out a styrofoam soup container from the bag Remmine had brought him."

Josie coughed, then took in a mouthful of air. Getting up had taken a great effort on her part, and she was beginning to weaken. Although she now refused to lie down, she did let Dieguito and Justin help her sit on the ground.

"Sonny poured what looked like menudo into a pot to heat up," Josie added. "That afternoon and the following day, I actually thought Sonny didn't know what he was doing when he reached out for the digitoxin vial and emptied it into the menudo. But now I'm convinced that he knew all along what he was doing."

"Do you have any idea why he would knowingly pour the drug into his menudo? I asked.

"I haven't a clue. I'm as much at a loss as you are. All I know is that he took the bowl of menudo into his bedroom. Because of the partition wall, I was not able to see what went on in there. I'm assuming he ate the menudo. I'm sure of one thing—he didn't come out of his bedroom again."

Ostensibly in pain, Josie groaned. For a while now, we had been hearing crunching and rustling noises, and I assumed that the sheriff and his men were on their way.

"Please, go on," Justin urged. "Tell us the rest. We don't have much time left."

"When I realized what he'd done," Josie said as she resumed her story, "I tried to get back into the house, but the door to the garden was locked. At that moment, I saw Randolph come into the house. He didn't force the door open, so I assumed that Sonny must have left it unlocked after Remmine left," Josie explained, then continued, "Anyway, Randolph came in, looking for Sonny. He sneaked a look in the bedroom and he went in for just a second, really. When he came out of the bedroom, he went to the kitchen and got the kitchen terry cloth. He began to wipe things clean with it. I assumed he was trying to erase his sister's fingerprints. Then

he went back to the kitchen area and washed all the dishes in
the sink."

Josie gasped and began to hyperventilate. After a brief
interval, she continued, "A short time after Randolph left, I
used my key to let myself into the apartment. I went into the
bedroom and saw Sonny lying on his bed. He looked so lifeless
that I was sure he was dead. For an instant, I hesitated, torn
between calling an ambulance or leaving things as they were.
I noticed the pair of scissors stuck in the mattress next to
Sonny. At first, I assumed that Randolph had intended to stab
Sonny with the scissors. But it occurred to me that he had
something else in mind. This wasn't just any pair of scissors, I
realized as I removed them and saw the piece of paper torn in
two. I immediately realized he was trying to implicate Carlota. I had no idea why this young man was doing that, but I
assumed that he had found out about his father and Carlota,
and that he blamed Carlota for what happened. There
couldn't be any other explanation for his behavior."

"You're probably right," Justin said.

"Anyway," Josie explained, "When I saw what Randolph
Stephens had done, I went into the kitchen and washed the
empty digitoxin vial and the scissors. I placed them inside the
pencil holder next to the FAX machine. Then I slipped away
without being seen."

Almost as if we had agreed beforehand, Justin and I
sighed then looked at each other. Justin hadn't found the digitoxin container, but we both realized that finding or knowing
about the vial wouldn't have made a difference. We would still
have looked for Carlota Navarro, still followed the same path
towards solving the case. Eventually, that path would have
brought us to this same time and place.

I wasn't sure which of the many intense emotions eddying
around my heart was causing my tears to well up again. But
to keep my wits about me, I walked to the other end of the

shed. The moon was clearing another hill. It now stood in the southeastern section of the sky, opposite the spot where I had first seen its amber countenance. I looked up the path Carlota and Ramón had taken and, for a brief moment, I thought I could still see their silhouettes climbing. Eventually, they became two specks of moonlit shadow at the top of the hill. The voices of the arriving sheriff and his men advised us to stay where we were and to keep our hands up. Just before they spoke, I thought I saw a hand wave at me. I waved back.

# Epicenters

I hadn't intended to fall asleep waiting for Justin on the chair outside the emergency room, or to have an erotic dream or a nightmare, but I had done all three things.

The hospital guard sitting outside Josie Baldomar's room eyed me with suspicion when I got up. A while before, the nurse had checked and re-dressed my injured shoulder. Like everyone else, I'd been advised not to leave the hospital ward until a deputy came to take us back to the sheriff's office to give our depositions. At that time, they would decide who was going to be arrested and what the charges would be.

I regretted having awakened, for memory refused to let go of the night's events. I couldn't begin to deal with the ambivalence within me, and I had the most urgent need to talk to María Baldomar. But what would I tell her—that I had helped one of her daughters get away but had shot and injured the other? To keep my mind occupied while I waited for Justin at the hospital in Sonoma, I asked the nurse if she would let me visit Remmine Stephens for a short while. Even though it was past visiting hours, after hearing my name, the nurse had agreed, as Remmine herself had asked to see me.

"Will the baby be affected by the jimsonweed?" I immediately asked Remmine.

"I'm way past my fifth month. But they'll have to keep monitoring the baby's heart and running tests until the end of my term, just to make sure," she explained. Unexpectedly, she added, "My baby and I owe you our lives."

I smiled and shrugged my shoulders to indicate it wasn't necessary to thank me.

She ignored my gesture and continued. "I know I'm carrying a girl, and I'd be delighted if you let me name my baby after you." I was taken aback by her offer, and for a minute words lumped in my throat, blocking my desire to speak.

"I am honored, but I have two favors to ask of you," I finally replied. "Would you mind naming your baby Luisa? She was my best friend, and she died last year." Remmine looked at me but didn't say anything. "She was a fine poet, and a very loving and caring person," I reassured her.

"Yes," she said after a while. "Luisa Remmine. It's a lovely name."

"For my second favor I need to clarify some things," I said.

Remmine looked at me and lowered her eyes. Then, to my surprise, she remarked, "I'm sure you think that I'm a terrible person."

"Why do you say that? I don't think you're a terrible person," I told her after I got over my surprise.

"Weren't you trying to ask me about my relationship with Phillipe?"

"No. Your relationship with Phillipe is really none of my business," I said.

Remmine looked at me attentively, as if she were expecting me to continue. I could see the moisture in her eyes beginning to gather.

I was exhausted and unwilling to discuss further anyone's actions and motivations. But I sensed that Remmine needed comfort and I wanted to give it, so I cautiously added, "I'm only sorry that Phillipe's unwise actions have caused you such grief and placed you and your baby in danger. But it is over, isn't it? You and Luisa Remmine will be just fine. You'll see." I reached out for her hand and held it between my hands.

With her other hand she reached out for a tissue and dried her eyes. She was quiet for a while, then she asked, "What was it you wanted to know?"

"You don't have to answer," I said, then stopped. But she signaled for me to continue. So I asked, "Was it you or your brother who tried to break into my house late Sunday night?"

"I'm truly sorry about that," she said. I gave her a reassuring smile, so she elaborated further. "It was Randolph. Randolph tried to break into your house. Both Mother and Grandma went to great lengths to make us believe that Father was a great man, that he had died of a broken heart when he had been unjustly accused by Josie Baldomar of raping Carlota. On her deathbed, Mother finally told us that she was sure Father had raped Carlota. She tried to comfort us by telling us that, nevertheless, he had been an exemplary father. I thought Randolph, like my sister Sandy and me, accepted the painful truth about Father. But I was wrong. As it turned out, my poor brother never really believed that our father had been such a...had been capable of such a despicable act. He went there to have it out with Carlota, to punish her for making up lies about Father. I didn't know about it until Sandy called me and told me about it. I'm truly sorry he hurt you."

"How did Randolph know where to find Carlota?"

"I'm afraid I'm to blame for that. I had talked to Ramón earlier in the evening. He had told me that Carlota was at your house in Oakland, and that he would try to arrange a meeting between her and me. If Carlota agreed to see me, he and Carlota would meet me at a shed between two mountains. He was staying there. Do you know the place?"

"Yes. Unfortunately, I do."

"I waited for a long time, but Ramón and Carlota didn't show up. I had already started up the hill towards Alta Vista Road when Phillipe's wife Josie showed up. She came at me with the knife. She was possessed, like a madwoman. And she..." Remmine checked the bandage wrapped around her head, then began to sob softly.

"It's all right," I told her. "You don't have to tell me the rest. I know what happened."

We were both quiet for a while. I was the first to break the silence. "Where is Randolph now?"

"He told me he was going back to Oakland earlier this afternoon. But Sandy says he didn't show up at her house."

"I have one more question. Josie told us that you gave Sonny a video tape when you went to see him. What made you do that?" I asked.

"A few days ago, I came across the video tape among Phillipe's things. Phillipe had told me what was on it when he first moved in with me. I was sure Josie had killed Phillipe. Not knowing what else to do, I went to see Sonny, hoping that he would help me prove Josie's guilt. I also foolishly thought that giving Sonny the film and the menudo would get me into his good grace. Was I wrong! All I managed to do was to get him angry!" she exclaimed. Then, she was quiet for a while. She seemed suddenly very tired.

"I know how hard this has been on you," I offered, not knowing what else to say. "But try to take care of yourself. We don't want anything bad to happen to Luisa Remmine." We chatted for a while longer about her plans. After we exchanged addresses, I left with Remmie's promise that she would send me a photo of the baby.

On my way back to the emergency room, I saw Dieguito walking towards the nurses' station. I was surprised to see him, since Sheriff Bell had taken him and Art to his office to give their depositions. When he saw me, he immediately handed me a message from María Baldomar that he had written on a sheet of typing paper. Then, he went to talk to the nurse at the emergency station.

I unfolded the paper and began to read María's message. It said, "I never asked you to look after my daughter Josie. I know you probably did what you thought best, and I thank you for sparing her life. Before yesterday, I don't think Josie cared much for anyone's life but her own. In some strange way, I may have gotten my daughter back now that neither of us has anyone left but each other. But I did ask you to look after Carlota, and you took care of her. Dieguito told me that. For that I am forever grateful."

Then Dieguito had written what I assumed María had said to him in Spanish. "For you, Sabina, light has always been and will always be born of darkness."

I felt tears welling up inside my lids, but I held them back. It would take me a long time to let them run freely, I knew.

When the emergency physician had patched up Justin, a deputy took us to the sheriff's office. Sometime after dawn, the interrogation ceased and the depositions were drawn and prepared for our signatures. Our stories coincided, "with some minor discrepancies," Sheriff Bell told us. With the exception of Josie, who had waived her right to legal counsel and had confessed to causing her husband's death and Remmie's and Justin's injuries, everyone else was told to go home. Since my testimony had been corroborated by others, including Josie, the sheriff decided not to charge me even with the unlawful firing of a gun. All of us, however, would be subpoenaed by the District Attorney's Office when they were ready to go to trial.

Throughout the sheriff's interrogation, I kept denying knowing Carlota's whereabouts. Yet in so doing, I felt as if I had taken an eraser and little by little deleted my last memories of her.

As we were leaving the sheriff's office, a green sedan pulled up, driven by the *migra* officer, who was still accompanied by the San Quentin guard. Justin and I looked at each other and chuckled.

By the time we got back to Quinta Selena, it was eight o'clock in the morning. Justin called Leo, then talked to Frank

Madrigal at the Oakland Police Department, informing both
of them of the night's events.

Art and Dieguito tried to get some sleep. Justin also
retired to his room.

Fitfully, I managed to sleep until eleven. Then, I got up
and walked to the bathroom to take a shower. The room that
Justin was occupying was across the hall from the bathroom.
The door was closed and I assumed he was still sleeping. The
door to the bathroom was ajar, but I heard the faucet running.
On a chair next to the bathroom door I saw the shirt Justin
had been wearing the night before, and I realized he was the
person using the bathroom.

I leaned on the wall and waited. A short while later
Justin walked out of the bathroom. Smiling, he greeted me
with a cheerful "Good morning." Although he looked more
rested, his eyes were still bloodshot. I put down my clothes
and towel on the chair.

"How are you feeling?" I asked.

"I'm so full of painkillers I don't rightly know how I feel
right now." He chuckled. Then he rubbed his eyelids gently.
"Except for my eyes."

"Maybe this will help," I said as I cupped my hands and
gently placed them over his eyes.

Justin leaned back to rest on the wall. Instinctively, I
moved closer. He raised his arms. I lowered mine. Suddenly
we were kissing, gently at first, then more passionately. I
closed my eyes. I felt his hardness.

"I do know what I feel for you," he whispered in my ear,
and bit my earlobe softly. "My room," he said.

Without letting go of me, he guided me to his bed and we
helped each other out of our bathrobes.

With the back of his fingers, he traced the contours of my
chin towards my ear. He then let his fingers slide down my
neck, and circle my breasts, my nipples. Beneath my lids,

desire was a midnight-red tree turning dark blue. Growing.
Budding into a thousand delicious sensations. I ran my fingers down his back, up his torso, his arms. I wanted him in
me. He tightened his embrace. I held my breath as long as I
could when he entered me, and concentrated on the waves of
pleasure between my thighs.

Our desire quickened. Deep underneath my third eye, the
image of the red tree turned ghostly white. My mind, my body,
and my soul anticipated the cresting of pleasure, the thrill of
the fall, the total abandonment to this savage power. It came
as expected, roaring and rolling, obliterating everything in its
path, first for me, an instant later for Justin.

Afterwards, we stayed quietly wrapped around each
other. Then, we began to feel again the painful cuts and
bruises. Unwittingly, we both groaned, then laughed.

After a brief meal with Art, Dieguito, and Robin Cardozo,
the quinta's manager, Justin and I left the Valley of the Moon.
Justin needed his rest. I offered to drive and advised him to
sleep all the way.

As we entered the Bay Area, the traffic on highways I-80
and 580 seemed unusually light for a weekday commute hour.
Then I realized that it was Tuesday, October 17. A large number of baseball fans had most likely taken the afternoon off
from work and had already crossed over to San Francisco to
attend the third game of the "Battle of the Bay," scheduled for
Candlestick Park.

The Bay shimmered as if myriad silvery fish sunbathed
on its surface, periodically brushed by breaths of wind. I
turned off the air conditioning and lowered the window to feel
the ocean breeze. It was a clear, crisp, and warm autumn
day—a perfect day, I thought to myself. Looking at the deep
blue, unclouded sky, I also thought about my mother and her
theory that earthquakes were preceded by mackerel-skies and
missing pets. I smiled. I hadn't realized how much I'd longed

to feel my mother's and my daughter's arms around me until that precise instant. Since they both joined me on Tuesdays for dinner, I now looked forward to our getting together later that evening. My daughter had announced that she would be bringing her friend, Maurice Trujillo. And my mother had insisted that Justin join us.

At about four-thirty, Justin and I arrived at my house. The first thing I did was to make sure that nothing had happened to Carlota's cactus. The nopal was still where I had left it, soaking up the sun. Then I called Myra Miranda to tell her that Art was all right and that I would be delivering Luisa's two manuscripts on Thursday.

Justin had come into the kitchen just as the phone rang. I asked him to answer. "Hi, Leo," Justin said, then listened attentively for a few seconds. "I see," he remarked as he heard what Leo had to say.

"Josie Baldomar died an hour ago," he informed me after putting the receiver back on the hook.

"Oh, my God," I exclaimed. A muscle on my right calf tightened. Feeling the painful zigzag of a cramp shoot down my heel and toes, I leaned on the kitchen table. "What happened?"

"She got hold of some pills and took them. It doesn't surprise me." He shook his head.

I had also suspected all along that Josie would sooner take her own life than spend any time in prison. "Has María been told?" I asked.

"Yes," Justin replied. "She's on her way to Sonoma now."

Neither of us had time to let the tragic news sink in further, for at that moment my mother, my daughter, and her friend Maurice walked into the house.

Still shaken up by the tragic news, I uncorked a bottle of merlot as my mother placed a pan of *mole* enchiladas in the oven. Tania and Maurice cheered as the players began to take their places on the diamond. "Who's pitching for the A's?" Maurice asked just as we felt the tremor's first ripple. It registered in my consciousness as if a fish had come up and snapped a dragonfly off the surface, upsetting for a second a limpid, quiet pool. The noise followed an instant later, a roaring sound like the growling of an injured beast, briefly preceding the clamoring of the crowd at Candlestick Park. "Ladies and gentlemen," a frightened sports announcer kept repeating, unable to finish the sentence. Then the transmission was cut off and all we could hear was the static on the screen. I caught a glimpse of my mother's eyes, which seemed to be saying, "*Te lo dije*—I told you so."

"Get under the dining room table. Hurry! Stay away from the windows!" I heard Tania tell Maurice, who, being from New Mexico, had never before experienced an earthquake. Outside, people blew their car horns. Their honking alternated with the intermittent sirens of the fire trucks rushing down the street and with the tinkering of the metal wind chimes in the back porch.

"The end of the world! Doomsday!" Maurice cried out, half in jest, as I heard glass shattering and doors slamming upstairs, then downstairs. Books tumbled out of the bookcases in Darío's office. The oven door opened and I staggered over to close it, but I was too late. The dish of hot enchiladas slid out and came crashing down, burning my hand as I tried to grab it.

"The gas," Justin said. I managed to turn off the burners and the oven. Wine bottles, pots, pans, cups, and plates flew out of cupboards and cabinets, crashing down all around us. I caught sight of Justin standing in the doorway between the dining room and the kitchen, trying to keep the kitchen door from slamming on him.

My mother and I were holding on to the table. But when a knife fell between her foot and mine we dropped to the floor and got under the table. Just then, a large piece of plaster came crashing down. My heart was pounding uncontrollably; for an instant, I thought it had stopped beating. Then I felt a prickling sensation around my waist and up my spine, making my hair stand on end.

For fifteen seconds, the noise was so loud my mother could hardly stand it and covered her ears with her hands. Hard as it was, I tried my best to keep the table steady, but it was becoming increasingly difficult. I had felt many earthquakes during my life in the Bay Area, but this one I instinctively knew was different. The tremor's centrifugal energy whirled us around while a second, opposing motion forced us up, then down, in some sort of macabre dance. Then, suddenly, it was over. Dead silence set in. We held our breath in expectation, but felt only the slight trembling of the ground, as if the strength of the beast's giant footfall grew weaker with every step.

The smell of wine, vinegar, and olive oil reached our nostrils. I saw the refrigerator door open, and the bottle of wine I had just uncorked and the salad spilled all over the floor. I noticed that the electric clock on the wall had stopped at 5:07 in the afternoon and its hands were no longer moving. A power blackout, I said to myself.

Almost as if on cue, all of us except Maurice, who was sitting on a dining room chair bewildered and speechless, stepped towards each other and hugged one another. No one spoke. No one dared stay away from one another for fear the ground would start trembling again.

My mother was the first one to break the silence. She began to tell everyone what to do and to pick up and put things back in cupboards and cabinets. Then she and Tania went through the upstairs rooms taking a quick inventory of windows and other things that were damaged. Justin made sure that the water heater was secured. I took out the container with batteries I kept in the refrigerator to put in the battery-powered radio-cassette-player.

"It's better if we eat whatever is left of this food," my mother suggested. "This was a bad one. Heaven knows when we'll be able to eat next."

We all helped her reset the table. But when we finally sat down to eat, we couldn't even begin to swallow a bite. Tania turned on the radio and we heard the announcer's instructions.

"The disaster emergency center advises everyone to stay off the phones and keep off highways and overpasses to facilitate mobilization of rescue units," the announcer instructed his listeners. Then with the steady humming of an engine in the background, produced most likely by a blimp, a second voice began to give a description of the damage to the San Francisco-Oakland Bay Bridge caused by the 6.9, fifteen-second-long "killer" quake.

For the next three hours, through dozens of light aftershocks and another of considerable strength, we kept ourselves busy cleaning and repairing what could be repaired.

When the sun set, we took charcoal and matches and went out in the yard. We lit the barbeque pit. To keep Maurice from having an anxiety attack, we told stories. We saw the moon rise. I remembered the events of the night before, but everything that happened in the Valley of the Moon seemed so strangely distant.

As we were walking back into the kitchen, we heard the radio announcer say: "It is awesome, folks. The double-deck of the Cypress structure in Oakland is now a pile of rubble and twisted steel. It looks as though a giant played hopscotch on it and crushed it. There is no way of knowing how many cars are trapped under the structure. But we do know that only two cars fell into the collapsed section of the Bay Bridge. And San Francisco burns again...an awesome sight."

As if to remind us that it wasn't over, another strong aftershock shook us again. The announcer's voice broke off. My heart began to beat faster as I thought that the transmission had been cut off. I was relieved when I heard the announcer's voice again. "Those of you all over the world who are watching us—we need your prayers, folks." Until that moment, I hadn't realized that millions of eyes all over the world were watching what was happening to us.

About two o'clock everyone except me had fallen asleep. I went upstairs and from a rear window saw the San Francisco Marina District fires still glowing in the distance.

Being literally in the dark, we in the Bay Area couldn't begin to fathom the extent of the damage that had been done to vehicles and dwellings. Nor did we know the number of lives lost. As I kept listening to the grim news reports, I realized that for the next few days all of us would be praying for the relatives of persons missing as they kept vigil, waiting, hoping, yet dreading the news. Unable to sleep, I went downstairs and out to the yard. It had been a long time since I'd seen so many stars, and I stayed outside a long time, star-gazing. Then I stirred the coals in the barbeque pit, hoping they would last till morning, and warmed some water for tea. As I put down the teapot next to Carlota's cactus, I realized I had been secretly fostering the false hope that Carlota would come back, though I knew I would never see her again.

"Tomorrow, or when this is over, I will plant the tiny nopal at the foot of Luisa's grave," I promised aloud, looking up at the morning star punctuating the canvas of the night.